MW01537937

FARDOOR

DANIEL TASCONA

Copyright © 2011 Daniel Tascona
ISBN-13: 978-1461109174
ISBN-10: 1461109175

fardoor.blogspot.com

For my family.

CONTENTS

Chapter

One 1

Two 13

Three 30

Four 48

Five 55

Six 68

Seven 81

Eight 95

Nine 102

Ten 114

Eleven 139

Twelve 160

Thirteen 175

Fourteen 191

Fifteen 200

Sixteen 210

Seventeen 230

Eighteen 242

Nineteen 257

CHAPTER ONE

"Are you paying attention Becks?"

Will glanced over his shoulder at his cousin Rebecca, who clearly wasn't paying attention. His other cousin Thomas watched as a pretty little bird with a black beak and bright blue crest hopped from tree to tree, landing on the large maple next to her.

"Oh look – a blue jay!" she exclaimed.

"Oh look – a blue jay!" Will mocked. He turned to Rebecca. "Focus, focus! You are the Queen of the Isles, and you must pick the bravest knight to slay the dragon that has terrorized your kingdom and taken your daughter."

"And then what? I get to play my daughter? *Oh save me, save me!*" she teased. Both boys glared at her, so she cleaned off a flat boulder and sat down to watch. At the same time, she patted her hair and straightened her color-coordinated outfit.

Thomas rolled his eyes. His sister used to be just as eager to play games as they were. Lately, however, she had been less interested in games and more interested in brushing her long, brown hair. Thomas called this 'a disturbing trend'.

"Are you paying attention now Becks?" Will asked again. He broke off two tree branches and threw one to Thomas.

"Yes, just get started already! And remember to fight fair!"

"Doesn't matter," said Thomas. "You probably learned how to

swordfight at your fancy British boarding school!"

"I hate that school! I only go there because I have to! But I *may* have picked up a trick or two."

"I choose the winner anyway," said Rebecca. She gave her brother an encouraging look.

He could tell she thought he was going to lose. It was a safe bet: Thomas was the smallest ten-year old in his class, while Will was two years older and much bigger. Rebecca was eleven, but she too was a couple inches taller than Thomas already (a fact that pained him). Still, people often mistook the Day children for twins - certainly their hazel eyes were almost identical.

"Draw your sword sir, that mine may find a quick home in your chest!"

"Thank you for that image," said Thomas with a sarcastic smile. Will returned it. "But first," he continued "we must bow to the Queen," - they bowed, and this time Rebecca rolled her eyes - "and now to each other, and on the count of three -" he looked at his sister, who started counting:

"One, two…"

"AAAAAAAH!" yelled the cousins as they ran at each other, branches held high. A swordfight ensued, with Rebecca watching and hoping that Thomas would - for once - come out on top. Within short order, Will had him pinned against a tree, their crossed branches/swords between them.

"You really should practice your swordplay," he stated.

Thomas stuck out his tongue and pushed Will off him. The fight continued for another thirty seconds, until Thomas's branch was knocked out of his hand, and the tip of Will's branch held at his throat.

"Give up?"

"Funny, I was about to ask you the same thing!"

Will raised an eyebrow. "I think we better let the Queen decide this one. Who is the winner, Your Majesty?"

Rebecca stood up from the rock and pointed her finger at them.

"You both are the losers!" she proclaimed. "The dragon is actually under my control and I think I'll have him eat you both!"

"I protest, m'lady!" joked Will in a haughty accent.

She laughed, and then smiled at Thomas. "Come on, I'm tired of this game. Let's do something else."

"Like what?"

"Like look for more birds!"

"Boring!" the boys exclaimed in unison.

"I know! Let's go exploring!" said Will.

"It's already eleven o'clock, and we have to be back home for lunch at twelve," she reminded them.

"Good. That leaves just enough time to check out the caves."

Every year since his mom had died, Will had come and stayed with the Day family for the summer. And every summer he had talked about investigating the series of caves near their house. The furthest any of them had ever gone in was the entrance, but this year Will seemed intent on really exploring them; he had already mentioned it several times since arriving.

"Will, you know we can't go in there – there are *bears!*" said Rebecca.

"Nonsense! That's just what parents tell their children so they won't have any fun! Are you with me Thomas?"

He shrugged.

"Great. Let's go get the torches."

Rebecca was just about to announce that their family did not keep torches when her brother interrupted: "That's British for flashlights."

A quick rummage through the house and the children were making their way through the woods, flashlights in hand. Thomas tested his. "Shoot! The batteries are dead in this one!"

"Mine's okay."

"Mine too."

"You guys go on ahead. I'll go back and get batteries, then run and catch up."

"No, we'll wait here," said Rebecca.

"He knows the way. Well, come on then!" Will grabbed her arm and started leading her through the woods. Thomas turned around and ran back to the house.

"I know the way too, thank you very much!" she announced while yanking her arm from his grasp. Will could be arrogant and bossy, but she forgave him because he was also loads of fun. Quickly she fell behind her much faster cousin, and did a little trot to catch up. He looked back at her and grinned.

"Another exciting adventure for Hastings and Day!"

"Day and Hastings," she corrected. "There's two of us!"

Once again Rebecca thought about how happy Will seemed to be. She knew he'd had some trouble at school again this year, and when he arrived for the summer he was in a pretty bad mood. She even thought she heard him crying in the bathroom one time. Then a couple weeks into his visit he'd come out and asked her parents if he could stay with their family after the summer ended. They said they'd speak to his dad and ever since he'd been positively beaming! *'He never sees his dad anyway,'* she thought. He also rarely spoke about him except to say he was an important businessman. The Day children had never even seen their uncle except in photos. His wavy blond hair and blue eyes resembled Will's, but the face was always unsmiling.

They continued their journey through the forest. Here the woods were cool and mostly quiet, save for an occasional birdcall or insect hum. Muskoka woods offered a good mix of deciduous and evergreen trees. Poplars, maples and pines all stood next to each other, their interlacing branches offering a speckled shade to the children below. White birches were Rebecca's favorite because their paper-like bark was fun to peel off, although her mother gave a disapproving *'tut, tut'* if she was seen doing it.

Thomas had a hard time finding batteries, and was nowhere to be seen when they arrived at the caves ten minutes later.

"We should wait for Thomas. THOMAS!" Rebecca yelled, and an assortment of birds scattered out of the trees. "Ooh – a cardinal!"

"We'll do a five-minute tour and be back before he gets here," said Will. Noticing that she was still watching the cardinal, he hastily added, "I promise we'll look at all the birds you want this afternoon."

"I'm waiting here," she said.

"Well I'm going in," he announced before turning around and entering the cave.

"Fantastic!" she heard him exclaim moments later from within. Rebecca groaned and then entered the cave herself.

Turning on her flashlight, she saw what Will was marvelling about. The walls of the cave were a dark grey that sparkled with the appearance of a million diamonds. Further in, she could see pointy stalactites hanging down from the ceiling, and their stalagmite siblings trying to reach them from below.

"Do you hear that?" he asked.

Rebecca strained her ears and just made out the faint sounds of moving water.

"There's an underground river here!" he exclaimed. "Let's try and find it!"

He started off before she could object. Rebecca reluctantly followed, giving an absentminded glance back at the entrance.

Finding the river was easier said than done, for the cave split into three different directions fairly early. Each of these then offered choices of their own. After a couple false starts, they learned to listen very carefully to which path had the louder gurgling. A few minutes more and they had found it. Rebecca made sure to memorize the route they had taken: left, middle, right, left.

"Mission accomplished!" Will proudly announced. They were now in a small cavern about ten feet in all directions with a swift current of water taking up half. The children ran their flashlights over the walls, Will halting his on the far side.

"What's this?" he asked.

"What?"

"It looks like writing!"

On the other side of the river, his light fell upon a faint inscription that was unmistakably some sort of writing, albeit none that either of them had seen before.

"Cool!" said Rebecca. "It looks like Native writing. There used to be lots of them in this area."

"Cool," Will agreed.

"Let's go get Thomas so he can see it. He knows a lot more about

Natives than I do."

"Hang on, I want a closer look." He moved up to the underground river's edge.

"Will don't get too close!" she said as she grabbed his arm.

It was too late. The edge had been made quite slippery by the sloshing water. As her cousin stepped closer, one foot slid right down into the river. The rest of his body had no choice but to follow the errant limb. As Will fell in, Rebecca was caught off balance and slipped in too.

She gasped. The icy cold water was like pointy daggers poking her on all sides. She couldn't breathe.

"Will!" Rebecca tried yelling, but her mouth filled up with water so only a funny gargling noise came out. The two of them tried grabbing hold of the rock, but the current was too strong and pulled them both along on its journey downward. Yes, Rebecca definitely felt as though they were moving downward. She wondered how long they could survive in this water. There wasn't much time to wonder: after less than thirty seconds, the river threw the children off a three-foot waterfall and onto the bank of what could only be described as a meadow.

Rebecca lay still on the soft grass for a moment. She heard Will ask, "You okay there Rebecca?"

"Uh-huh," was all she could manage. She continued to lay with her eyes closed, but heard him rustling beside her.

"Fantastic!" he said. "What is this place?"

Rebecca opened her eyes expecting to be outside, but found she was still underground. They were in a large cave, much larger than any they had been in before. Where the waterfall fell, the river ended in a frothy pool. The rest of the ground was soft, and covered in pale grass that came up to her hip. In the centre of this meadow was a tree with long, wide branches, and a broad trunk. Its coarse bark was chocolate brown, but its branches were thick with leaves as pale as the grass below. Although it grew at least forty feet tall, there was a good fifteen feet more above the highest branch to the ceiling of the cave. The tree was unlike any of the ones Rebecca had seen growing in the woods above.

"Did you know about this?" he asked. The look on her face told him she hadn't.

"Will, where's your flashlight?"

He checked his empty hands. "Must've lost it in the river."

"Me too. So where is this light coming from?"

It was a good question. Although neither child had a flashlight, the cave was lit. Not very bright, mind you, but lit all the same. Both Will and Rebecca looked around for a source - a crack in the ceiling perhaps that was admitting some light from outside. They could find none. It was as if the cave itself was suffused with light – as if everything in it was *glowing*.

"That's odd," said Rebecca.

"What? The light?"

"Yes that, and…Will do you feel cold?"

"Well actually, no. That is a bit funny. I'm dripping wet and underground – I *should* feel cold, but I don't."

"Me neither."

In fact, a warm breeze moved through the cavern, rustling the tree and drying the children off nicely.

"It's an odd sort of place, isn't it?" he asked.

"It's beautiful. But how are we ever going to get out? We may be stuck down here for days until someone finds us!"

"Where *is* your sense of adventure Becks? We've just found a place where probably no one's been for a century! Besides, Thomas knows we're in the caves." He looked at her earnestly, but couldn't hold it. His face broke out into a large grin. "Come on, let's have a look at that tree!"

"*You* look at the tree, while *I* try to find a way out – we obviously can't leave by the way we came!"

"Deal," he said.

So as Will made his way to the centre, Rebecca began searching along the walls that lined the cave's rather large circumference. She placed a hand on the dark stone. It was warm. Starting by the pool, Rebecca walked slowly around the cave's periphery, tracing her hand on the wall, feeling its rough outline. She scanned up and down while walking, looking for a hole where this cave might join up with another. The task was difficult as it was much darker here at the edge of the cave; most of the light seemed to be surrounding the tree in the centre.

She continued this job for the better part of fifteen minutes. Occasionally she would hear Will say things like *'Fantastic!'* or *'Brilliant!'*, but she herself remained silent until her hand felt an area of rock that had been smoothed over. "Hmmm," she said.

"Found anything yet?" Will asked loudly.

"I think…maybe," she responded.

"Well I've found loads. Come here and look!"

"Just gimme a sec." Rebecca felt the contour of the smooth rock, which jutted out from the wall a bit. It was a step. She backed up a little and scanned the surface of the wall more carefully. Her heart leapt. There was a whole staircase carved into the side of the rock face! Thirty-odd steps curved up the wall and ended in a small opening she could just make out. The small size of the steps, combined with the dark stone and the dim light, easily camouflaged the staircase against the surrounding wall. She reasoned this was why she hadn't noticed it previously. Excited, she ran the hundred feet over to where Will was sitting by the tree.

"I found a way out!" she panted. "There's a staircase up the wall! Will you're a mess!" She had just noticed his appearance: blonde hair in tangles, grass stains on his clothes, dirt on his hands and face.

"I've been *searching*," he explained. "Anyway, well done on the staircase Becks. Now have a look at what I've discovered!"

Will motioned for her to sit down beside him, which she did. He had made a small clearing in the grass, and now he showed her his prizes.

"First of all, there are *these*." He scooped up some stones with both hands, each about two inches long, and flat. All of them were brown, and very smooth. Rebecca took one and flipped it over.

"Will!" she exclaimed, "There's more Native writing!"

Indeed, as she took each stone in turn she saw that each of them possessed one or more of the curious symbols.

"I wonder what they mean?" she said. "Were they all in a pile here when you found them?"

"No, they were scattered around the tree. There's probably more; this grass makes it hard to find things. Four of them is a good find, though, wouldn't you say?"

"Terrific," she agreed. "But we really should try to get back now that we've found a way out. It's probably almost twelve, and Mom will start to get worried. Thomas has probably already gone home and told her we're missing."

"Hang on, I also found *this*!" Will triumphantly produced an object from his pocket and handed it to her.

"Oooooh," she cooed. "What is it?"

His blue eyes danced with this major discovery. "Don't know. But I found it in the grass around the tree, just like the stones."

Rebecca examined the object more closely, turning it over repeatedly in her palm. It consisted of a frame formed by two curved twigs, tightly bound to each other at both ends with some leather twine. At one end the twine pulled out to form a small loop as if for hanging. The other end boasted a small white feather. More leather twine was wound between the frame in a criss-cross pattern, at the centre of which was a pale violet stone, almost clear. Its stay on the ground had dulled it, but she was sure the stone would sparkle wonderfully if polished right.

"It's fantastic, isn't it?" he asked. Will had been silently watching her look at the object for a minute, so now he eagerly offered his own insight. "See that loop at the end? I think it must have been hung like a necklace of sorts, probably for a Native princess."

"A Native princess," Rebecca repeated absentmindedly. "It's beautiful, Will. Can I keep it?"

"Sure. But if you find any arrowheads give them to me, alright then?"

"Deal."

She reached out and shook his hand before remembering how soiled it was.

"There's dirt on your hand," he said.

"Yeah, from you!" she replied, then wiped her hand on his shirt. Laughing, he did the same.

"Now put that somewhere safe," he instructed, nodding at the object in her palm.

She smiled and dropped it in her pocket.

"And remember, all arrowheads to me."

"Yep, but we're heading back now right?" She paused. "Unless...you've found anything else?"

Will ticked off a list on his fingers. "Let's see...stones, jewellery...oh yeah!" he continued "I've found food!" Rummaging in the grass behind him, he pulled out a large, pale yellow apple. "Just one, mind you. There's more in the tree, but they're too high up. I found this one on the ground."

"An apple?" Rebecca questioned. She was eyeing it suspiciously. "Will, I don't think we should be eating anything that grew in a cave."

He rolled his eyes. "It's just an apple Becks. We need energy for our trek back." She still looked wary. "I'm hungry," he added.

Will rubbed the apple on his shirt – "Your shirt's just as dirty," said Rebecca – and then took a large bite.

"Mmmm, it's delicious!" he stated with his mouth full. "I'm serious Becks – it's really sweet."

"Okay," she said, "I'll try some." Rebecca reached out for the apple.

"Uh-uh - you don't want any, remember!" he taunted, pulling the fruit away from her grasp.

"Stop teasing!"

"If you want it, come and get it!" said Will as he got up and ran to the other side of the tree. Rebecca quickly followed, and around its trunk in circles they went, both of them laughing at her inability to catch him. After a few times around, she stopped.

"Fine, I don't want any," she announced while trying to catch her breath.

"Liar," Will said, and then took another bite. "Mmmm, it's *rahhhly* good!" he pronounced in his snobbiest English accent.

"Are you done yet?"

"Oh, I guess so. Here you go."

He leaned across to hand her the apple, placing one hand on the tree to brace himself. As soon as he touched its rough bark, however, the tree's glow increased magnificently. Rebecca turned her head to shield her eyes, and within a couple seconds it returned to its former luminosity.

"What was that, Will?!" she asked. After such a bright light, her eyes had not yet adjusted to the relative dimness of the cave. She did not see that he was gone.

"Will?" she tentatively asked again, after receiving no reply. She ran around the tree. "Will! Where are you?!" she yelled. Her voice echoed around the spacious cavern several times, emphasizing her solitude. She touched the tree. Nothing happened. "Will!" she yelled again, looking wildly around the cave. *'He ate the apple,'* she thought. *'That must be it.'*

She quickly scanned the ground for the apple Will had held in his hand, but concluded it must have gone with him. Looking up, she could see several of the golden fruit far beyond her reach. "Maybe I can shake one down," she muttered aloud. As the trunk was so wide, Rebecca jumped up and shook a low branch instead. Dozens of small, silver butterflies fluttered out from the leaves, but none of the apples budged; they were just too high up. She briefly thought about climbing the tree, but didn't feel confident she could make it to the highest branches where all of the apples were. Instead, she decided to search through the grass for another that might have fallen. "Perhaps Will missed one," she reasoned.

Rebecca kneeled down and started hunting through the deep grass. Will's activity had already pressed down the region surrounding the tree somewhat, but there was a very large area to look through as the branches were so wide. The task was made more annoying by a few of the butterflies which insisted on fluttering about her face instead of returning to the tree with the rest. "Stupid butterflies!" she exclaimed while swatting them away with one hand and searching the ground with the other. "I wish this grass wasn't so high and thick," she said to no one in particular. "I can't find anything in it!"

A couple minutes on her hands and knees did turn up two more of the curious stones, but no apple. She stood up. *'I should get help,'* she thought. *'But who knows how long it will take to get back? And no one will believe what happened!'*

While pondering what to do, Rebecca noticed that the butterflies were no longer bothering her. Out of the corner of her eye, she could see that they had settled on a spot some fifteen feet away. Forgetting her quandary, Rebecca walked over to the butterflies and bent down to have a look. And there it was – a yellow apple as big as the first, hidden beneath the grass. Heart pounding, she picked it up. The butterflies scattered, and then resumed their previous fluttering around her. This time, however, she did not swat at them, or even take notice. She just looked at the yellow apple in her hand. Suddenly she took a large bite and swallowed. Then she walked straight at the tree and placed her hand on it.

CHAPTER TWO

Once again a tremendous light emanated from the tree, only this time it felt different. Although equally bright as before, she could look through it and not shield her eyes. The light was...warm. And as it surrounded her, she had the strange sensation of moving and not moving at the same time. Slowly it receded and Rebecca found she was standing outside under a clear blue sky with her hand on a tree. It appeared she was in another meadow. This one looked just the same – same size, same tree in the centre – only greener. Instead of encircling rock, this meadow was ringed by forest. Down at her feet she saw Will's discarded apple core and two more beside it of a different color. *'Wow,'* she thought *'he sure ate those quickly!'*

"Oy, Rebecca! Over here!"

"Will!" She spun around and saw a familiar dishevelled boy walking towards her from the edge of the meadow, golden hair glinting in the sun. A wave of relief swept through her. "Are you okay?" she yelled.

"Of course I'm okay - except I've been waiting for *hours*!" He ran the rest of the way over to her. "What took you so long?" he asked.

"But you've only been gone a few minutes!"

"Not true. I've already had time to look around this place over and over. I was going to go into the forest, but I thought I should wait for you. That was ages ago, and I've just been *waiting*! Really, Becks, I thought you'd have figured it out sooner!"

"I'm serious, Will! I saw you disappear from the cave less than five minutes ago!"

"Oh, come off it!" he laughed. "Five minutes!"

She flashed her cousin a look that told him she wasn't joking.

Comprehension dawned on his face. "Five minutes…really?"

"Less than five minutes."

He slowly put his thoughts together. "Well then wherever we are, time must move differently."

"Where *are* we, Will?" She looked around at their surroundings – they looked normal enough. "Maybe it's just another part of the forest," she suggested.

"I don't think so. Those woods over there aren't like any I've ever seen around your place." He paused in reflection. "I think that the tree in the cave acts as a portal to a different world - *this* world. The Natives must've known that, but their secret went with them when they died out."

"Maybe they didn't die out, Will. Maybe they came *here*."

"Yeah…maybe. At any rate, I tried searching through this meadow for more stuff, but didn't find anything."

Will swung at the grass with a stick he had picked up to emphasize the point, and then sat down for a rest. "Have a seat Becks."

She sat down beside him and started playing with a blade of grass, twisting it over and over between her fingers. It felt good to be off her feet.

"So tell me, how *did* you get here?" Will asked.

"Well I figured it must be the apple right away, so I tried shaking the tree, but then none of the apples fell and all these stupid butterflies flew out to annoy me."

"I didn't see any butterflies."

"They were hidden in the leaves. Anyway," she continued "I found one on the ground that you missed. Actually the butterflies found it." He gave her a quizzical look. "Then I just took a bite and touched the tree, like you did."

"And then – "

"Next thing I know you're running towards me complaining about the time!"

"Hmmm," was all he said.

Rebecca went back to twisting the blade of grass while Will lay back to look at the sky. Both children were silent as they pondered the situation.

"If we are in a different world," she said after a while "have you considered how we're going to get back?"

"I imagine you just have to eat one of the apples from this tree, and then touch it. There's a lot more on this one."

Looking around, she could see this was true. Not only were there more in the branches, but there were also several red apples on the ground.

"It looks like you already ate two of them," she pointed out.

"Yes, but I was careful to not touch the tree."

"Why not?" she questioned. "I was worried!"

"What, and miss the opportunity to explore this?!" he said, gesturing grandly. Will looked genuinely shocked that she would ask such a question. "Plus, I knew you'd figure out how to get here eventually."

"Well thank you for that! Now haven't you done enough exploring?"

"Who knows if we'll be able to come back here, Becks! Plus it looks like we can spend hours in this world and not much time will pass in ours."

"We don't know that. Anyway, I thought you said you were hungry."

"I'm fine," was his curt reply.

Rebecca was silent again as she considered whether to go back alone or stay with her cousin. She thought she'd make another attempt to sway him.

"Will, we need to go back and have lunch." She gave him a once-over. "You need to have a shower, and I need to brush my hair," she said, patting the tangled mess on her head.

He scoffed. Her suggestion of hygiene had been the wrong tactic. "You go back - I'm staying." Defiantly, he got up and began to walk off.

"What about Thomas?"

"I'm sure he'd want me to explore. He'll probably want to come here himself, if we can find it again."

He was displaying his legendary stubbornness. *'No consideration for what I want,'* thought Rebecca. She wanted to go back, but also didn't feel good about leaving Will here by himself.

"Please Will, please come back now?" She looked earnestly at her cousin, who stopped walking and turned around.

He softened. "Don't worry Becks. I'll probably be back at the house ten minutes after you." Walking over to the tree, Will picked an apple off the ground and handed it to her. "Here, have a bite. I'll watch you go through."

Reluctantly she took the red fruit, then hesitated slightly before biting into it. A nagging voice in Rebecca's head told her to grab Will and touch the tree, but she did not. Instead she slowly chewed the apple and walked over to the tree by herself. Looking up she saw that Will was waving at her. She smiled weakly and waved back. Then she touched the tree.

A brilliant light surrounded her and Will was lost from view. The uneasy feeling of moving and not moving at once occurred again, and then the light diminished. She was back in the cave with her hand on the tree. For a moment while the light was still receding, it looked as if several butterflies were frozen about her. But then their wings flapped furiously again. *'I wonder if they moved at all while I was gone?'* she thought.

Rebecca backed away from the tree. She could not believe what had just happened: they had just found a portal to *another world!* "Although maybe it wasn't another world at all," she muttered. "It looked pretty normal." She kicked at the grass, remembering that her cousin made her come back alone. "Stupid Will! Doesn't care about anyone but himself! Well I'm not waiting for him."

From where she stood it was difficult to discern the staircase against the wall of the vast cave. She determinedly walked in the direction where she knew it ought to be. The butterflies decided not to follow, but flew back up to hide in the abundant leaves once more. Her new resolution was to get out of the caves, find Thomas, eat lunch, and not talk to Will for a week. She pounded down the high grass with each step to emphasize her newfound determination. Reaching the cave's periphery, she found the steps to be just where she had left them. Without hesitation she started to climb the staircase, gripping the adjacent wall for support. Once again, it was surprising to feel such warmth emanating from the rough stone.

At the topmost stair Rebecca stopped to look around. At this height she was now level with the top of the tree, and found she had a more complete view of the whole cave: small waterfall and pool on the far side, large tree in the centre, and tall grass that covered every other square inch right up to the walls. From this vantage she could also clearly see the sweeping breeze that gently flattened the grass and rustled the leaves. Every so often it would move across the cave, but each time in a different direction.

'It's a very odd wind – always changing directions like that. I wonder where it's coming from?' she thought, forgetting how strange this place was already.

There were only two entrances to this cave that she knew of: the waterfall, and the passage at the top of the stairs to which she now had her back. "The wind can't be from behind me or I'd feel it," she reasoned aloud. "And I don't think it's coming from the river's entrance either." She watched it a bit longer. "Well wherever it comes from, I think it's picking up."

This was true. The wind did seem to be getting somewhat stronger as she stood there watching. However, Rebecca gave it no further consideration, but rather turned around and walked into the passage.

The light from the cave only penetrated a few feet into it, and she soon found herself in total darkness without a flashlight. She had never been claustrophobic, but her heart started racing nonetheless at the prospect that this route did not offer a way out. It was large enough to stand in, but steadily narrowed. It also seemed to be taking her upwards. *'Well that's a good sign!'* she thought.

Rebecca continued to walk blindly, now crouching a bit, feeling the way around her with her hands. The stone had ceased being warm a few steps into the passage.

After a very long minute of walking she came to a barrier of loose rocks. She quickly set about moving them, wondering if the Natives had perhaps put them there intentionally.

A dull grey beam of light pierced through the barrier as one of the top rocks was removed. Excited, she worked even harder at moving the rest despite her fatigue. In short order she had disassembled them all. Behind the rock barrier the passage abruptly narrowed to a tunnel no larger than a crawl space. *'And that's for someone* my *size! The Natives must have slid flat on their stomachs to make it through!'*

Accepting the fact that she was already completely filthy, Rebecca climbed through the small opening and continued on her hands and knees. The grey light let her see the end of the tunnel, which was only a few metres away. She raced towards it, and fell through the opening with great relief.

* * * *

Thomas thought he heard a sound behind him. He had now been sitting on a log at the entrance of the caves for thirty minutes, and was currently debating whether to even speak to Rebecca and Will when he saw them. The sudden noise from within the cave had startled him out of this debate, however, and now he whipped around with flashlight at the ready, new batteries in place. Although he had never really believed there were bears inside, his heart raced at the possibility one was already approaching him. His darting flashlight was quick to show the real cause of the sound, as it passed over his own sister picking herself up off the ground. She dusted off her clothes and then hurried over to him.

"Thomas, I'm so glad to see you!" she exclaimed.

"What happened to *you?*" he asked. His normally impeccably kempt sister was covered in dirt from head to toe, her long brown hair in tangles.

18

She gave a little cough. "You wouldn't believe it even if I told you."

"Fine, I'll ask Will." He shone his flashlight into the cave behind Rebecca, expecting to see his cousin making his way over. "Where is he?" he asked upon seeing this wasn't the case.

"He's still in the caves. Well...sort of. Is that food?" Rebecca had just spied the plastic bag in his hand and her hunger had leapt to the surface again.

"I asked Mom if I could bring some sandwiches so we didn't have to come back right away."

"Good thinking, Thomas!" she said while reaching for the bag.

He hid it behind his back. "First I wanna know what you've been up to. I've been waiting *forever!*"

"I w*ill* tell you, but I need a sandwich first – I'm really hungry."

"Okay," he sighed and handed her the bag. "I already had mine."

Rebecca opened it and found two ham and cheese sandwiches, two drinks, and some chocolate chip cookies. She grabbed a ham and cheese and took a large bite. "Mmmm," she said, sitting down on the log beside her brother.

Thomas patiently waited for her to finish the sandwich and down the drink before giving her a look that said it was time to start talking. He decided to start first anyway: "Is it safe for Will to be in there by himself?" he asked.

"No, but he's so stubborn!" Thomas nodded in agreement. Excitement suddenly took hold of Rebecca as she remembered what had happened in the caves. "It was *amazing*, Thomas!"

She proceeded to recount her story, telling him all about how she and Will had found an underground river and then fallen in, how it took them downwards then plopped them in an immense cave with an underground meadow in it. She told him how everything was bathed with pale light, especially a large tree at the centre of the spacious cavern. Details then quickly flew out of her mouth: the staircase in the wall, Will disappearing, her following soon on eating the apple and touching the tree, the outside meadow to which it took them, and the discrepancy in time. She concluded the story with Will's insistence on staying but her decision to return and take the passage at the top of the staircase, which was followed until it landed her at the entrance of the caves.

Thomas listened to all of this without interrupting. Of course he thought she was putting him on. She had made stuff up in the past, for sure – once she'd not only told him he was adopted, but actually printed out a fake adoption certificate on the computer to give him! He had learned to be less gullible as a result. But as he listened to the implausible story, he *almost* believed her: there was genuine sincerity in the way she told it.

He had listened without interruption, but now it was his turn to speak. "Show me the stones," he said.

"Oh…I don't have them."

"Then show me the cave."

"I will. Just…" Fantastic as her story may be, Rebecca actually hadn't anticipated any skepticism. She *should* have brought the stones. All of a sudden, she realized she had something even better. "I *will* show you the cave," she said. "But first, look at this!"

She pulled the Native object out of her pocket and handed it to Thomas. Fortunately, it had not been damaged while she was crawling around.

He peered at the beautiful decoration intently. "It looks like it's meant to be hung," he said.

"That's what we thought, too."

He stared at it for a couple more seconds and then handed it back over. "You can find stuff like this at any tourist shop around here," he announced.

Rebecca was hurt. "We found it *in there*," she said, gesturing at the caves.

"So a tourist bought it in a shop, and lost it *in there*," said Thomas, mimicking his sister.

"Uggh! You're so annoying! Listen, you like reading about history and Native stuff. What do you know about the Natives that were in this region?"

Thomas waited a second to judge the sincerity of her question. This was the first time she had ever asked him about History, one of his favorite subjects. "Well there was more than one tribe. Both the

Algonquin and Huron people lived in this area."

"That's all of them?"

"Actually, there was supposedly a third tribe that disappeared before the Europeans made contact with them – the *Eechawey*." Thomas saw that his sister was giving him a *'See – there you go!'* look. "They were probably all killed in a fight with another tribe, if they existed at all," he said.

"I don't know about that. Some tribe obviously knew about the cave. Will and I think they may have gone through to the other world to stay."

"Come on, Rebecca. *Another world?* Do you honestly believe that?"

Rebecca ignored the question. Instead, she looked back at the caves and asked, "I wonder where Will is?"

"I just asked you that a few minutes ago!" he exclaimed.

"I know, but if time really does move much faster in the other world, then he should be back already. Maybe he's having trouble finding the way out – I didn't have a chance to show him."

"Then let's go get him," said Thomas, rising from the log.

Rebecca looked at her clothes and then at her brother's. "I was gonna get cleaned up!" she pouted.

Thomas crossed his arms and raised his eyebrows at her. Changing outfits was clearly not a priority to him.

"What about the food?" she said. The bag dangling from one hand still contained an uneaten sandwich, drink and cookies.

"We'll take it with us," he suggested impatiently while pulling her up off the log and turning her in the direction of the cave. "You lead the way. And if this is just you and Will playing a trick on me, you're both in a lot of trouble!" Somehow, though, he didn't think this was the case.

"It's not a trick, and don't push me! What's with you guys always pushing or pulling me in some direction?!"

Rebecca entered the caves for the second time that day. It was the same entrance she and Will had used before, only now the faint sounds of rushing water seemed to be gone. She strained her ears even more. "Before, Will and I could hear the river from here."

Thomas listened carefully. "I don't hear it."

"Me neither."

"Well do you remember how to get there?" he asked.

"Yeah, but we're not going that way anyway."

She motioned for him to shine the flashlight on the spot where she had dropped out a few minutes ago. About six feet up the wall was a small, nondescript hole in the rock face – large enough to crawl into if you could reach it, but easily unnoticed in its surroundings. "That leads directly to the underground meadow."

"No wonder you're so filthy. But how will we get into it?" Both of them were less than five feet tall.

They walked over to the hole to better assess its height.

"I'll give you a boost, then you reach down and help me up," Rebecca decided.

"Okay, let's try it."

She placed the bag and flashlight on the ground, and then offered her hands as a step for her brother.

Manoeuvring up to the hole was not easy. "You've got to keep your hands more steady!" Thomas laughed as the hand-step gave way and he fell for the third time.

"Sorry!"

A couple more tries and he managed to brace himself between the wall and his sister, then climb into the hole. "Okay, now hand me that food and the flashlight," he ordered.

Rebecca complied and then put up both her hands. "Pull me up!" she said.

"Just a sec." Thomas laid flat on his stomach and spread his legs between the adjacent walls for support. He reached down and grabbed the sides of her arms. "Unnnh! You should be pulling *me* up!"

"Just keep pulling!"

With him holding her arms, Rebecca was able to 'walk' up the wall and into the hole. "See – it worked!"

Thomas resumed his crouching position. "Now what?"

"Now we start walking in that direction." She pointed into the darkness behind him. "You have to lead, 'cause I can't get around you."

He nodded and carefully turned around. Then Thomas started doing the sort of shuffle that's only possible when crouched down low. Rebecca followed close behind with the bag of food, thankful for the flashlight her brother held.

"Last time I didn't have any light, you know." Her voice sounded strangely muted in their cramped environment.

"Oh yeah, I forgot to ask: where's your flashlight?"

"Will and I lost them in the river."

Saying his name reminded her that they were looking for him. "WILL!" she yelled. "ARE YOU THERE?"

Thomas grabbed his ears and winced. "Ow Rebecca! That was right in my ear!" he scolded.

"Sorry. You yell for him then."

"I think he would've heard that. Let's just keep moving."

They quickly came to the point where the passage abruptly enlarged – or narrowed, depending on which direction you were travelling. Rebecca had already cleared the rocks away, but she made a point of how it had previously been blocked, " - probably by the Natives."

They continued to walk, now standing up.

"Thanks a lot Rebecca – my ears are ringing from all that yelling," Thomas remarked.

"That's not ringing – I hear it too. It sounds like wind."

Indeed, a soft, high-pitched howling sound permeated the passage. It steadily increased as they approached the large cave. By the time they reached it, the noise was so loud they had to shout just to speak to each other. Thomas, of course, wasn't trying to speak at all. He stood with mouth agape at the top of the staircase looking down on the meadow below. Rebecca had been telling the truth! It was just as she had described it: tall grass, small waterfall, and large, broad tree in the centre. Although, she hadn't mentioned the gale-force wind that violently beat down a path across the cave and threatened to knock them from their perch.

Instead of the random movements Rebecca had previously witnessed, the wind now churned in a circle with the tree at its centre. Its wide branches followed the circular movements of the wind, making the tree look as if it was doing a funny sort of dance.

Both children were bracing themselves against the wall. Rebecca was saying something, but he couldn't make it out.

"WHAT?" he yelled.

"I SAID - IT WASN'T THIS WINDY BEFORE!"

"WHAT SHOULD WE DO?"

"LOOK FOR WILL!"

This was a hard task, as the wind blew their hair in their faces and made their eyes well up. Tears streamed across Rebecca's cheeks giving the impression she was crying; Thomas supposed he looked the same.

"I CAN'T FIND HIM!" he yelled.

"JUST...KEEP...*LOOKING*!"

Rebecca said this last word so loud that it was quite a shock to poor Thomas when the wind abruptly ceased just prior to her screaming it. He winced again as it reverberated around the cave.

"Sorry," she said in her normal voice. "Are you okay?"

"Yeah." He let go of his ears. "What was with that wind? Where was it even coming from?"

"I don't know. It was much softer when Will and I were here, but I did notice it picking up when I left."

Now that the tree had stopped moving she could see several of the small, white butterflies fluttering out of its branches. They danced around the trunk for a bit, then returned to their hiding place. She tapped her brother on the back. "Look, Thomas! Did you see them?"

"What?"

"The butterflies!"

He had started down the stairs though, and hadn't been looking. "No, where are they?" he asked, now looking around.

"They've gone back in the tree," she said disappointedly.

"Oh." Thomas continued down the stairs, and Rebecca followed. "This place is so cool!" he exclaimed at the bottom. "I just hope that wind doesn't start up again." No sooner had he said it, than a gentle breeze rippled across the grass. "I suppose that much is fine," he remarked.

"Sure..." Rebecca was only half-listening: she was more concerned with the fact they were obviously alone in the cave. "I guess Will isn't here," she said. "I hope he's okay."

Thomas shared her concern. "That tree *really* took you to another world?" he asked.

"Yes."

"*Really?*"

"Yes!" was her emphatic reply. "C'mon I'll show it to you!" And she ran towards the tree.

Thomas followed close behind, pushing the high grass out of the way as he made his way towards the centre. This place fascinated him. Most of all it was the soft light that seemed to come from the plants themselves. '*So strange...*' he thought to himself. The flashlight was still in his hand, just in case. "Show me those stones you were talking about!" he panted, coming to a stop.

"Oh – I hope they haven't blown all over! Will had them in a little pile over...there." Rebecca pointed to a spot on the ground beside her brother. Bending down and pushing away the grass, she could see that only one of the five stones remained. "Here you go," she said, handing it to Thomas. "Help me look for the rest." But a small sweep of the surrounding area only turned up one more.

Thomas felt the smooth stones between his fingers. They were both brown, and both had a single curious symbol carved on one side. By the way he was looking at them, Rebecca thought he might recognize the writing. "Do you know what it says?" she asked.

"Of course not. I've learned about the Natives – I don't know how to speak their language!"

"Well *sorrrrry!*" she said sarcastically.

"You should be sorry."

"I am."

"Good."

"Great."

They both smiled, and Thomas pocketed the stones. "Is it all right if I hold on to them?" he asked.

"Sure. Now what?"

"I dunno." He craned his neck to look up at the tree. "You said there're apples?"

"At the very top."

"I see 'em." He looked down. "Looks like a couple more fell to the ground from that wind."

"Oh good, 'cause I left mine somewhere in the grass when I came back and it's probably lost now."

"Does that mean we're going to...*the other world*?" He said these last words very softly.

Rebecca reconsidered what she had said. "Oh I don't know if we should..." She bit her lip, looking worried.

"But you said Will's probably still there, right? So shouldn't we go after him?" Although he said this, Thomas was himself apprehensive about it.

"I guess, but Thomas – I'm just eleven and you're only ten. We should get help."

This irritated him. Yes he was ten years old and the smallest kid in his class. But mentioning it only increased his resolve to show he *didn't* need help.

"Who knows how long that'll take. And no one will believe us."

"You believed me."

"*After* I saw it. Our parents aren't going to climb through a crack in the wall of a cave!" He paused. "I'm gonna take a look at that tree!"

"Don't touch it!" she exclaimed as her brother walked towards the tree.

"You said nothing happened until after you ate the apple."

"Yes, but still..."

"Relax," he said confidently. Inside he was a lot less sure, and rather hesitantly reached out to touch the trunk with the tip of his index finger. "See – nothing."

Both children breathed a sigh of relief. Reassured, he placed his whole palm against the side. He looked back at Rebecca. "Maybe you're right. Maybe we should get help. Or maybe Will is back already and found another way out." Somehow he didn't think this was the case, and neither did she. But his original apprehension had returned.

Before she could answer, however, the butterflies flew out of the branches again. This time there had to be at least a hundred of them, and all were descending upon Thomas. He still had one palm on the tree and now wore a look of shock upon his face.

"The butterflies!" Rebecca cried.

He saw them. A hundred butterflies with silvery-white wings dancing around him, only he was pretty sure they weren't all butterflies.

Rebecca laughed at his expression. "They're harmless!" she said.

He didn't move. "Uh, Rebecca…did any of them look…*different* to you?"

"What - like different sizes?" She had no clue what he meant, but she did think it odd how they continued to flutter about him in such a mad way.

"Not exactly…"

From what he could see, most of them were butterflies. But here and there he caught glimpses of what could only be described as… *fairies*. They had the same silvery-white wings, but a bit bigger. And attached to these wings were tiny, little, human-type bodies. With all the frenzy surrounding him, at any moment he could only briefly see an arm or a leg – or most startling, a tiny head with its tiny eyes staring right at him.

"*Who are you?*" he whispered. More mad fluttering.

Rebecca walked towards him and made a motion to swat them away.

"*WHO ARE YOU?*" he yelled, and at once the true butterflies flew up into the tree, leaving five small fairies hovering behind.

"We are the Sprites of Laurea, Guardians of the Tree!" five squeaky voices announced in unison.

Rebecca's jaw dropped. Both children stared at the curious things, speechless. Now that the fairies were still, Thomas could see them more clearly: they could not have been more than two inches long, and were hard to tell apart. Each had very pale skin and long silvery hair. Each wore a light dress that seemed to be made out of the same material as their wings (which were now beating quite fast to keep them hovering in one place).

Quickly turning their attention from Thomas, all five zipped over to Rebecca and began speaking in rapid succession:

"You came here before!"

"You followed the boy to Laurea!"

"The boy has changed everything!"

Rebecca found the courage to speak. "Who, Will?"

"*Will* has not come back!"

"*Will* is in danger!"

"Laurea is in danger!"

They now zipped back over to Thomas.

"You must save Will!"

"You must stop him!"

"Or Laurea is doomed!"

"And so is the boy!"

Now Thomas spoke. "Stop who?" he asked.

"The *Destroyer*!" they cried, and then turned to each other to speak. There seemed to be a disagreement.

"He is not ready!"

"He is!"

"Not yet!"

"He can do it!"

"Not alone!"

"He needs her help!"

At this they flew back over to Rebecca.

"He needs your help!" they announced.

She didn't know how to respond to this, so instead she shot a *'What-in-the-world-is-going-on?'* look at her brother. Thomas, for his own part, seemed to have already accepted the fact that multiple fairies were flying in front him. He stepped forward.

"This...*Destroyer*. It threatens Will?" he asked.

"And Laurea!"

"Laurea is the other world?"

"Laurea is the Forest! Fardoor is the Land, the Sky, and the Water!"

"Is Fardoor on another planet?"

At this, the fairies seemed stumped. They clearly did not know what he meant and shot quizzical looks amongst themselves before turning back to him. "Save Laurea!" they cried together.

"And Will!" added one.

"And Will!" the rest cried.

Rebecca stepped forward, having almost come to grips with the strange situation herself. "What are we supposed to do?"

All five zoomed right up to her face, startling her. "Find the Forest King!" they said. "And stop the Destroyer!"

"Yeah, we got that part," Thomas muttered.

The fairies gave each other frightened looks as the gentle breeze again swept through the cave.

"Hurry, time is passing!" one said. Then all five flew over to an apple that had fallen on the ground and each grabbed a hold of part of the stem. Together they lifted it up and carried it to the children.

Thomas and Rebecca looked at the perfect yellow apple hanging in mid-air, and then at each other. Both shared the same mixture of worry and excitement, and it showed on their faces. Thomas was the first to make a decision. He reached out and grabbed the apple, at which the fairies immediately let go. Staring at it for only a moment, he took a large bite and then handed it to Rebecca.

"Mmm, that's actually really good!" he said, marvelling at its sweet taste.

Rebecca shrugged her shoulders and bit into it. "Here I go again," she said.

CHAPTER THREE

"Not really that different, is it?"

They were now in the other meadow, having touched the tree and been transported by the extraordinary light that invariably ensued.

"What?" asked Rebecca.

"Don't get me wrong – it's pretty, of course, just kind of the same as what we already have back home."

"What were you expecting, Thomas?"

"Oh, I don't know. Maybe a purple sky and orange grass?" he said thoughtfully.

"Well it still may be Earth, after all."

He raised an eyebrow at her. It was a useful look that annoyed his sister, so he did it often. Rebecca wished she could do the same but her eyebrows would go only go up as a pair, giving her a surprised look – not what she wanted to achieve.

"Rebecca, those were fairies we just saw back there! I mean c'mon – *fairies*!"

"They called themselves sprites," she corrected.

"Fairies, sprites - whatever. You get the point." He paused. "I'd just like to say that it was pretty rotten of them not to come with us. Or at least send one of them."

"I know, but they seemed pretty insistent that they ha.. with the tree. At any rate, we should keep looking for more."

"Agreed."

It was warm out, and the sun shone low in the clear sky. Judging by the multitude of cottony seeds lifted up by an easy wind, Thomas felt it was probably late summer wherever they were. Back home, of course, the summer had only just begun.

Despite their seemingly normal surroundings and his casual demeanour, his heart was pounding with excitement. The whole thing was almost too much to believe. The two of them were still standing by the tree, but now Thomas felt the urge to express what he was feeling.

"*Whoohooooooooo!*" he whooped, rushing into the field.

Rebecca couldn't help but grin herself. "See," she said "it really does exist."

"It sure does! *Whoohoooooooo!*"

"Don't go too far! In fact, come back here!"

"Hmmm, I think we should also take an apple from this tree," she said to herself. She searched the ground for one of the red apples she had previously seen to add to the yellow one still in her hand. Thomas came running back, many of the fluffy seeds clinging to his messy brown hair and clothes.

"Thppt," he said while trying to remove one from his tongue. "Is this what it was like when you were here before?" he asked.

"There weren't all the seeds in the air, but other than that, yes." She bent over and picked up a red apple from the ground, then dropped it in the bag of food.

"So it was around late summer?"

She frowned. "It's hard to tell – I wasn't here long, you know."

"And Will's been gone for almost an hour our time, right? How long has he been here, then?"

"Probably several days. When I was gone for five minutes before, he said it had been a few hours already when I showed up. Oh, I hope he isn't hurt!"

"Those 'sprites' seemed to think he was in danger. Okay," he decided "we're on a mission to find Will, so we should get going."

Thomas started to walk but stopped, realizing that there was no clear path into the forest that encircled them. "Which way?"

"Last time I saw him he was headed into the forest over there," she said, pointing to a spot on the far side of the meadow. "Let's go."

He nodded, and both started walking in that direction.

"It looks like the sun is going to set soon," he observed. "You still got the flashlight?"

"It's in the food bag. Will will be happy to see we've brought food!" she said, adding "I hope he's nearby."

"Well the sprites said both he and the forest are in danger, so he's probably in the forest, right?"

"I hope so."

"Maybe the Destroyer is a forest fire," he suggested. "In which case, how do they think we can defeat it?"

"Let's just focus on finding Will."

They had reached the meadow's edge and were about to enter the forest. Rebecca looked back at the unassuming apple tree. "Hold on, Thomas. Perhaps Will couldn't find his way back here, since there's no path. We need to make sure *we* remember how to get back."

"Good idea, sis. But how…" Thomas put one hand on his hip and rubbed his chin with the other. "Aha! We could use the bread from the ham and cheese sandwich to make a breadcrumb trail *à la* Hansel and Gretel. Who knows, we might even meet a mean old witch living in a gingerbread house!"

Rebecca giggled and gave him a slap on the shoulder. "Don't make fun – we might, you know!"

He rubbed his shoulder and pretended to look hurt. "Fine. You think of something."

"How about we just look for some unique signs?"

"Like trees!"

"Well maybe an *unusual* tree, yes."

At that, the two of them started into the forest.

"Actually, they all look pretty unusual," she remarked after only a few steps.

"Yeah. Definitely not Muskoka woods."

The apple trees hadn't looked like they belonged in Muskoka either, but at least they had looked *normal*. The ones in this forest were completely different. Most had fat trunks that twisted in several directions and gave off low, meandering branches that tangled with those of adjacent trees. Long, feathery moss hung from these limbs as a sort of screen to whatever lay behind. The thickest limbs gave off vertical branches of their own that went straight down and penetrated the forest floor: a sort of tree on crutches.

"I know it's not a purple sky and orange grass, but still..."

"Yeah," said Thomas. "Weird."

"Smells wonderful, though. Very sweet," she said as they continued walking.

Indeed, the fragrant combination of flowers and cinnamon permeated the air. Thomas shivered a bit. It was considerably cooler in the forest than outside in the meadow, and he found himself wishing he had worn long sleeves. On top of this, the sun was having difficulty penetrating through the thick canopy of leaves from its low angle in the sky.

"We're gonna need that flashlight in an hour," he remarked.

"I don't know if I want to be in this forest at night, Thomas."

"Me neither. We should start calling for him now. Wait - not in my ears this time okay?"

Rebecca smiled and yelled "WILL!"

"WILL!" he joined in. Some birds scattered out of the trees and a round bush shook as a small animal scurried away, but no voices responded. The children continued yelling anyway as they ventured further in.

For forty minutes they walked, occasionally calling for their cousin. In between, Rebecca would carefully make a note of things she felt would help identify their way back. "See those funny red mushrooms in a patch right there?" she'd say, or "Remember we turned right at a tree that looks like an old man." After a little while, Thomas remembered he had his pocketknife on him and started making arrows on the trunks to point the way back.

Despite the thick tangle of branches above them, the forest floor was fine to walk through as the trees were fairly spaced, and there wasn't much underbrush to negotiate. The steadily increasing darkness, however, made it seem as though the way ahead was narrowing.

Discouraged at the fruitless search, Rebecca stopped and sat on a rock. "This is pointless!" she said. "He could be anywhere! And we haven't seen anyone or *anything* that can help!"

"Yeah, I really thought we would have come across more of those sprites or something." Thomas's initial excitement had faded now that it seemed they were really just going for a jaunty walk in the forest - something they already did all the time back home. "Well what do you wanna do?"

"We can't give up, of course. How 'bout we just rest here for a minute?"

"Sure. And I say we eat the rest of those chocolate chip cookies for energy. He'll still have the sandwich and drink."

"Sounds good to me!" said Rebecca, and she fished them out. "Four cookies left. Thank you, Mom!"

"Speaking of which, do you think she's worried yet?"

"I don't think so - all the time we've spent here has probably amounted to about a minute back home."

Thomas munched on his cookies. "Let's have a look at that flashlight; we're gonna need it soon."

"You put new batteries in it, right?" Rebecca asked as she handed it over.

"Brand-new, so it should last a while." He turned it on and off a couple of times. *"Should you hold the torch or shall I?"* he said in his best English accent.

"You hold it."

"OK. Ready to go?"

"Ready."

The Day children stood up and continued their trek. Occasionally they yelled for Will, but mostly they just walked. Within fifteen minutes almost all light had receded and what they could see of the sky above was a dark pink; the sun had almost set. Thomas and Rebecca drew closer as it faded completely. An eerie quiet descended upon the forest, as if all sound had disappeared with the sun. Pale moonlight did its best to illuminate the still and now silent surroundings. Nevertheless, it had become considerably darker.

Thomas turned on the flashlight and pointed in the direction they had been walking. "Do you think we should keep going this way?" he asked.

"Doesn't matter. Thomas I want to go home." She grabbed his hand.

"Me too," he said but started walking ahead anyway. Rebecca followed and held his hand even tighter. He squeezed it back to show he felt just the same.

He liked to think himself brave, but inside Thomas had his doubts. The idea of a whole different world had thrilled him; it still did. But he'd never planned on walking through an unknown forest at night. Actually, he had half-expected to come across Will right away and *then* go exploring. One thing was certain though: he sure was glad he had his sister beside him. Rebecca felt the same about Thomas. Both of them knew they had to find Will before leaving.

Huddling close together, the Day children slowly made their way through the forest. Rebecca tried to take notice of markers they could use to find a way back, but no longer mentioned them aloud. Thomas continued marking the occasional tree with his pocketknife. He still had hope that they would come across a sprite or some other creature that could help them. Certainly neither of them knew what they were looking for while wandering aimlessly, but they continued searching nonetheless. Rebecca was the first to notice the clearing ahead of them.

"Look over there," she said "there's more light between those trees." She redirected his flashlight-hand to where she was looking.

"I see it," said Thomas. "It must be a clearing."

It was only about fifty feet away, so the children quickly ran over. Sure enough a small, circular space revealed itself. A smooth, brown, rectangular stone dominated the centre, and all the ground was covered in short grass that spread partly into the forest before stopping abruptly. Rebecca stepped into the open space, marvelling at how surprisingly soft the earth was.

Thomas joined her. "Finally, something interesting," he said.

"That stone looks like some kind of altar."

"Or maybe a meeting-table."

"Hmmm," he said, running his fingers over the smooth surface.

While Thomas inspected the stone, Rebecca looked up at the starry sky above them. She gasped and grabbed her brother. "Thomas, look!"

He quickly looked up. "Holy cow!"

Two moons. They were definitely on a different world.

"Where *are* we?" Rebecca wondered aloud. One moon was grey-white and about the same size as Earth's, while the other was slightly smaller and a little more blue. It lay close to, but not right beside the first.

"This is so cool!" said Thomas. "I wish I'd brought a camera!"

"Yeah, that would have been a good idea. Who knows what else we'll find."

They stared at the two moons for a little while longer, then Thomas remembered he hadn't finished looking at the altar stone. He resumed his inspection.

"Maybe we should stay here until morning," Rebecca proposed.

"I'm not tired yet, and we can always come back here. I say we keep moving, just let me finish looking at this thing."

"Okay," she agreed and turned her head up to the sky again.

The light of the two full moons made the clearing fairly bright, but from what he could see the altar did not appear to have any markings on it; it was just a smooth stone. Although it *was* a familiar shade of brown... Thomas took out the stone he had in his pocket and compared it to the large one in front of him. Both their color and texture matched. On a hunch, he bent down low to inspect the altar stone's base. "Take a look at this Rebecca," he said "there's some writing carved into it."

"Oooh - is it like the writing on our stones?" she asked, bending down to see for herself.

"It looks similar. And the stone itself matches the brown one we found in the cave." He handed one over so she could compare.

"You're right!"

"I guess this proves the Natives did know about this world, and even came here."

"So what you're saying is that maybe Will and I were right about that one tribe coming here instead of dying out?" She gave him a wry look.

"I *suppose*...okay, want to start moving again?" he asked quickly, changing the subject.

"Sure."

The children started into the forest, continuing on their original path. Finding the clearing had invigorated them, and now they journeyed with a renewed sense of purpose. Rebecca had begun humming softly when all of a sudden Thomas was yanked off the ground beside her. "Whoooa!" he exclaimed as a rope trap pulled him up and left him dangling by the feet above his sister.

"Get me down!" he hissed.

" HEL-" Rebecca started to yell.

"Shhh! Whoever set the trap may come, and that may not be someone we want to meet!"

"Well what am I supposed to do?"

Thomas thought for a moment and then checked his pants. Both pockets were empty. "Get my pocketknife - it fell out of my pocket. I'll cut myself down. And see if you can find the stone too - it also fell out."

"Okay," Rebecca whispered, and started searching the ground.

"Do you see it?"

"Not yet. Oh wait - there's the knife," she said, picking it up.

"Okay. Now I'm gonna drop the flashlight down to you, and then you throw me the knife."

"Just a sec." She put down the food bag and pocketknife so she could use both hands to catch the flashlight. "Hold on, I see the stone."

It had flown a bit further, and now she stepped over to pick it up.

Flppppt! Rebecca was caught in a similar trap – '*Like being shot from a slingshot!*' she thought – and was left dangling from the adjacent tree.

Thomas had a surprised look on his face. "Well that was unexpected," he said, trying to stifle a laugh. The sight of his sister

37

being flung upwards had been a shock, and now the sight of both of them upside down and twirling slightly was somewhat comical. "What do we do now?"

"Shhh!" she hushed. "I think someone's coming."

He stopped moving and listened hard. All was quiet.

"What did you hea-"

"Shhh!" she hushed again.

Only a minute ago he had been the one telling her to keep it down. He listened. Somewhere close by a twig broke, followed by soft steps that gradually got louder. Both children froze as something emerged from below.

Short and round was the best way to describe its body. And every part of its face looked like it was made for someone else: its eyes were too small, nose too long, mouth too wide. Wispy hair grew out of its head in patches with a substantial amount also protruding from its rather large ears. It wore a funny-looking garment not unlike a nightgown, with the exposed area being covered in rough, wrinkly, grey skin.

Humming to itself, the creature waddled on its broad, bare feet over to the bag of food. It picked the bag up with its stubby fingers and started rummaging. "Hmmm!" it said, taking out the ham and cheese sandwich. It carefully unwrapped an edge and sniffed it several times. It then took a small bite and chewed it far too slowly in its gigantic mouth. Deciding it was safe to eat, the creature engulfed the rest of the sandwich whole and swallowed. The children remained quiet through all of this, but Rebecca was considering asking for help. Thomas debated whether to throw the flashlight at it. They both decided to watch a bit longer.

The creature now noticed the pocketknife and picked it up. It turned the unopened knife over several times, and sniffed it twice before dropping it in an unseen pocket. Returning to the bag of food, it took out the red apple and inspected it very closely, once again sniffing it with its long nose. Something dawned on the creature, and an enormous grin threatened to split its face in half. The red apple was carefully replaced into the bag and the pale yellow one removed. This apple was eyed suspiciously. The red apple had been whole, the children having picked it up on their arrival in this world. The yellow apple, however, was the one that brought them here and had two bites out of it as a testament.

Thomas decided to speak before the creature made off with their things. "Hey you!" he cried. "That's our stuff!"

The creature looked up. Its tiny eyes widened. "Human children! Oh my, my!" it said.

Rebecca decided to take over from her less diplomatic brother. "Can you help us down, please?" she inquired.

"Oh yes, yes. Jorka help human children down," it replied. The creature made no movement, however, other than to scratch its head.

"The thing in your pocket," said Rebecca. "Pass it up!"

"Oh yes, yes," it repeated, then reached in its pocket and pulled out Thomas's knife. With the blade folded in the creature clearly did not know what it was, but rather sniffed it again before tossing it up to her.

"Thanks."

Rebecca set to work on cutting herself free. For his own part, Thomas had observed the whole exchange in silent wonderment. It *looked* like Rebecca was conversing with the creature. But when it spoke, all he heard was stuff like *"Gorgobs slat plargs,"* and similar gibberish.

"Rebecca!" he whispered. "You understand that thing?"

"Don't you? It's speaking English," she whispered back.

"More like 'crazy-forest-creature-from-another-world' talk. I couldn't understand a word!"

"Well that makes no sense. How come I can understand it?"

Although they were whispering, the creature had overheard their entire conversation -not surprising at all considering the size of its ears. "It must eat fruit," the creature said. 'It' clearly referred to Thomas.

Rebecca stopped cutting and shook her head. "The apple? We both had a bite."

Now the creature shook its head. "The fruit!" it said, pulling out the red apple.

"Ohhh," said Rebecca. The creature was right. Only she had

eaten the red apple - when she returned home after her first visit here with Will.

"What is it?" asked Thomas.

Rebecca shushed him. "The apple helps me understand you?" she asked it.

"The Fruit of Laurea," the creature solemnly stated. "All who eats it understands."

"Hmmm." She returned to cutting the rope and said to Thomas, "The red apple makes you understand its language, I guess. I ate some the first time I was here."

"Well give me some, then!"

"Wait till you're on the ground!" and with that, the rope holding up Rebecca split and she went crashing down. "Aaaah!"

The creature took one step and caught her.

"Thanks," she said, dismounting. "I really should have thought that through better!"

It nodded slightly. Rebecca closed the knife and threw it up to Thomas. He managed to hold on to the rope while cutting it, so that he could drop down feet-first.

"Okay," he said "let's see that apple."

Rebecca reached tentatively for the bag in the creature's hand. To her relief, it was happily relinquished. "Thank you," she said, and the creature gave another small nod.

Their food bag now only contained the two apples and the drink - a can of grape pop.

"I hope it enjoyed Will's sandwich," he muttered.

Rebecca handed him the red apple.

"Here goes nothing!" said Thomas.

"Gragor korpug!" said the creature.

He bit into it, once again delighting in the apples' taste. This one was tarter than those of the cave, but just as delicious. He would've eaten the whole thing, except the creature interrupted after the first bite.

"Jorka has some fruit?" it inquired.

"I understand you!" exclaimed Thomas. "Well, except for the Jorka part."

40

"I think that's its name Thomas," said Rebecca. "Is that your name - Jorka?" she asked.

The creature smiled and nodded. "I Jorka, you human children."

"That's right. I'm Rebecca, and this is my brother Thomas."

"And this *my* brother..." It looked around and frowned. "I Jorka," it repeated.

"Incredible," said Thomas. "I can see that it - *Jorka* - is not speaking English, but I still understand him, uh - it."

"Yes, yes - Jorka understands you, you understands Jorka." It gave a pleading look. "Jorka has some fruit?"

"Sure, *Jorka*." She gave a hand-it-over look to her brother, which he did.

It/he (both children had decided it was a 'he') excitedly took the red apple and opened wide. Rebecca thought he was about to engulf the whole thing as he did with the sandwich, but instead he took a small bite to match Thomas's and handed it back. He chewed as best he could with that enormous grin of his, beady eyes happily darting between his two companions. It was an amusing sight that abruptly ended when he began walking again in his original direction.

The children looked at each other, unsure if they should follow. After a few steps though, Jorka turned around and motioned for them to start moving.

"Come, come," he said "human children follow me. Not safe at night anymore."

Thomas and Rebecca caught up and started walking on either side of the fat creature. Jorka put his arms around them, locking them in place.

"We're looking for the Forest King," said Thomas. "Can you take us to him?"

"Yes, yes, in morning. Not safe at night anymore. Shadows try to trap Jorka, but may be happy with human children."

He wasn't quite sure how to reply to this last part so Rebecca spoke up instead.

"Well actually, we're trying to find our friend Will. Have you seen him?"

Jorka looked confused, so she added, "Another human child.

Have you seen another human child?"

"Oh no, no," said Jorka. *"Rebecca* and *Thomas"* - he looked proud to say their names – "are first human children in many years."

"Hmmm," she said "I guess he didn't come this way."

Thomas leaned forward so he could see his sister and talk around Jorka's considerable belly while they walked. Rebecca did the same.

"Maybe these 'Shadows' caught Will," he suggested.

"I don't even want to think about that."

Jorka, of course, overheard. "Shadows try to catch *Jorka,*" he corrected.

"Why?"

"Shadows can't find Forest King, but Jorka knows where to find him!" he said proudly.

"Why are we even afraid of these 'Shadows' when all they've got are stupid rope traps?"

Jorka looked hurt. "Rope traps are for Jorka to catch Shadows!"

"Oh, uh – sorry," said Thomas. Rebecca gave him a stern look. "Sorry!" he mouthed at her, and then stood up properly so he couldn't see his sister anymore.

"Tell us more, Jorka," she said as brightly as possible.

He looked grave. "Shadows use bad magic. But Shadows can't catch Jorka because Forest King hides Jorka's home for him!" His smile returned.

"What do they look like?" asked Thomas.

"Jorka never sees one. Bad, nasty Shadows!"

Throughout the conversation, Rebecca had neglected to keep track of their surroundings as they walked. And now they stopped in an area of the forest that looked the same as the rest. Thomas hadn't thought of using the flashlight, as Jorka seemed sure of where to go in the dim light. Since they stopped, however, he decided to turn it on to check out where they were.

Jorka immediately reacted to the bright flashlight. "Turn off bad light! Shadows will see!" he exclaimed while reaching for it.

Thomas complied and held it out of Jorka's reach, lest he throw it at a tree. This seemed to calm him. In any case, the quick light hadn't revealed any sort of dwelling.

Jorka turned his attention to the two trees in front of them and closed his eyes. One hand was raised before him. Then to the children's astonishment, a soft green glow shot out of the extended hand and circled the trees - which promptly dissolved to reveal a small thatched-roof house! Jorka opened his tiny eyes and grinned.

"The Forest King shows Jorka how to hide his home from Shadows!"

"Was that *magic* we just saw?" Rebecca asked no one in particular.

"Incredible!" said Thomas. "You'll have to show me that trick sometime!"

Jorka smiled wider, obviously pleased with himself. He opened the small door (a perfect size if homes were made with children in mind) and ushered them inside.

The first thing Thomas noticed was the wonderful aroma of some sort of stew cooking over a fire in the corner. "Mmmm," he said "what's for dinner? I'm *starving*!"

"Thomas!" Rebecca scolded under her breath. "What a...um, lovely home you have, Jorka," she said.

It certainly was interesting. They had entered a circular room with wooden walls and low ceilings. Scattered all about the room were many different cabinets, shelves, countertops, and tables. Scattered all over these was an incredible array of pots, pans, rocks, figurines, loose paper, and other assorted items. Apparently, Jorka liked collecting things. The floor itself was devoid of any clutter, reminding Rebecca of their dad's favorite quote when their rooms got messy: *'The floor is for walking on.'*

Jorka insisted on giving them a full tour before anything else. As there was only one other room, this did not take long. He showed them his tiny bedroom, which – like the first room – had walls with many small windows of every odd shape and color. It seemed the windows were cut out to accommodate whatever irregular panes of glass could be found.

"Where does he go to the bathroom?" Thomas mumbled when it became clear the tour was over.

Jorka took them back to the first room, which seemed to double as both a kitchen and living area. "Rebecca and Thomas want stew?" he asked.

"Yes please!"

He grinned and motioned for them to sit by the fireplace, then searched the clutter for three sets of bowls and spoons, and a serving ladle. Jorka daintily portioned out their meals, clearly delighted at having guests.

The children eagerly ate the stew. Whatever was in it, it tasted good. Jorka sat in between them with his happy grin and gladly served them more when their bowls were empty.

"So Jorka," Thomas ventured after finishing his second helping "who is this Forest King, and how do we find him?"

"Oh yes, yes. Forest King is King of Forest. Forest King does good magic and is very kind to Jorka. Helps Jorka hide home from Shadows!"

"Do you think he'll help us?"

"Oh yes, yes – Forest King helps Rebecca and Thomas. Rebecca and Thomas are Jorka's *friends*." He gave them a big squeeze to emphasize the point.

Rebecca popped herself out of his arm and patted down her hair. "Well that's some good news. So he'll know where Will is, and then we can get out of here."

"Or maybe Will's already with him!" offered Thomas.

"Great!" she said. "So let's go see him!" She looked at Jorka, who was listening intently.

"Oh no, no. Must wait for morning. Only safe during day now!" He trembled a bit. "Maybe not safe during day anymore!" he said in a hushed voice.

Rebecca flashed her brother a worried look. Thomas just raised his eyebrow. Truth be told, he found Jorka's ominous warnings a bit amusing. At any rate, their new friend's enormous grin returned same as before as he exclaimed, "Rebecca and Thomas sleep here and Jorka will take them to Forest King in morning!"

The matter seemed to be settled, so Rebecca helped clear the dishes. There didn't appear to be a sink anywhere, but Jorka motioned for her to put them down on some counter space he had cleared off. He then grabbed a small, woven satchel from one of the cupboards and sprinkled a bit of powder from it on each dish. *Poof!* Any remnants of food disappeared in a cloud of orange smoke.

"My mom would love to get some of that!" said Rebecca.

With the dishes done, Jorka turned himself to the matter of their sleeping arrangements.

"Rebecca and Thomas sleep *here*," he said, motioning to the small amount of space by the fireplace.

The bare wooden ground didn't look very comfortable to the children.

"Um…okay," said Thomas. "Do you have any blankets?"

"Rebecca and Thomas get cozy bed," was his reply.

Jorka began rummaging through the knick-knack-laden cupboards and counters, humming to himself while the confused children looked on. Suddenly, he saw what he was looking for at the bottom of a particularly cluttered pile of glass jars, silver instruments, carved wood, and ragged paper: "A cozy bed!" he announced, then picked up most of the pile in one swoop and perched it precariously on an adjacent mountain of curious junk. A small purple box was left on the table. Jorka brought it over to the children, pulled out a tiny handful of hay and carefully placed it on the ground. He turned the box upside-down and a miniature blanket fluttered down onto the hay. Jorka grinned, and then went back to rummaging through the cupboards.

"He's nuts," Thomas decided.

Rebecca shrugged. "It does look cozy!" she joked.

Jorka came back with the same small satchel he'd previously used with the dishes, then pinched a bit of the powder and sprinkled it on the hay. "A cozy bed!" he said for the third time.

The pile started to grow as if hay was being added from beneath it. More and more blanket pushed up through the centre. It happened slowly at first, so that the children weren't really sure if they were seeing it right. But then it picked up speed, and in less than fifteen seconds a pile of hay and blankets big enough for one person lay on the ground in front of them.

"Cool!" said Thomas, while his sister felt the soft bed.

Jorka was less pleased. "Hmmph!" he said and sprinkled a bit more of the powder on it. Rebecca jumped back as it suddenly expanded so that it could comfortably sleep two.

"Thank you, Jorka," she said.

"Yeah, thanks!" agreed Thomas as he jumped on it. "I guess we're sharing a bed tonight, sis!"

"Just keep to your side. And take off your shoes."

"Goodnight, Rebecca and Thomas!" said Jorka.

"Goodnight Jorka!" they repeated in unison.

Jorka turned around and walked to his room, careful not to knock over any of the tables along the way. He put the satchel back in the cupboard just before leaving them.

"I'd love to try using some of that!" said Thomas. Both of them were now in the bed with their backs to each other. Sharing a bed was something they were often made to do when visiting relatives; it was never a pleasant experience for either of them.

"What, the magic powder?" asked Rebecca. "I saw him use it to clean the dishes earlier. Who knows what it can do!"

Light from the dying fire danced across the funny room, casting bizarre shadows on the walls. Rebecca pulled the blanket tighter. "What do you think about Jorka?" she asked.

"Well it's a good thing we ran into him, but he sure is strange! This whole place is strange!"

"Yeah..." she agreed.

"I wonder..."

"What?"

"Well, if that apple, excuse me – *Fruit of Laurea* – can make us understand Jorka, then why does he talk so funny? I mean, shouldn't it sound like proper English to us?"

"Hmmm. Maybe he's not speaking his own language with proper grammar and stuff," she suggested.

"I never thought of that."

The children went silent, and listened to the crackling fire. After a few moments the faint sounds of snoring could be heard from the next room. Rebecca was getting a bit sleepy. She tried closing her eyes.

Thomas rolled over and tapped her on the back. "What do you think Mom and Dad are up to?"

"I don't know. It's probably only been a few minutes since we left," she said without opening them back up.

"Oh yeah." He rolled back over. More silence. "I hope we find Will tomorrow," he said through a big yawn. "Then we can all explore this place together."

"I hope so too."

Thomas closed his eyes, and both children fell fast asleep.

CHAPTER FOUR

Something startled Thomas awake. He remembered a large crash in his dream, but whether it had actually happened was unclear.

"Rebecca!" he whispered "Did you hear that?" Her soft and slow breathing suggested she was still asleep. Jorka's snoring could also still be heard. He wondered for how long they'd been sleeping. Judging by the scattered glowing embers in the fireplace, he guessed about two hours.

It was very dark in the room (*Even with two moons overhead!*) and Thomas debated whether to get up. He listened intently but heard nothing out of the ordinary. "Must've been my dream," he determined, and closed his eyes again. The rush of being startled awake kept his heart pounding though, and he found himself still awake after several minutes. Through his shut eyes, he sensed that the room had become a bit brighter. Opening them, he saw a dim blue light bathing the surroundings and casting no shadows.

'It can't be dawn already,' he thought. Although really, he realized, it could – they had no idea how long night lasted in this place.

The blue light increased. It seemed to be coming from all around them. Thomas decided to check it out, but not to wake his blissfully unaware sister. *'She'd probably tell me to go back to sleep!'*

He quietly got up, slipped on his shoes, and tiptoed to the door. Getting there was like going through an obstacle course, but he managed not to knock anything over. Although Rebecca did stir a bit when the door was opened, she didn't get up. He stepped outside into the dark forest, now softly lit by the same blue light. He gently shut the door behind him so as not to wake Rebecca. A soft little 'Pop!' was heard just as it closed – either from the door itself or from the entire house as it suddenly disappeared.

"What the - ?!" exclaimed Thomas. The forest now surrounded him completely. The same two trees they had seen upon arriving to this area once again occupied the space where Jorka's home had been. *'It's an illusion,'* he thought and tried feeling for the sturdy wall he knew was there. Except it wasn't. The house was gone, the trees were real, and Thomas found he could walk right between them.

"Rebecca! Jorka!" he yelled, close to tears at his own stupidity. "Let me in, I'm outside!"

The blue glow began rapidly increasing, now accompanied by a high-pitched screeching noise that also gained intensity.

"REBECCA!" he yelled again, covering his ears. It was getting so bright he couldn't see. And the noise was unbearable. He doubled over in pain as it drilled through his skull. Panic set in. Just when he thought he might collapse, a hand reached out from behind and yanked him back in the house. It was Rebecca, and Jorka was with her. Blue light poured through every window. The noise had stopped, leaving only deafening silence in its place. After a few seconds, the light disappeared too. His unadjusted eyes could no longer see Rebecca and Jorka, but he sensed their presence.

"What were you doing out there?" asked his sister.

"I, I thought I heard something. I didn't want to wake you." His head hurt. "What *was* that?" he asked.

Jorka looked very upset. "That was Shadows! They almost catch you! Now they know Jorka's home nearby, maybe find it soon!"

"Apologize!" Rebecca whispered and pinched his arm.

"I'm sorry Jorka."

"Jorka never told you not go outside. Jorka sorry too."

Rebecca looked at their strange new friend. "What now?" she asked.

"Now Jorka sleep in this room with human children tonight, and ask Forest King for help tomorrow." With that, he turned around to get the bed from his room.

"Wait," said Thomas "what was that horrible noise?"

"I didn't hear a noise," said Rebecca.

"Just now, when I was outside with all that blue light. You did see the blue light, right?"

"Yes we saw the light," she said "but there was no noise. Wait - is that why you looked like you were in pain?"

He wondered what was wrong with him. *Why hadn't they heard that awful sound?* "Yeah, there was a really loud screeching noise. I thought my head was going to explode!"

"Any ideas Jorka?" asked Rebecca. He shook his head 'No'.

"Well are you okay now?"

"Yeah, I'm okay."

Actually, he was far from 'okay'. His heart was pounding, ears ringing, head throbbing, and he couldn't shake the awful feeling that he had only narrowly missed meeting something very bad.

"I just need to get some more sleep," he said.

Jorka offered to sprinkle some powder from the woven satchel on him, saying it would help him rest. Thomas politely declined – there was no way he would let any of that crazy stuff touch him! So instead Jorka collected the mattress from his room and plopped it right down in front of the entrance, after moving some of the tables out of the way.

Rebecca and Thomas climbed back on their pile of hay. Looking at her face, Thomas could see that his sister was enduring a magnificent struggle between anger and worry for him. All she said before turning her back was "Goodnight." Anger had won.

"'Night," he replied.

* * * *

Although his mind had a lot to think about, Thomas felt totally drained by the whole experience and was able to fall asleep right away. He awoke the next morning to a sunlit room and the excited whispers of Jorka.

"Ooooh! A yellow fruit…of Laurea?"

Rebecca whispered back in much quieter tones. "Yes, well this one came from our world, but brought us to yours."

"Ooooh!" he repeated, barely whispering now.

"Shhh! Jorka, he's still sleeping!"

Thomas sat up. "What's going on?" he inquired.

Jorka and his sister were sitting at one of the tables, which had been partially cleared. Another uncertain mountain of odd items stood on a nearby counter. On display in front of them were the remaining contents of their plastic bag: the flashlight, pop, and the two partially-eaten apples.

"I'm just showing him our stuff. Did you sleep alright?"

"Yeah, you?"

"Fine except both of you were snoring for a bit."

Rebecca and Jorka were smiling at him. Last night's events seemed a mile away in the sunny environment.

"Thomas hungry?" Jorka asked.

"Sure. What's for breakfast?"

"Oh yes, yes. Get some breakfast." He got up and started looking for a bowl. Thomas sat down at the table.

"We already ate," explained Rebecca.

Jorka came back and set a bowl full of what looked like porridge in front of Thomas. He looked at his sister. "Is it…?"

"Porridge," she affirmed.

He dug in. "Mmmm - with brown sugar!"

Jorka then gave Thomas a glass and poured what looked like orange juice in it. Again, he looked at his sister.

"Definitely not orange juice," she said.

"You're fooling!" He took a large gulp and promptly spat it back in the cup. "Uggh! It tastes like pickles and spinach!"

She laughed. "I told you!"

"Blech!" he exclaimed, taking large bites of oatmeal to cover the taste. "How about some of that grape pop, then?"

"Good idea," she agreed. "We should let Jorka try some too. Do you have any more cups?"

"Oh yes, yes." Jorka got up again and came back with three squat glasses. He looked very happy to be a part of whatever they were doing.

Rebecca opened the can and poured equal amounts of the fizzy purple drink in each glass. The children eagerly drank theirs down. Jorka was more cautious with his - first sniffing it a bit, then taking a small sip. His face contorted as he swallowed it.

"What's the matter Jorka? You don't like it?" asked Rebecca.

He looked embarrassed. "Oh no, no. Jorka like Rebecca and Thomas purple drink *very much*. Maybe...seasoning?" he tentatively offered.

Jorka pinched a bit of powder from the satchel and sprinkled it in the glass. Immediately, the grape pop turned the consistency and orange color of the disgusting drink he had been serving. He gulped it down. "Mmmm!" he said, licking his fat lips.

"What a waste," Thomas muttered.

"How does that stuff work, Jorka?" asked his sister.

Jorka scratched his head.

"I mean, how can it clean dishes, enlarge hay piles, and turn grape pop into...whatever that stuff is?"

He still looked confused.

"Maybe he just makes a wish in his head or something," suggested Thomas. "Can I try some?" Jorka looked hesitant. "Just a little bit, I promise."

"Okay." Their new friend handed over the satchel, but still looked wary.

"Thank you."

"What are you going to do?" asked Rebecca.

"Ummm...I'm gonna turn this porridge into scrambled eggs!"

Thomas squeezed a tiny bit of powder from the satchel. It tingled in his fingers. He then closed his eyes and thought hard about scrambled eggs while scattering the powder onto his remaining breakfast. He heard a little "Poof!"

"Well?"

"Open your eyes and see for yourself."

He opened one eye a crack and peered out. Something had changed. He opened both eyes wide and looked in his bowl.

"Hey, where's my porridge?"

Rebecca burst out laughing. "It cleaned your bowl for you!"

Jorka grinned widely to see her laughing so hard. Thomas slumped back in his chair. "Oh, I was sure that was gonna work," he said dejectedly. "Are you almost done?" he asked Rebecca, who was still laughing.

She sighed and wiped away a tear. "Yeah."

"Well, where does this stuff come from, anyway? No wait – let me guess. The Forest King?"

"Oh yes, yes. Forest King give Jorka present and show how to use."

"Maybe he'll show us how to use it too," said Rebecca. "Not that you need to have it explained, Thomas."

He stuck his tongue out at his sister.

"So what are we waiting for?" she said excitedly, rising from the table. "Let's go see the Forest King!"

"Good idea. Shall we go, Jorka?"

"Oh yes, yes. Jorka gets some food."

The children collected their things while their friend packed a small bag with some bread and cheese. He returned the mattress to his bedroom, but left the pile of hay as it was. All three met at the front entrance.

"Thanks for the accommodations Jorka," said Rebecca before opening the door.

"Yeah, thanks," agreed Thomas. "And I'm really sorry about what happened last night."

A rush of guilt filled him as the same scared expression momentarily flashed across Jorka's wrinkled face. His wide grin quickly returned, however. "Forest King will help!" he said.

With that, all three stepped outside. Thomas was the first one out, and he turned around to look at Jorka's home before the door was shut.

"Oh – now I understand," he said. Jorka appeared to be closing a door in the middle of the forest. Through it, he could clearly see the circular room they had just exited. On either side, however, were the two trees Thomas had assumed to be an illusion last night. Jorka closed the door, and a soft little 'pop' was heard as it disappeared. This was no illusion. This was real *magic*.

"I suppose that's why you couldn't get back in last night," suggested Rebecca as they started walking.

"Yeah, it definitely would've been good to know about that ahead of time! It's a good thing you woke up, or I would've never gotten back in." He shuddered on remembering the awful, high-pitched sound.

CHAPTER FIVE

The forest in the morning was a much friendlier place. Sunlight poured through the canopy of leaves from above, and a soft breeze carried more cottony seeds in the air. Once again, birds chirped in the strange, twisty trees that were starting to look less unusual to the Day children. The gentle fragrance of flowers and cinnamon greeted them just as it had when they'd first entered the forest the day before.

"How far is it to the Forest King?" inquired Thomas after only going a short distance.

"Not far."

"Is there a Forest *Queen*?" asked Rebecca.

"Oh yes, yes. Forest *Queen* also help Jorka. Forest Queen very wise."

"Good. I'd hate to think only men have the power around here."

"For all we know, the Destroyer could be a woman," said Thomas. "It could even be a twelve year-old girl!" He gave her a serious look. "Remember, Grandpa always said we *destroy* a bit of the environment every time we litter in the forest."

"Oh yeah, well do you remember him saying anything about vanishing homes on worlds with two moons?"

"Hmmm. He *might* have. I wasn't always listening carefully."

The three of them continued walking while the Day children asked questions about the Forest King and Queen. "What do they look like?" wondered Thomas. "How long have you known them?" asked Rebecca. Jorka's answers were scarcely helpful. He mostly just responded with assertions that the Forest King and Queen were good friends to him, and "- help Jorka very much." When it became clear they weren't going to get any useful information out of him, Rebecca turned to looking for some of the markings they'd made note of previously; at some point they would be needed to get back to the meadow. Thomas busied himself with his pocketknife.

Soon they came across the place where Jorka's carefully laid rope traps had left them swinging upside down from the trees. Their jolly friend insisted on resetting them, *"To catch Shadows."*

"I don't see the point," muttered Thomas. "I don't think these would've trapped whatever was coming after me last night!"

The frayed rope ends could be seen dangling high up. Only a small portion of each was left poking out of the branches, as the children had cut a good chunk off (including the noose) in order to get down.

"How can we help, Jorka?" asked Thomas.

"Set trap for Shadows!"

"Okay..."

Jorka found the hidden ends tied down at the ground and began pulling the rest of the two ropes out of the trees. Rebecca located the cut ends and brought them over. Jorka, however, started retying one of the loops used to grab the person's ankle before yanking him upside-down.

"I wonder why he doesn't just magically reseal these on, using some of his powder?" she wondered out loud.

"Good question."

Jorka didn't answer, but continued to busy himself tying one end, and then the other. He hummed a pleasant tune while he worked, and never once stopped smiling.

"Why is he always grinning like that?" Thomas whispered to his sister.

"I think it's because he's happy," she whispered back, then went up and tapped Jorka on the shoulder, asking, "How can we help with these rope traps?"

His face brightened. "To catch Shadows!" he exclaimed. First the second loop was finished, and then he showed the children how to set the trap. This involved securing the rope to the ground before winding it taut through some tree branches.

Thomas was about to volunteer to climb the tree, when all of a sudden Jorka sped up it himself. Their squat friend was surprisingly nimble! After watching the placement of the first trap, he set the second one under Jorka's guidance.

"I'm gonna set one on Will once we get back home!" he said excitedly.

As a last step, the three of them rearranged the leaves on the ground to hide the traps. Then, they were ready to resume their walking.

Once more, Rebecca looked for the markings they had left behind. *'We should definitely see them now since this is before we met Jorka,'* she thought. And indeed, she did spy one of Thomas's carved arrows shortly thereafter.

"Aha! Look Thomas – one of our markings!" She pointed triumphantly to a tree where some of the rough bark had been removed, and a shoddy arrow hastily inscribed.

"Oh yeah! Maybe we should follow it a bit and make sure we left a good path." He turned to Jorka. "Do you mind if we take a little detour on the way to the Forest King?"

"Jorka doesn't mind. Rebecca and Thomas take detour!"

"Okay, let's see," said Rebecca. "This arrow points left - I wish I knew what compass direction that is - so off we go. Everyone look for another arrow!"

The three companions turned left. Jorka took this opportunity to open up the dark bread and cheese he'd brought. He offered the first bit to Thomas. Thomas, for his part, was more wary after the 'orange juice incident'. He cautiously nibbled a corner, and then engulfed the rest after finding it to be similar to rye and cheddar.

"Over there," he said with his mouth full.

"What? I couldn't understand what you said!" Rebecca was

about to call him a pig for shoving so much food in his mouth at once, but noticed Jorka had done the same thing. Instead she patiently waited for her brother to swallow.

"I said, *over there!* I see another arrow." He gestured to a nearby tree.

"Oh – good eye!" she said, walking over to it. "Hmmm." She traced the arrow with her fingers and then looked at her brother dejectedly. "You're not going to like this!"

"What? What is it?"

"This arrow tells us to go back the way we just came!"

Sure enough, the tree boasted a carved arrow that pointed to the right.

"We must have gotten so turned about last night, we made arrows all over the place!" She sat down with a new feeling of hopelessness. Sensing the children's concern, Jorka stopped grinning, but continued his loud chewing.

Thomas tried to comfort his sister. "Well it was a good plan, Rebecca," he said, sitting down beside her. "And maybe the rest of our path isn't so screwed up." He had an inspiration. "Plus, remember we're about to see the Forest King. He'll be able to help us back for sure!"

She brightened at this last suggestion. "You're right," she said "we probably don't even need our own path! Okay Jorka, no more delays! Let's go see the Forest King and Queen!"

The children leapt to their feet, expecting to set off walking again.

"Okay!" Jorka exclaimed, but made no move other than to rummage through the large pockets in his frock. (Although it looked like a nightgown, 'frock' seemed a more appropriate term as it was clearly daytime and he was still wearing it.)

"What are you looking for, Jorka?" asked Thomas.

"The key!" More rummaging. "Aaah!" He pulled out a small green gemstone, then turned around and pointed it at a large thicket of which the children had taken no notice.

"I guess that means we're already there," Rebecca muttered.

Thomas didn't respond, but rather watched in anticipation as

Jorka closed his eyes. Their new friend raised his arm as he had done the previous night when revealing his home, this time holding the gem in his closed hand. Shortly, a green glow leaked out through the cracks between his fingers. Even more remarkable, the thorny branches of the thicket bush began to move!

"Cool," said Thomas as they continued to rearrange themselves. The branches stopped moving once an opening large enough to crawl through had been revealed. Jorka put the gem back in his pocket and grinned.

"I suppose that's the door," said Rebecca. "Shall we go in?"

Thomas bowed his head and made a sweeping gesture with his hand. "Ladies first," he said.

Jorka, however, made the first move toward the opening. Just as he was about to enter it, several colorful 'butterflies' zoomed out and flew off in different directions.

"Oooh! More sprites!" said Rebecca before eagerly following Jorka. Thomas went in last, and was quite unprepared to find himself suddenly sliding downwards.

* * * *

"Wheee!"

Thomas slid down the twisty tunnel with its smooth floor and earthy walls. He barely registered the light behind him ceasing as the thicket branches moved to conceal the opening. Another light shone from below in the distance. This was the longest slide he had ever been on!

"Thomaaaaaaaas!"

He could hear Rebecca, but couldn't see her as she was already so far ahead and there seemed to be many turns. The light was getting significantly brighter though, so he reasoned they must be approaching the tunnel's end. He was right, as he soon heard Rebecca go "Ouch!" – presumably as she was thrown from its exit. *Plop!* A few seconds later Thomas was also ejected, landing right on his sister just as she was getting up.

"Get off me!" she exclaimed.

"Whoops! Sorry about that." He stood up and gave a hand to Rebecca, who was face down on the ground. "You okay?"

"I think so. Maybe warn us next time we're going to be hurtled downwards, okay Jorka?"

He gave a small nod and turned the children around. "Home of Forest King," he announced.

"Incredible," said Thomas as they took in their surroundings: an underground environment three times as big as the cave back home, and brimming with life. Soft, green grass lined the ground, and brown, earthy walls with reinforcing roots formed the dome. Many large trees like those of the forest above were scattered about, their thick, green foliage belying the fact there was no sunlight here. There was, however, a glow like that of the cave – only many times brighter. Some of it was coming from the inhabitants themselves: thousands of sprites that fluttered all around, popping in and out of holes in the dome much smaller than the one they had just come through.

"It's so pretty!" said Rebecca. Unlike the forest above, all the trees here boasted beautiful yellow and pink flowers. More were sprinkled in the grass below. She breathed in the wonderful fragrance.

"Look how different all the fairies, er sprites, are," said Thomas.

"Many different sprites in forest," agreed Jorka.

Indeed, they were all sorts of varying colors and sizes. One might have pink skin and multicolored wings, while the next could be entirely blue from head to toe. Most had variously shaped butterfly wings, but some resembled those of a dragonfly. The largest sprites were the size of a child's hand; the smallest, a fingertip. And all of them gave off a bit of light.

"I can't wait to meet the King and Queen!" said Rebecca, and then surveyed her appearance. "Oh – I'm a mess!" she exclaimed. Her fall to the ground had left her clothes covered in dirt. She tried brushing some of it off in a vain attempt at making herself more presentable.

"Uh, Rebecca?" Thomas pretended to brush some dirt off his cheek.

"It's all over my face too, isn't it?" She wiped her face with the still-dirty shirt, and then patted down her tangled brown hair. "It's no use," she decided.

"Well, I'm a bit of a mess myself, Rebecca. I'm sure they won't mind."

"Look," said Jorka. "Sprites come to greet Rebecca and Thomas!" He pointed above, where dozens of the tiniest white sprites were slowly descending upon them as if softly falling snowflakes. These 'snowflakes' stopped and hovered a few feet above their heads. The children craned their necks, watching and waiting for something to happen. And then something did: a shower of shimmering sparkles was released by the sprites. It fell upon the three companions and magically cleaned them top-to-bottom. Rebecca saw that the dirt was gone from her clothes.

"Amazing!" she said. "I feel like I've gone through the laundry!" She ran her fingers through her now-sleek hair.

Thomas reached up and felt his own head. The normally messy brown hair had been carefully combed and parted to one side. "How do I look?" he asked.

"Very respectable."

"How does *Jorka* look?" asked their friend.

The children assessed him. If there was a change, they couldn't find it: his head didn't have much hair to brush (not counting the hair coming out of his ears) and his brown frock had hid whatever dirt it may have had on it previously.

"You look great."

"Yeah, top-notch."

He gave a great big grin and thanked the sprites, which were now coming down for a proper greeting. These ones were very small, and all white. They looked like children.

Rather than stopping in front of them, the sprites hovered all around. Many took up spots on Thomas and Rebecca themselves, resting on their shoulders without saying anything.

Rebecca took the opportunity to speak. "Thank you, um…forest sprites," she said, aware that several of them were walking on her head. "I'm Rebecca and this is my brother Thomas. Jorka has brought us here to see the Forest King."

None of the sprites responded. One of them did fly right up to Thomas's nose and try to reach around either side with its outstretched arms. He made himself very cross-eyed trying to look at it. *'I hope it doesn't fly up my nose!'* he thought. It didn't, but rather sat upon the very tip and waved several of its friends over. Now five of the sprites examined his face. They were so tiny that Thomas squinted to see them better. One sprite promptly lifted his right eyelid. Others prodded his cheeks, tugged his ears and danced in his hair. Excited chattering seemed to be taking place amongst the sprites, although not a peep could be heard.

Thomas allowed this to occur without saying a word himself, for fear a sprite might zoom into his mouth if it opened. He did make a curious humming noise to let his sister know how uncomfortable he was.

Rebecca watched the show and tried not to laugh. Jorka made no attempt to communicate, and still had that stupid grin on his face. She cleared her throat and spoke again: "Can you please take us to the Forest King?"

The sprites she could see started clapping their tiny hands. Jorka clapped his as well. One of them flew up to her and began speaking rapidly, except it was more like the sprite was mouthing the words: she still couldn't hear a thing. It stopped talking and waited for her to respond.

"I'm sorry," she said "I can't hear what you're saying."

Over by Thomas, the sprites inspecting his face had all relocated on top of his head and were watching to see what would happen next. The sprite talking to Rebecca was clearly frustrated, a tiny flush of pink filling its cheeks. Suddenly it zoomed into Rebecca's right ear and started chattering again. Now she could definitely hear something: a high-pitched tinny sound like the ringing of a glockenspiel. "Ow!" she said.

The sprite flew out of her ear and waited for a response again, this time with crossed arms and silently tapping its foot in mid-air.

"I'm sorry, I still couldn't understand you," said Rebecca.

This was clearly not to the little sprite's liking. It threw its hands up in exasperation and zipped back into the crowd, who all seemed to be making fun of it.

"They're very small; they haven't found their voices yet," said someone from behind the nearest tree.

A head not unlike that of a garden gnome popped out from behind it. A second later the diminutive body followed. The sprites, all of whom had turned to the tree as soon as the gnome had spoken, flew off as a group. They danced in the air like real butterflies before settling on the far side. Thomas checked his body to make sure none of them were left sitting on him.

The tiny fellow walked towards them. "Those were our youngest sprites," he said. "Not very mature at all. They don't like me on account of my scolding them sometimes. Nice to see you again Jorka," he finished, stopping in front of them. Jorka smiled and gave a little bow.

The two-and-a-half foot gnome turned to the children, adjusting his blue vest and pointy red hat. "Welcome to the underground home of the Forest King and Queen," he announced. "M'name's Noggin. The wife and I tend the grounds here. She wanted to come greet you but she's busy sorting out, um…something. Hope you don't mind."

Thomas crouched a bit to get closer to the gnome's height. "Not at all," he said. "I'm Thomas, and this is my sister Rebecca."

"So nice to meet you," she said, copying the little bow Jorka had made.

"Rebecca and Thomas need help from Forest King."

"Yes I know," said Noggin. A tiny flash of concern appeared on his face as he gave his white beard a couple good tugs. "Okay then – follow me." He turned and started walking. They followed, Thomas and Rebecca still marvelling at the beauty of their surroundings and its wonderful glow.

As they walked, sprites continued to fly above them and through the trees. Most ignored the children, but some flew up close for a better look before flying off again. One even sat on Jorka's head, staring at Rebecca. He didn't seem to notice and she tried not to either.

"Hey Noggin," said Thomas "how come we didn't see any

sprites above ground?"

"Oh – they mostly stick to the trees. If you look really hard you might spot one on occasion." He pointed to the ceiling, where lots of bare roots were hanging down. "They don't need to come through the big entrances like you either. The sprites know the secrets of the trees of Laurea. They pop in and out of them as they please, and know exactly which ones lead here."

"Cool," said Thomas. "I'll look harder next time."

A few more steps and they had entered the edge of a large clearing marking the heart of the underground wood. A gurgling stream encircled it, and many of the sprites with dragonfly wings could be seen congregating around the water - some diving in and out of the stream, others skipping along its surface. Soft earth and green grass covered the rest of the space, as it did between the trees. A brown altar stone stood at the centre. The effect was very similar to the clearing they had stumbled upon above ground the night before. Although a noticeable difference was the two large, wood chairs on the side opposite them. It wasn't as if these chairs were *made* of wood – it was more like they had *grown* there. Sturdy roots anchored them to the ground, and little twigs and flowers served as decorations. They were obviously seats for the Forest King and Queen – who were nowhere to be found.

"Hmmm," said Noggin. He looked embarrassed. "Everyone should be here. I'll go see what the, um…hold up is. Please have a seat." He ran off into the trees again.

"I guess he means for us to sit in the grass," said Rebecca; there were no other chairs around. Both she and Jorka plopped down on the ground, while Thomas decided to inspect the altar.

"Thomas, come sit down!" she ordered.

"Hang on, I just want to see if it has the same writing on it as the brown one we saw last night." He bent down and traced his fingers over the bottom. "Yep, here it is." Satisfied with his discovery, Thomas joined Jorka and his sister sitting cross-legged on the soft grass. "I'd almost forgotten about the clearing we came across yesterday."

"Yeah, me too. We must have come very close to it when we

were walking here this morning."

"Jorka, do you know what the altar is for?"

As usual, Jorka had been eagerly watching their conversation, waiting to be spoken to. "Oh yes, yes," he said "for *spells and incantations*."

"Cool! What about the one we saw above ground – you have seen that one too, right?"

He nodded. "From when humans shared Forest of Laurea."

"Oh, more humans!" Rebecca said excitedly. "The Eechawey!"

"How long ago was that?" asked Thomas.

Jorka scratched his head and pondered. "Many, many years. Eight hundred."

"Eight hundred years ago!" both children exclaimed.

"Must've been a different Forest King," muttered Thomas.

"Oh no, no. *Same* Forest King."

"Eight hundred years and it's the same one?" he asked incredulously. "I can't wait to meet him."

There was still no sign of the King or Queen, however. Meanwhile, Rebecca noticed that more and more of the colorful sprites were hovering high above them. *"Waiting to see what happens, no doubt,"* she thought. She tapped Thomas on the shoulder.

"Yeah, I saw," he said.

"Many sprites come to see Rebecca and Thomas," observed Jorka.

As they watched, the sprites began descending with the slow movements of falling flower petals. Soon they were hovering all around again, this time keeping a respectful distance from the children.

"Oh, I wish Noggin had told us how to address the King and Queen!" Rebecca worried aloud. She had always been more concerned with social etiquette than Thomas.

"No time now," he said "I think I see them coming!"

He definitely saw Noggin approaching from the far side with another gnome Thomas presumed to be his wife. A little shorter and just as round, she looked like Noggin would if you shaved his beard and put him in a dress.

"I see them too!" said Rebecca as she stood up. "Everyone on their best behaviour!"

Thomas groaned as he and Jorka got to their feet. "Do you see the King and Queen yet?" he asked. Jorka nodded.

"Actually, no," said Rebecca, squinting her eyes. "I see two sprites with them – but if those are the King and Queen then they definitely need some chairs that fit!"

Two gnomes and two sprites crossed the stream and entered the clearing. Noggin gave the children an anxious smile. His wife was avoiding eye contact altogether. Something seemed amiss, and even Jorka sensed it: his ever-present grin had been replaced with a look of confusion. Thomas wanted to ask him what was wrong, but the party had almost approached the wood thrones; he decided to wait.

Noggin and his wife took a position to one side of the altar. Many more sprites descended all around, and the two that had accompanied the gnomes floated gently onto the thrones. Then something unexpected happened: their glow intensified magnificently. The children shielded their eyes until it dissipated, at which point they saw a beautiful man and woman sitting where the sprites had been.

"May I present King Irith and Queen Dalea of Laurea!" announced Noggin. He still looked anxious.

After hearing the King was over eight hundred years old, Thomas had been expecting a decrepit old man with a cane. Instead, here was a young King that looked no more than twenty-five, as did the Queen. They both had soft features and wore flowing robes of green and gold. Their hair was brown, their eyes a piercing green. Their skin too had a greenish tinge. Each wore a crown of golden petals on their heads, and neither had wings in their present form.

Unsure of what to do, Rebecca performed a little curtsey and Thomas did an awkward bow. Jorka just stood there looking confused. Rebecca had been counting on him to make the introductions, so she spoke up instead.

"Your Majesties, my name is Rebecca, and this is my brother Thomas," she said.

Thomas gave a little wave, "Hello."

Queen Dalea smiled but looked at them with sad eyes. King Irith was not smiling at all. "I will not help you," he said.

CHAPTER SIX

The children were stunned. Jorka was clearly surprised as well. "Forest King," he said "Rebecca and Thomas are Jorka's *friends*."

"Not mine!" he responded. The sprites, who had stirred a bit at the King's opening line, now twittered madly all around. Jorka looked hurt.

"*Irith*," said Queen Dalea softly, putting her hand on his shoulder. He continued anyhow.

"Jorka, you are my friend. But these human children cannot be trusted!" He stared at them. "Five years ago the girl came with another boy. She left him behind and he was taken by the Destroyer. Now the Destroyer threatens us all, and SHE IS TO BLAME!" He pointed a furious finger at Rebecca, who was close to tears.

None of what the King was saying made sense to her. Five years?! How could that possibly be true? A few minutes back home had meant a few hours here before. How could an hour back home mean five whole years had passed? Had Will been stuck in this world for *five years?*

The Queen still had a friendly look upon her face, and it gave Rebecca hope. "Please, Your Majesty," her voice trembled. "We found a cave with a tree; it brought us here. I wanted to go get my brother but our cousin Will insisted on staying. I shouldn't have left him, but I only went back for an hour!" Her voice strengthened. "When we returned to the cave, some sprites told us Will was in danger, and we came right here. They told us you could help us save him!"

The King was not amused by Rebecca's boldness. "It has been five years," he said sternly "and he cannot be saved."

"I was only gone an hour! I swear!"

"It's true," offered Thomas.

"FIVE YEARS HAVE PASSED!" the King roared, rising from his chair. He sat back down. "I know this cave of which you speak. Tell me, was it windy there?"

The children were frightened by the King's outburst, but he seemed to want an answer. Rebecca was bravely trying to hold back tears, so Thomas decided speak for her.

"Not initially, right Rebecca?" She nodded. "But then yes, it was very windy for a bit."

"Those are the Winds of Change," said the King. He looked satisfied. "They've slowed for now, but the stronger they are in *your* world, the faster time moves in *ours*. Five years have passed," he solemnly repeated. "There is nothing I can do for you or your cousin. The Destroyer has already caused much strife in Fardoor, and shortly he will come to this forest – the Forest of Laurea. I must prepare for our defence."

Queen Dalea spoke softly again. "Irith please help them. Maybe their cousin can be saved, and all of Fardoor as well."

"It's too late. They may seek him out at their own peril, but any power I give them will surely end up in the hands of the Destroyer." He looked at the children with stern eyes. "Follow the path of the larger moon if you wish to find your cousin. But be warned: you will probably die."

The children were quiet. They looked around for support, but found none. Both Noggin and his wife were avoiding eye contact, as was Queen Dalea now. Jorka still looked hurt, and none of the sprites had spoken a word. Clearly, this was not the Forest King they were used to.

Thomas thought he'd try one more time to explain. "Please –"

"That is all," interrupted King Irith. He waved his hand and the world around them dissolved. When it rematerialized, Jorka and the children found themselves in the forest above once more.

Rebecca let go of her restraint and the tears poured out. "How could he be so *awful* to us?" she cried. "We just wanted to find Will and *leave*!"

Thomas put an arm around his sister. "What a jerk," he said.

A few tears also ran out of Jorka's tiny eyes and down his wrinkled, grey cheeks. "Jorka thought Forest King help Rebecca and Thomas," he said to himself. "Oh no, no. Forest King mean today. Forest King not help at all!"

All three of them sat down. "Do you really think it's been five years?" asked Thomas.

He nodded. "Many years since last human child in Laurea."

"Does that mean he's seventeen now? I wonder if we'd even recognize him! Or maybe he hasn't aged – Jorka, do humans age in Fardoor?" Again he nodded.

Rebecca had stopped crying and was valiantly trying to regain composure. Trembling lips betrayed her, though. "Jorka," she asked "Did you *see* Will when he was here? I mean, five years ago, did you see him?"

"Oh yes, yes. Jorka met *Will* in forest. Jorka took Will to Jorka's home. Old home," he corrected himself.

"And what happened?" asked Thomas.

"Will upset because couldn't find Tree of Laurea. Will ate apple but couldn't find Tree again. Couldn't get home."

"And? Did you take him to see the Forest King?"

Jorka scratched his head. "Will not stay, Will went into forest and Jorka never see again."

"So he never made it back to the Tree..."

"...and sometime later he was taken," finished Rebecca. "That settles it," she decided. "We have to see if *we* can find the Tree again, and then we have to get help."

"I agree," said Thomas.

They both looked at Jorka, who still had a few tears running down his forlorn face. It was apparent he'd really felt stung by the actions of King Irith. Rebecca leaned over and wiped his cheek with her hand. "We need your help, Jorka," she said softly. "Will you help us?"

He brightened a bit. "Oh yes, yes. Jorka help *friends* Rebecca and Thomas."

"Great!" said Thomas, slapping him on the back. He smiled and then Jorka broke out into his usual grin.

Although their current situation was less than ideal, and the whole thing with Will was alarming, it felt like they had a renewed sense of purpose. And a plan – they were going to find the Tree of Laurea and they were going to get help. What kind of help, neither of them knew. Perhaps some sort of rescue team, with police and such. They had no idea what they were up against, but this didn't seem to matter. As long as they got back before those "Winds of Change" started up again.

"Okay," said Thomas "Can you take us to the Tree?"

Jorka scratched his head and then shook it 'no'.

"Um, why not?"

"Jorka doesn't know where Tree of Laurea is."

This was unexpected. "You have seen it though, haven't you Jorka?" asked Thomas.

"Oh yes, yes. Forest King showed Jorka many years ago."

"Well we're not going back to *him* for help!" said an exasperated Rebecca. "I guess that leaves the path we made last night. It seemed a bit mucked up this morning, but I bet most of it is okay if we can get past the last part."

"It's all we've got," her brother agreed. The children stood up, pulling Jorka to his feet as well.

Thomas looked at their current surroundings. "Do you recognize where we are, sis?"

"Hmmm. Oh look – there's that bush we went through to reach the Forest King!" They had rematerialized close to where they had been. "That means we're already close to the path. Both of those trees with arrows are nearby. The problem is, which one do we follow?"

"Let's just pick one," suggested Thomas.

"Okay, the first tree. 'Cause it seems like we'll be backtracking a bit if we follow the second one."

"Let's go."

The first arrow had directed them to the area with the secret underground entrance. They walked to the bush and continued past it. With each of them carefully noting each tree they passed, they shortly came across another with an arrow.

"Oh good!" said Rebecca. "It tells us to go left!"

"Why's that so great?"

"Because it's not telling us to go back the way we came!"

They turned left and kept a keen lookout for more arrows. It was now early afternoon and the sun was at its peak. Bright shafts of light pierced through the canopy of leaves, casting shadows on the forest floor.

"Look!" said Rebecca "There's the tree I said looks like a ballerina! That means we're going the right way!"

"Are you sure?"

"Pretty sure."

Thomas looked at the tree and thought he recognized it as one she had pointed out, but still didn't see how it represented a ballerina. Like the others in the forest, it had thick branches held up by their own struts that penetrated the ground. Two large branches emerged from either side of this particular tree and gently curved towards each other. They sort of looked like arms, he guessed. And this tree's trunk was more slender than most.

"If you're sure, but I still don't see a ballerina," he said.

"It's doing a plié," she announced matter-of-factly, and continued walking. Jorka looked as confused as ever, but followed anyway.

The children walked with their Fardoor companion in this way for over an hour, carefully taking note of the signs and markings they had left the day before. There were a couple more instances of arrows contradicting themselves, but both times they made a choice and kept moving - and both times they seemed to be right; it did not appear that the group was walking in circles. It did appear, however, that they were walking for too long. After almost two hours Thomas abruptly halted and sat down.

"What are you doing?" asked his sister "We don't need to rest yet!"

"No, but we need to figure out what's going on. I really think we should've come across the Tree by now."

"Well, we had a couple detours," she explained. Inside though, she'd had the same nagging feeling.

"I know that. But we still should've come across it. We're moving much faster than we did yesterday."

It was true. Although they were keeping a careful lookout today, they had been much more cautious yesterday on account of their new surroundings and the dwindling light.

Rebecca had to agree. "You're right," she said "something's wrong. There must be magic involved." She sat down, defeated.

"This must have been what happened to Will," said Thomas. "He went into the forest thinking he could find his way back…"

"…but the Tree of Laurea is only easy to *leave*, not find!"

"Exactly." He rested his chin on his hand and thought. "It was a stupid plan anyway – going to get help in our world. No one would've believed us, and who knows how much time would've passed by the time we got back here!"

"So what do you suggest we do?"

"I don't know."

Jorka had sat down too and begun taking out the remaining food. Although they hadn't eaten in hours, Thomas found he wasn't hungry. Jorka insisted he take a piece of bread. He reluctantly accepted and nibbled slowly while scanning the trees.

Rebecca noticed what he was doing. "What are you looking for Thomas?" she asked.

"I don't know. A sprite. Noggin said if you look hard enough you might find one."

"Good idea."

Rebecca started scanning the trees as well, but her brother was the first to notice something unusual. It was a flicker amongst the leaves that caught his eye.

"Hey!" he yelled. "Hey you! Sprite! Please come here!"

"Did you see something?"

"Shhh!" Thomas hushed. He squinted his eyes and was fairly certain he saw a couple of wings. There was no more movement, however.

"Hey you! Sprite!" he repeated. "I see you!"

Thomas's suspicions were confirmed as a tiny white sprite popped its head out and flew down from above. It was one of the very young sprites and it was giggling madly. It flitted between the three, its mouth rapidly moving. Of course, this one was as impossible to understand as the rest. Before they could respond, however, a larger yellow sprite descended from above. '*That's a relief!*' thought Thomas: he wasn't eager to deal with the first.

The yellow sprite silently scolded the little white one, which made a quick departure. It then turned to the children. "There is only one path to the Tree of Laurea!" it said in a pipsqueak voice that at least they could hear.

"Oh yeah," said Thomas "what's that?"

"There's no time now," it said. "You must return to Jorka's house before it gets dark." The light had diminished somewhat in the last little while.

Rebecca gave it a suspicious look. "Who are you?" she asked, "And why didn't you help us earlier?"

The sprite gave a nervous look around before speaking. "I have followed you since you were sent away by King Irith. You have friends in this forest, but we had to gauge your intentions first. We are ready to help, but it must wait until tomorrow!" There was a genuine urgency in the way it spoke. "Go to Jorka's home and we'll meet again in the morning!"

They still looked unsure. Seeing the open bag, the sprite flew over to it and shook itself. Showers of sparkly dust landed in the bag.

"That should help," said the sprite. "Now go!" It gave them one more urgent look before flying off.

"Sprite dust?" inquired Rebecca. "Is that your magic powder Jorka?"

"Oh yes, yes. Good for magic." He took up the bag, which fortunately had had all the food removed already.

"Well, I guess we should head to your place Jorka, before it gets dark," she said.

"I've still got the flashlight," commented Thomas "but I suppose the dark itself is not really a concern." He turned to Jorka. "Do you know the way back from here?"

Their new friend looked around and scratched his head. "Jorka know the way."

"I wonder what the sprite means for us to do with its magic dust?"

Jorka grinned, happy to be of service again. "Sprite dust good to move *fast*," he said, then grabbed most of the powder in his hand. He sprinkled some on each of the children and the rest on himself. "Now follow Jorka."

And with that, he started walking. Slow at first, then picking up speed once he was sure the children were keeping up. The odd thing was, they kept getting faster and faster, beyond what should have been a reasonable speed for the children. They broke into a light jog. It seemed to Thomas that every step he took covered the space of five. Trees began to blur, and still they gained speed. Colors melted together. Now each step was like ten, now twenty – until there was no meaningful way to determine just how much ground they were covering. Yet still the children followed their friend, who was always just a little ahead.

They stopped at the two trees that hid Jorka's home about seven minutes later.

"Amazing!" the children cried in unison.

"Let's do it again!" said Thomas. "Later, of course," he added.

Jorka held out his hand and concentrated, same as before. Like a vanishing mirage the two trees went wavy and disappeared, to be replaced by the odd stone and wood house once more. The three of them entered Jorka's home and into its familiar cluttered mess.

"Strange…" said Thomas "I know we've only been here once before, but it feels good to be back. Safe, you know?"

"Yeah, I have the same feeling. I guess it's because we know the house is hidden by magic."

"Yeah…"

Jorka had already moved over to the fireplace and started a fire. He hung a large pot over it and began putting in the ingredients for a stew.

"Good idea Jorka! I'm *starving!*" Thomas rubbed his stomach, only now acknowledging its rumbling.

Jorka looked at Rebecca. "Rebecca hungry?" he asked.

"Yes, very."

"Good. Jorka make big stew." He continued preparing the ingredients.

Soon a delicious aroma filled the circular room. Rebecca and Thomas had offered to help, but Jorka had insisted they rest. Both of them sat at the table instead and watched him work.

"I wonder what the sprite has planned for us tomorrow?" questioned Rebecca.

"It said we had 'friends in this forest'. Maybe they'll all be there to greet us."

"Whoever *they* are."

The children were silent as each contemplated who these "friends" could be. Maybe it was a risk for them to reveal themselves: it was unclear whether the King's refusal to help them forbade others from helping as well.

The last remaining sunlight glinted through the variously colored and shaped windows of Jorka's home.

"Look, we made it back here with plenty of time to spare," remarked Thomas, changing the subject.

"With some help from the sprite dust. Amazing stuff."

"Yeah," he agreed. "Maybe it can help us find what we're looking for."

"Will…"

"And the Tree of Laurea."

"I've been thinking about that," said Rebecca. "Finding the Tree, I mean. We still have one of its apples - I wonder if it could somehow be used to show the way."

"With magic, perhaps," added Thomas.

"Exactly."

"Good thinking Rebecca! We should ask the sprite tomorrow."

On the table in front of them was the plastic bag the children had been carrying for over a day now. Its current contents were only the two apples and the flashlight. Thomas grabbed the bag and removed the red apple taken from the Tree of Laurea, turning it slowly in his hands. Two bite marks glistened white where he and Jorka had sampled the fruit. His stomach growled. He briefly considered taking another bite, but thought better of it. Placing the red apple on the table, he next removed the pale yellow one they had taken from the Tree in the Cave. This apple also had two bites out of it, and they too revealed the white fruit underneath. Thomas came to a realization.

"Look," he said "they haven't spoiled at all!"

"You're right!"

Rebecca remembered how quickly an exposed apple would turn brown. Their mom used to pack their apple slices for lunch in vinegar to prevent this from happening. The apple from the cave hadn't turned at all brown in over a day; the bite marks looked like they had been made moments before.

Thomas finished examining it and handed the apple to his sister. "I guess we really shouldn't be surprised by anything anymore," he said.

"No, I guess not." She put both apples back in the bag. "We better keep these safe," she announced, but left the bag on the table. As long as they always knew where it was, she reasoned that would be okay.

Jorka had finished making the stew and was just letting it simmer. He put a bit more wood in the fire, which was now the only source of illumination in the room. Flamelight flickered across the walls and its darkened windows, creating an effect that was more eerie than comforting. Sensing this, Jorka found a couple lamps and lit them. He brought one over to the table and sat down.

"Stew smells good," Thomas commented. What he really wanted to know was when it would be ready.

"Almost done," said Jorka, reading his mind. He grinned and got up again.

"No, let me," said Rebecca. She rose from the table and rummaged through the mess until she found two bowls on one table and three spoons and another bowl on a shelf.

Jorka thanked her and ladled some delicious stew into each bowl, handing them back. When all three had a full portion in front of them, they dug in.

"Ouch! Hot!" laughed Thomas, careful to blow on the next spoonful.

The stew was hearty and gave their bare stomachs a nice, weighty feeling. They took turns refilling the bowls until the large pot was almost empty, talking and laughing the whole time. Jorka told them about life in the forest and the children told him about life back home. He found the concept of school to be especially interesting, and had a hard time comprehending that no one knew magic in their world. Rebecca and Thomas also told him about their cousin Will, and all three wondered what sort of meeting would take place the next morning. Throughout the entire conversation, no one mentioned King Irith or the Destroyer. All of them felt the need to be happy and light-hearted – at least for the time being.

Sometime during their second helping of stew, a soft, blue glow began to appear outside. It slowly but steadily increased through their third bowl, and was first noticed by Thomas during the fourth.

"That's like the blue light I saw last night!" he said, pointing to the window. "That's how it began!" His heart quickened a bit.

"It's the Destroyer, isn't it?" exclaimed Rebecca. She looked at Jorka, and was not reassured by the worried look he returned.

"If we stay in here we'll be safe, right?" asked Thomas. "I learned my lesson last time! Still, it has started much earlier tonight."

"Do you suppose it knows where to look now?"

Jorka didn't respond. The blue light continued to increase. He got up and took out his satchel of magic powder. "Rebecca and Thomas come with Jorka to safe place," he announced.

"I thought *this* was a safe place!" said Thomas as he and Rebecca hurriedly followed Jorka into the next room. Their forest friend threw aside his mattress and counted three wooden floorboards from the wall. On the third one he sprinkled some powder from the satchel, then took out the emerald stone he'd used earlier and rammed it into the board. A green glow appeared from the stone and soon surrounded several square feet of the adjacent flooring.

"Oh wait – the apples!" Rebecca suddenly remembered. She ran back into the circular room and Thomas quickly followed. Blue light poured through the windows. Looking at the table, she could see that the bag was no longer there.

"They're gone!" she exclaimed.

"Check the floor!" said Thomas. "The bag might have fallen when we got up!"

Both children got on their hands and knees to search.

"Rebecca and Thomas!" Jorka yelled from the other room.

"Just a second!" yelled Rebecca. She had a feeling that the apples would be very important to have in the future, and didn't want to leave them. The bag was spotted on the floor under a counter.

"I found it!" she exclaimed. "Let's go!"

Rebecca grabbed the bag and made her way back to Jorka, Thomas close behind. The light was now so bright that it was difficult for them to keep their eyes open. She reached Jorka without realizing that Thomas had stopped. A stable green glow in the centre of the floor of Jorka's bedroom was nearly washed out by the intense blue light.

Jorka looked at her. "Where Thomas go?" he asked.

She turned around. "Oh my God, I don't know! Thomas!" she yelled, and went back to the circular room. The glare was incredible, but her brother could be made out hunched over on the ground with his hands on his ears.

"The noise!" he exclaimed. The same tremendous buzzing noise filled his head as it had the night before, making him incapable of doing anything other than try to block it out. Unfortunately, covering his ears didn't seem to help at all.

Rebecca heard nothing, and Thomas did not hear her calling his name. Then two things happened in quick succession: the door burst open and a hand grabbed Rebecca from behind. She barely had time to register several dark figures entering Jorka's home before she found herself pulled down and backwards. The hand had been Jorka's, and he'd pulled her into the secret hole he'd created in the floor, leaving her brother behind. They landed on soft earth a few seconds later.

"Thomas!" she cried.

* * * *

Three shadows moved through Jorka's home, searching. They did not emit the blue light but rather seemed to absorb it. At any rate, it dissipated fairly quickly after they'd entered the house. The hole in Jorka's bedroom floor had closed soon after he and Rebecca had entered it. Now there was no trace it had ever been there. The shadows noticed the displaced mattress, though, and two of them began an incantation. The third moved through the circular room, upending tables with a look in place of a touch.

They seemed to be searching for something, but found nothing of interest. The two shadows in the bedroom ceased their incantation, unable to reopen the secret entrance. All the while, Thomas remained crumpled on the ground. The noise in his head was excruciating. It stopped only when he passed out.

Their search ended, two of the shadows collected the now unconscious Thomas and took him out the door. The remaining shadow stayed behind, chanting something unheard. Jorka's home burst into flames and the shadow departed.

CHAPTER SEVEN

"Thomas!" Rebecca cried again. "We have to go back and get him!"

"Too late, cannot go back," said Jorka. A tremendous sadness filled his wrinkly face.

"WE HAVE TO GO BACK!"

Tears flowed down her cheeks. She couldn't believe she had now lost both Will and Thomas! The memory of the dark figures entering Jorka's home replayed in her mind. "What were those things?" she asked between sobs.

"Bad things. Shadows. *Nasrati:* Henchmen for Destroyer."

"Well they're going to kill my brother!" Rebecca was becoming hysterical.

He shook his big head. "Shadows take Thomas, not kill him."

"You don't know that!" yelled Rebecca wildly. Jorka grabbed her arm and tried to calm her.

"LET GO OF ME!" she screamed, yanking it back. Jorka began to cry as well.

"I, I'm sorry Jorka. I didn't mean it like that," she said softly. "I just…don't know what to do." She tried to control her sobbing and looked around. Their current setting was very familiar. "Where are we?" she inquired.

"Forest King lair," he answered, confirming her suspicions.

"What? Why?" she asked, becoming more agitated. "He refused to help us before! He might've prevented this!"

"Rebecca and Jorka safe here."

"So we're just supposed to wait and let King Irith not help us again? Forget it!" Without thinking, Rebecca grabbed some powder from Jorka's satchel and sprinkled it on her head. She moved towards the large hole they had previously used to enter the lair.

"Rebecca! Not safe tonight!" yelled Jorka behind her.

She didn't respond but rather kept on running to the exit, hoping the magic powder would help her move fast like it had earlier. A large group of sprites was fluttering towards her. Rebecca ignored them and entered the hole in the wall.

It was a steep incline and the low ceiling required her to crouch. However, she was able to move up it quite quickly and with ease – evidence that the powder was having an effect after all. The obscuring bush parted as she approached the top of the passage, then closed up again after she had exited into the forest.

'No going back now,' she thought to herself; she didn't know how to reopen the secret entrance.

The forest surrounding her was dark and quiet. And more than a little scary. But Rebecca had a purpose, and she often found frightening situations to be less so when you have a purpose to be there and a goal to attain. Her plan was simple: use the magic powder to move fast and catch up with whoever *(whatever?)* had taken Thomas. She assumed they would be taking him to the Destroyer - so according to King Irith, all she had to do was follow the larger moon. This she was able to find even between the leaves above.

She headed off in the direction of the larger moon, and was pleased to find herself building up speed nicely. Once again, trees blurred and colors melted around her. She was moving very fast now. Where, she had no idea. She just desperately hoped she would be able to do something when she came across Thomas and his captors. They didn't seem to affect her like they did her brother, so that was a start. Maybe she could quickly grab him and head back before they even knew what happened! She wondered how long the powder would last.

Rebecca continued to ponder her options while running through the forest; she found she didn't have to think about her path at all. Laurea was big, but she was moving through it at an incredible speed. After a few minutes, she came to the forest edge. Laid out in front of her was a large grassy plain. *Vast.* The only defining feature she could make out were some mountains in the distance. Both moons shone through the cloudy sky overhead: a large full moon in front and a smaller crescent one to the side. In the absence of trees, this enormous plain was flooded with moonlight. She started running again, still following the larger moon. Speed built up quickly, but only for a few seconds to her horror. Then she was simply running as fast as an eleven year-old's legs could go.

"No, no, no!" she exclaimed, still running. "It can't stop working yet!"

Looking behind, she could see the short burst of speed had taken her about three hundred metres from the forest, no more.

Rebecca kept running. Somewhere inside she knew it was probably futile: she could see for miles on the flat grassland, and couldn't make out any other figures. Still she ran. *'What choice do I have?'* she thought wildly.

In times of desperation, humans can do extraordinary things – even an eleven year-old child. Rebecca continued running for longer than anyone would think possible. When she could no longer run, she walked. At some point, though, exhaustion caught up and her legs gave out. She collapsed on the grass.

The mountains were still far away, and now so was the forest. Rebecca was utterly spent and totally lost on a giant plain in some strange land called Fardoor.

"Thomas! Will!" she cried out loud. And with her last ounce of energy: "Somebody help me." Then she passed out.

* * * *

Who knows how long Rebecca lay on the ground? Probably not

long: when the Nasrati came and collected her the small moon had only moved a little. The larger moon hadn't moved at all. (Although, it never really seemed to move much, did it?)

There were two of them this time. Rebecca regained consciousness for a moment and saw the dark figures coming towards her, but the knight that accompanied them stayed out of view. Her eyes closed again.

* * * *

"Rebecca!" said a hushed but excited voice. "Rebecca!" it repeated.

She stirred. "Huh?"

"Rebecca, wake up!"

She opened her eyes to find herself in a small, cylindrical cage bumpily moving across the plain on the back of a large, unusual animal (*'Like a giant, shaggy ox,'* she instantly thought). It was morning.

The cage was only a few feet wide, but tall enough to stand in. Thick metal bars held her in, and a metal roof blocked out the sun. There didn't appear to be a door. Thomas was in an adjacent cage waving dramatically at his sister.

She was about to yell his name in joy when she noticed he was motioning for her to talk quietly. "Thomas!" she said instead in a joyous whisper. "You're okay!"

"Yeah, I'm okay. Are you?" he whispered back.

She checked herself. "I'm dirty, tired and hungry, but I'm feeling better now!" She smiled and Thomas smiled back.

"There's food in there. I tried mine and it seems fine," he said.

Rebecca spotted the half-loaf of bread and jug of water on the floor of her cage. "If you say so..." She began wolfing both down. "What happened?" she asked between mouthfuls.

"I don't know. I just woke up in this cage about an hour ago and you were in that one. I've been trying to get you to wake up this whole time. What happened with you?"

Rebecca paused from eating. "After we found the apples, I didn't notice you'd collapsed until I reached Jorka. I tried to go back for you but he pulled me down the hole he'd created in his bedroom floor."

Thomas was listening attentively with his hands on the bars and his face pressed up between them. "And? Where did you end up?" he asked.

"The lair of the Forest King."

"Him?"

"That was *my* reaction!"

He let Rebecca have a few more bites of bread before pushing for more details. "So, what happened next?"

"So, I kind of went ballistic on Jorka. I feel bad about that. Anyway, I grabbed some magic powder from his satchel and just started running. I ran out of the underground lair, out of the Forest of Laurea and onto these plains. I figured those things were taking you to the Destroyer, so I just followed the larger moon like King Irith said."

"Did the powder help you move fast?"

"Uh-huh. But it stopped working when I reached the plains. Then I just ran on my own until I passed out."

"I wonder how you ended up here?" said Thomas.

"Well, I think I remember two of those *Nasrati* coming towards me. That's all."

"Incredible. So Jorka took you to King Irith after all that."

"Yeah – he said it would be safe there. I really blew up at him, so remind me to apologize next time we see him – hopefully at his place."

Thomas looked down at the ground. "Uh...I think Jorka's home was destroyed by the Nasrati. I think I remember opening my eyes and seeing it on fire."

"What? Oh no! Poor Jorka!"

"Yeah."

Thomas continued his downward gaze. "And it's all my fault, too. I don't think they would've found his home if I hadn't gone outside the night before. *We* wouldn't be in this mess either!"

"Oh Thomas, don't say things like that! We have no idea if that's true," encouraged his sister, who'd abandoned her food for the moment.

"Well, it probably is."

She decided to change the subject. "Those Nasrati are horrible things. I wonder where they've gone?" she said, noting that the animals were being driven by a less imposing, hunched over figure riding a horse in front of them. He held the reins to their two animals and a third beside Thomas that carried an empty cage. *'Probably for Jorka,'* she thought.

"I have no idea where they've gone," said Thomas. "I'm just glad they aren't here. And I want to know why you don't hear that awful sound they make!"

"Don't know." Rebecca rubbed her stomach. The combination of her quick meal and the bumpy ride was making her feel ill. "Oooh…I don't feel so good," she said, rubbing it some more.

"You don't *look* so good," said Thomas. "Maybe you should lie down."

"I think I will."

She lay down in her cage, her body curled up so it would fit. It was a curious feeling, being trapped in a cage: something of a mixture of anger and helplessness.

"You don't have to get up," Thomas instructed "but I think I see another one of those stone altars in the distance."

"So I guess they're not just in the forest," she said without much enthusiasm.

He decided to wait a few minutes before talking to her again. "Feeling any better?" he asked.

"A little." Rebecca rolled over and saw that her brother was now sitting down in his own cage, watching their driver carefully. "What's the deal with him Thomas?" she asked.

"What, the driver? I don't know. I haven't seen his face 'cause he hasn't turned around once since I woke up. At one point I tried yelling for his attention, but he wouldn't even acknowledge me."

"That's strange," she said, eyeing the driver. He was short – probably shorter than Thomas. His broad back was severely hunched over and sported a tattered, brown hooded vestment. Weak, tiny legs fell to either side of the horse, but large, powerful arms held its reins and those of the animals behind it.

"Maybe if we both yell?" she suggested. Rebecca started shouting at the driver: *"Hey you!", "Turn around!", "Where are you taking us?"* Thomas joined in, but the driver didn't even flicker. They returned to their quiet speaking voices.

"Well, he's better than the Nasrati," said Thomas.

"Agreed. Although we are still stuck in cages on the way to the Destroyer, aren't we?"

"Yeah, well – that part's not so good."

Silence followed, interrupted by the occasional animal grunt.

On such a sunny morning the atmosphere seemed less frightening than at night, despite the fact they were in cages. Mentioning the Destroyer, however, had sent a shiver down both children's spines. Each pondered what was in store.

"I wonder what the Destroyer plans to do with us," Rebecca finally said.

"Me too," acknowledged Thomas "but I think his biggest prize was supposed to be Jorka. That empty cage was probably meant for him."

"I was thinking the same thing. But why does he want Jorka so much?"

"That's easy," said Thomas matter-of-factly. "Because what the Destroyer really wants is to get at King Irith; if he was defeated it would probably mean the downfall of Laurea." He sat up and continued speaking animatedly. "But for some reason, the Destroyer can't find the King's lair. So he needs to get his hands on someone who knows where it is!"

"Jorka," offered Rebecca.

"Jorka."

"Thomas, we also know where the Forest King's lair is now."

"Yeah, but we don't know how to get in - Jorka did that for us. Plus, I imagine King Irith would be able to change the entrances."

Rebecca sat up, her stomach a bit better. "He should just catch himself a sprite, then," she said.

"Yeah, there must be some reason why he wants Jorka

specifically. Maybe he needs that green rock."

Now Rebecca pressed herself up against the bars as Thomas had done. "Well I for one am not looking forward to meeting him. At least not trapped in a cage." She lowered her voice even more. "What do you think the chances of us escaping are?"

Thomas rubbed his chin. "Hmmm...I'm gonna go with nil to none. Rebecca – there's no door to these cages."

"What?" She looked around hers: solid metal roof, solid metal floor, and sturdy metal bars all around. There was no lock to pick, no door to open. "So we're just supposed to sit here?"

"I don't like it either, but what choice do we have? Neither of us knows any magic!"

She gave her brother a serious look. "Just...don't give up yet, okay?"

"Of course not!" he exclaimed in surprise. "Plus, this may be our best chance to find Will! Once we have him the three of us can make our escape together."

"We're clever – we'll find a way out," said Rebecca, her spirits rising.

"That's what I'm saying!"

She sat back down and looked at their unusual driver. "Now if only *he'd* give us some information," she said, thumbing her nose at him. He had barely shifted position the entire time they'd been speaking. Occasionally the driver would tighten the reins held in his meaty hands, but that was really their only clue he was even alive.

"Thomas, can you imagine if we did escape and he had to run after us on those little legs?" she giggled.

"He'd probably fall over and start rolling 'cause his top half is too big! Of course, he'd also probably just chase us on his horse."

"Oh right - well at any rate, it'd be great if he would just TELL US WHERE WE'RE GOING!" she said, yelling the last part.

"I think we're heading to the mountains, Rebecca."

"Well I realize that, stupid."

Although still a ways off, the mountain range loomed much larger now than when she had first stepped onto the plains.

"I meant where are we going *exactly*." She was about to scold him some more when something caught her eye. "Hold on," she said "I think I see people up ahead!"

"I see them too!"

Several figures on horses were heading towards them from only a hundred metres away.

"Did you notice them before?" she asked.

"No. They can't have been riding towards us all this time or we would've seen them much earlier."

"I know, but what are you suggesting – that they just materialized in front of us?"

Thomas had no chance to answer her question; the riders had nearly approached. Both children stood up in their cages.

There were five of them, tall and neatly dressed in dark metal armor. The central one rode slightly ahead with a black cape and a silver crest on his breastplate. He bore no weapon, whereas the other four did – savage ones like clubs and maces.

"Halt," said the central rider when they had nearly reached the convoy. This was an order both the driver and riders obeyed.

The children waited in anticipation to see if these knights were there to rescue them. The central rider removed his helmet revealing a blond-haired, blue-eyed handsome young man. Rebecca recognized him instantly.

"Will!" she cried. "Is that you?"

"Rebecca Day!" said the youth in a familiar British accent. "How nice to see you again! You too of course, Thomas."

"Will?" Thomas offered tentatively.

"That's right cousin – it's me," he said grandly. "Oh it's been too, too long! Five years I believe."

Thomas remained silent. There was something he didn't like about this person claiming to be Will. Something...menacing. Rebecca, however, seemed to have already accepted his claim.

"Will!" she repeated. "You're so much older!"

"Five years older."

"But it's still you, isn't it! Can you get us out of these cages? We think we're being taken to this *Destroyer*," she said, whispering the last part.

"We heard you were taken by him, or it," said Thomas.

"But obviously he wasn't!" she interjected. "Or maybe he escaped - and now he's okay!"

"Yes, I am okay Rebecca. Although I *was* taken by the Destroyer, in a way."

"But you escaped!"

"Well, not *exactly*."

"I don't understand," said Rebecca.

The young man's smile decreased a bit. "Well then let me *explain*. You see, when you left me in Fardoor, I didn't realize it would be for so long."

"Will I only went back for an hour in our world, to get Thomas – " she hurriedly began.

"I said let *me* explain," he interrupted, his voice more threatening. Rebecca was taken aback.

"As I was saying," he continued "I didn't realize I'd be here for so long. I wandered into the forest. Not too far: I wanted to stay close to the tree portal so I could get back of course. The thing is, even though I memorized the short path I had taken, I never was able to find that tree again. I couldn't *ever* get back." His voice became steelier. "I spent days in that wretched forest. I met Jorka – I believe you've become acquainted with him? Well I thought he was too stupid to be of any help. I've changed my mind on that matter."

The children continued to listen, their hands gripping the metal bars tightly. The young man paused for a moment to choose his words.

"All the time I was in the Forest of Laurea, I believed you would find me and we'd go back together. However, my hope diminished as the days passed, and I became weaker. Eventually I wandered out of Laurea and onto these very plains. I made it all the way to those mountains," he said proudly. "I don't know why. Because they were there, I suppose."

"Will – " Rebecca started.

"NO INTERRUPTIONS!" the young man yelled, startling both children. He composed himself again. "Let's see, just when I thought I was going to die – *when things looked bleakest*, you might say – I came across a marvellous stone in the walls of one of the mountain's caves. The stone gave me certain...powers, which I learned to control and use. I realized I needn't ever go back home." He looked at them intently. "The stone helps people do bad things, Thomas and Rebecca."

"You mean – "

"The *stone* is the Destroyer – AND I AM ITS MASTER!"

He flew off his horse, hovering in the air in front of them with both arms raised. Darkness began to form a dome around them.

"Will!" exclaimed Rebecca.

"What are you doing?" shouted Thomas.

He dropped his arms, the dome of darkness complete. A cold, blue light dimly lit the occupants.

"I've become quite powerful these last five years. Fardoor lives in fear because of me. However, King Irith has so far managed to rebuff my attacks on the Forest of Laurea – and I'd very much like to have it." He looked at them as if inviting questions, but the children said nothing; they were in shock. The young man continued instead. "I've never even seen him, you know: King Irith, that is. But I'm certain I would have much less trouble conquering Laurea if I could find his lair and destroy him."

The children clenched the bars even harder, a mix of fright, anger and pity rising in both. The young man eyed them suspiciously. "Now I know what you're thinking," he said "*Why not just capture a sprite?* Unfortunately, they have a nasty habit of dying under my interrogation methods. Much too small." He nodded at the empty cage. "That one was for your fat friend. I've been trying to catch him for a little while now because I know he can give me the information I need. Imagine my surprise to hear the Nasrati report a human boy and girl in Laurea when they were looking for Jorka's home. I just knew it had to be you two, after all these years. Thank you Thomas, for opening Jorka's door and showing us exactly where he lived. Although I had been closing in you know. It's really too bad he escaped, but I guess you can be my consolation prize."

Thomas felt a surge of guilt. He'd had enough. "You must be Will, 'cause you're the same arrogant jerk from before, only older!"

he yelled.

"Now Thomas - that hurts. And I don't take pain, I give it."

A familiar buzzing noise started in Thomas's head, very faint. "No!" he cried out.

Rebecca couldn't hear the noise but realized something was happening. "What are you doing?" she exclaimed.

"I've invited the Nasrati! They like the dark, as you may have noticed. The stone helped me call on them shortly after I acquired it."

Several shadowy figures began emerging from the black surroundings. The buzzing in Thomas's head increased significantly, and he doubled over in pain.

"Stop it!" screamed Rebecca.

He ignored her and spoke to Thomas. "That noise you hear is the Nasrati communicating. Only young people can hear it, and even then not all of them can. A shame you can't, Rebecca."

There were three Nasrati present and more were emerging.

"AAAH!" screamed Thomas.

"Remarkable, isn't it?" said the young man. "I've never heard it myself, of course, but I've been told it can be quite excruciating!"

As if to emphasize the young man's point, Thomas collapsed onto the floor of his cage and began convulsing. About ten Nasrati were now gliding about the dark dome he had created. They really were 'shadows' as Jorka had called them. Their bodies were dark wisps that absorbed what little light came their way. Although she couldn't see any faces, Rebecca could feel them looking at her. She was terrified.

"Stop it!" she cried. "Please!" But the young man claiming to be Will simply laughed. "YOU WERE THE ONE WHO WANTED TO STAY!" she screamed.

This got his attention. His smile quickly faded and he motioned for the Nasrati to depart. They turned to the dark walls and melted into them, disappearing. Thomas stopped convulsing but remained on the ground. His rapid, shallow breathing at least signalled he was still alive. Rebecca glanced over to make sure he was okay and then returned her gaze to the blond-haired youth hovering before them.

He was looking at her with contempt.

"Don't worry," he said "I wasn't going to kill him; I've got other plans."

Emboldened by her success and the departure of the Nasrati, Rebecca gave him a steely look of her own. "You were the one who wanted to stay," she repeated.

"Yes I wanted to stay, to explore what we'd found. But you should've stayed with me! Maybe I would've gotten back, then."

Rebecca thought the young man – *Will* - actually sounded sad. For a moment she saw the boy who always looked hurt when told he had to go back to boarding school after spending his summer with the Day family.

He reasserted himself. "I guess we'll never know how I might've turned out, will we?"

"Will, there's still hope, there's still a chance – "

"No, there's no hope, no chance. I *like* what I've become now." He floated backwards onto his horse. "Unfortunately I must depart. Business, you know. But I'll see you later, and I'll leave this nice young gentleman to accompany you in the meantime." He motioned at one of the knights, who then trotted his horse over beside the children's cages.

"Will you don't have to do this!" exclaimed Rebecca. He looked right at her before putting his helmet back on and disappearing, along with the three remaining knights. The black dome receded too, and the children once again found themselves in bright sunlight. The driver (who still hadn't shown his face) started the convoy on its original route towards the mountains. The only difference now was that a horseman rode alongside to Rebecca's right. She took note of his terrible-looking club.

Thomas still lay on the ground, his breathing slowed. "Thomas!" said Rebecca in a hushed voice. She glanced nervously at the knight, who continued to look ahead. "Thomas!" she said again, a bit louder. He stirred a little but was silent. *'I guess I should let him sleep,'* she decided.

Rebecca sat down and turned her thoughts to the young man they had just encountered. Thomas may have had his doubts, but she was certain he was their cousin Will Hastings. *'Or at least he was at one time,'* she thought. Now he was a frightening person that the people of Fardoor called the Destroyer.

Will had always been arrogant, but never cruel. She shuddered to think of what his 'plan' for them may be after what he had just done to Thomas. And yet, she somehow felt – *knew* – that part of him was still their Will, and if she could only reach that part... *'This must be what the sprites meant about 'saving Will','* was the last thing she thought of before the exhausting ordeal sent her back to sleep.

CHAPTER EIGHT

A midday sun in a cloudless sky bore down on the children. It had passed the point of being directly above their cages, and now formed angled slats of burning light as it passed through the bars. Rebecca woke up, uncomfortable in the heat. She looked around to find nothing much had changed; not any of the knight, driver, or Thomas had shifted position. The mountains seemed mildly closer. Rebecca reasoned that she'd only been asleep for a couple hours. The large animal beneath her gave a heavy grunt in agreement.

Under any other circumstance, thinking of ways to escape would have been her top priority. In this case, however, her thoughts immediately returned to how she might get through to her cousin. *'And anyway,'* she acknowledged *'escape seems to be an impossibility for now.'*

Famished, she munched on her remaining bread, happy to have not eaten it all earlier. She was about to take a swig of water when she noticed the knight move his head out of the corner of her eye. He, apparently, had noticed something behind their convoy. The knight stopped and turned his horse around while the rest of them kept moving. Rebecca also turned to have a look, and her heart leapt at what she saw: a multi-colored flock of 'butterflies' was fast approaching. Three figures ran beneath the flock, two of them very small.

"The sprites!" she exclaimed. "The sprites! Thomas wake up! We're being rescued!" He didn't budge. Although she was very thirsty, Rebecca took the remaining water in her jug and splashed it on her brother through the cage. This woke him up.

"What? What's going on?" he asked, looking startled.

"Thomas we're being rescued!"

"Huh? Where's Will? The last thing I remember – "

"I'll explain it all later!" she interrupted, noting that he had called the young man 'Will'.

Thomas looked confused.

"Just – get ready."

"Okay. I'm ready."

"Um, good," she said, turning her head back to the scene behind them. He did the same. They had now travelled a hundred feet from where the knight had stopped, and the sprites were another hundred feet on the other side of him. Nothing had happened yet.

"Look he's raising his club!" said Thomas. "How does he expect to hit a bunch of sprites with that?"

Rebecca didn't answer, but watched as the knight lifted the large, black club in the air, then swung it down hard on the ground. Where it struck, an arc of blue light exploded from the earth and swiftly moved towards the sprites. The entire flock moved up as one and the arc just missed.

"Oh, I hope they can keep doing that!" she said.

Their driver sped up, throwing the children back against the bars. He then apparently changed his mind and made a sharp turn back towards the knight. The large animals protested such sudden movements, and the ropes holding the cages to them threatened to come loose.

"Whooah!" said Thomas as he was tossed about the cage. "I guess our driver decided to help after all!"

The convoy rushed back towards the knight, who was raising his club again. It struck the ground, causing another explosive arc of light to speed towards the advancing flock. This time it split in two as it approached them, catching some of the sprites off guard. Those hit fell to the ground.

"They're getting killed!" said Rebecca.

"But they're fighting back too – look!"

A green vine had wrapped itself around the knight's feet. Another one shot out of the ground and caught the knight's right arm just as it was going to strike with the club again. Instead, the club did a sideways glance off grass and the feeble arc that resulted missed wildly. A bolt of ivory light shot towards the knight and knocked him off his feet.

"Fantastic!" said Thomas "I think that's Noggin and his wife!"

They were now close enough to make out the two gnomes and the third person whom neither recognized. Much taller and human-looking, the ivory bolt had shot out of her hands.

With their opponent lying on his back, Noggin's wife touched a wooden staff she was carrying to the ground. More vines sprung up and wrapped themselves around the knight. He struggled for only a moment before easily breaking free and standing up. A second ivory bolt shot from the unknown woman missed. The knight struck his club to the ground and a dozen smaller arcs of blue light exploded towards the party. Several more sprites were felled. One of the arcs just missed Noggin's head, who exchanged a frantic look with his wife. The unknown woman was not so lucky – she tumbled down after being hit in the leg.

Meanwhile, their hunchback driver had let go of the animal's reins and sped the rest of the way alone on his horse. He charged right at the gnomes who had no choice but to ignore the knight. At any rate, the sprites had reached him and were busy trying to pull off his helmet. He was trying to keep it on with one hand while using the other to swing at them with his club.

Rebecca and Thomas were of course still trapped in their cages. Now freed from the driver, the animals below had taken to grazing the field.

"Come on you stupid animals! Do something!" shouted Thomas. "Go trample the knight!" He kicked the cage.

"They'd probably just as likely trample Noggin," said Rebecca.

"It looks like our driver already had that idea. Watch out Noggin!" he yelled as the driver's horse threatened to crush him.

Noggin ducked out of the way and gave another frantic look at his wife. She was retrieving her staff, which she'd lost while trying to avoid the knight's attack. She tapped the ground twice once it was in her hand. More of the green vines sprung out to entangle the horse's legs, and the driver leaped off his steed as it fell. On foot he still posed a threat. His hunched back combined with giant arms and tiny legs forced him to do a sort of gorilla-run as he charged the gnomes. But he also looked as strong as a gorilla. A vine jumped up and caught his arm. The driver easily snapped it without even slowing down. He raised a large fist to pound Noggin. Noggin, however, blew an orange cloud of smoke from his hand into the driver's face. He suddenly went rigid as a statue and toppled over, arm still raised.

The sprites had by now succeeded in removing the knight's helmet and were currently whirling around his head. His movements slowed and the knight crumpled to the ground.

"Yaaaay!" shouted the children simultaneously. Noggin breathed a sigh of relief, then looked up at the children and waved. His wife was already tending to the human woman who hadn't yet gotten up. Noggin went to help her while the sprites flew over to the children's cages: first to Thomas's, where they formed a swirling spiral around one of the solid bars. Showered with silvery strands from the sprites, the bar twinkled then disappeared.

The flock moved over to Rebecca's cage, but one of them stayed behind. It was the yellow sprite who had greeted them in the forest the day before. It looked at him without speaking.

"Er - thanks for the rescue," he said as the sprite flew up close to his face (something he was getting more used to). It gave him a sad half-smile.

"You're welcome. Are you hurt?"

He checked himself. "No, I'm okay."

"Good, we must get going." It sped off and rejoined the flock, which had just freed Rebecca.

Thomas stepped out of the cage and jumped to the ground as his sister ran over to hug him. He hugged her back. Noggin walked up to meet them and Rebecca hugged him too.

"Thank you so much for rescuing us!" she exclaimed. "You guys were great!"

Noggin blushed. "Oh - well, sorry we didn't help earlier. Are you both okay?"

"Yeah, we're fine," said Thomas "Is she?" He pointed to the woman on the ground who was now sitting up with the help of Noggin's wife.

"Velarr? She will be. She was hit in the leg."

"Oh – that's good." Both children felt relieved; they had been afraid she'd died trying to save them.

"And the sprites that were hit?" asked Rebecca. "Will they be okay too?"

Noggin shook his head sadly. "No, I'm afraid they're dead. Sprites are too small to sustain any sort of hit from those weapons."

"Oh – I'm so sorry Noggin!"

Thomas looked at the ground. "Yeah, I'm sorry too."

Rebecca was hugging Noggin again. "This is awful! They died just to rescue us!"

"It's all right," he said "they died to save Laurea. And you two aren't the only ones rescued just now. Follow me."

They followed him over to the knight, who was still face down on the ground. Noggin flipped him right side up and the children were surprised to see he was another teen-aged boy.

"He's so young!" said Thomas.

The boy had light brown hair and a tan complexion. His smooth face made him look no more than fifteen.

"What do you mean we're rescuing him?" asked Rebecca. "Didn't you notice how he was trying to kill you?"

"He was under the influence of powerful forces and could not control his actions," was Noggin's reply. "His family will be happy to see him again."

He began pulling up the boy but saw the children's confused looks. "It will all be explained to you shortly, but we really must be leaving before the Destroyer shows up again."

'The Destroyer,' thought Rebecca. 'Will.'

Noggin jogged her out of contemplation. "Would you two mind

holding him while I help Velarr and Brufa?" he asked.

"Um, sure," said Thomas. Together, he and Rebecca held the boy in a standing position. The job was somewhat difficult considering the boy was almost a foot taller than either of them. It was clear, however, that Noggin and his wife were having an even tougher time: they were so short that the hurt woman had to press down on the tops of their heads for support. In this way the three of them walked over.

"Look Rebecca – I thought she was human but I don't think she is," Thomas quickly whispered.

"I don't think so either," she whispered back. "The blood on her wound is blue and her skin's a bit blue too, isn't it?"

He didn't answer because they had almost approached.

The slender woman took her hand off Noggin's head and adjusted the white toga she was wearing. Blue streaks of blood coursed down the front from a nasty-looking wound on her left leg.

"My name is Velarr," she said gracefully "and no, I am not human."

The woman pulled back her golden hair to reveal pointed ears.

Rebecca was embarrassed that she had overheard them, but her brother didn't seem to mind. "Are you an elf?" he asked.

"I am not familiar with that term," said Velarr. "I am an *Uru*."

"I don't believe you've been properly introduced to my wife Brufa, either," interjected Noggin.

Brufa managed a smile and a "Hello", but was evidently having a very hard time now that most of Velarr's weight was being placed on her head alone. Velarr sensed this and put her other hand back on Noggin.

The sprites, who had been circling high above, came down lower. The same yellow one zoomed over to Noggin.

"We must go!" it said.

"We're ready; just give us a good sprinkling."

"Wait…what about the sprites who died?" asked Rebecca.

"Look!" said Thomas. He pointed to the ground, where no sprite bodies could be seen. Instead, a tiny flower had sprouted where each one had fallen.

"All set?" asked Noggin. "Don't worry – you'll find him much easier to carry once you've got the sprite dust on you."

Just as he said that, the entire flock began to shake themselves vigorously over the group. When they felt a sufficient amount had been given, they stopped. Thomas noticed their wings were beating a bit slower.

"Okay then, let's start moving," said Noggin. "Thomas and Rebecca – you follow us."

Noggin, Brufa, and Velarr started running back the way they came, while the sprites flew overhead.

Rebecca and Thomas followed with the boy between them. Neither looked back at the still-unconscious driver or the grazing animals with their now-empty cages. These were left behind along with the Will they once knew, at least for the time being.

CHAPTER NINE

Moving very quickly is a funny thing. It gets you places much sooner, of course. But sometimes you might wish you'd had more time to think before arriving.

This was Thomas's dilemma: they had already travelled at least a hundred miles back into the forest and he had barely begun to digest their encounter with the Destroyer and their subsequent rescue (Thomas having been unconscious between the two events).

On the other hand Rebecca had a list of questions ready to ask, starting with why they hadn't been told their cousin was the Destroyer.

The rescuers slowed down and so did the children. No longer were the sprites flying overhead, but were now only a foot off the ground. They looked exhausted.

The party entered a clearing and the sprites immediately spread themselves out on the grass. Thomas saw the brown altar stone at the centre. "We've been here before!" he said.

"No dear, you haven't," said Brufa. "There are several of these places in Laurea." She bowed. (With difficulty since half of Velarr's weight was still on her head.) Noggin and Velarr followed suit, and that's when Thomas took notice of the other people standing by the altar: Jorka, an old man and two gnomes he didn't recognize, and

Queen Dalea at the centre. Rebecca had apparently just seen this too, as she and Thomas quickly bowed simultaneously.

"You are hurt, Velarr," said the Queen softly.

"I'll be all right Your Majesty. The boy will wake up shortly, however."

"Yes, indeed." She turned to the children. "Thomas and Rebecca I'm happy to see you well. Please bring the boy here." They carried him over the best they could now that the sprite dust had worn off. Jorka meanwhile placed several large bowls of what looked like spun sugar in front of the sprites. They sluggishly flew onto the food and began eating. *'Just like real butterflies,'* thought Rebecca.

"Lay him on the grass," instructed Queen Dalea.

The children laid the boy down gently and were happy to see the Queen smiling at them when they looked up again.

"I'm sure you must have many questions," she said. "Brufa and Jorka, please answer their queries and explain our situation while Hezzoroch and I tend to Velarr and the boy. Noggin, I will need you to give me details of the rescue effort."

The gnomes set Velarr down with obvious relief. Then Brufa and Jorka led the children to an area on the other side of the clearing where platters of food had been laid out. Noggin could already be heard explaining their rescue.

"- just one guard then?"

"Yes. I don't think we could've handled more than one."

"I recognize this boy. His name is Ochim."

The unfamiliar old man had spoken the last part.

Jorka started talking, drowning out the other conversation. "Jorka very happy to see Rebecca and Thomas!" he beamed.

"We're happy to see you too, Jorka," said Rebecca "I'm sorry for running off like that."

"Yeah, and I'm sorry about your home."

"That not important as Rebecca and Thomas safety," he replied, which made Thomas feel a little better.

"Please, have something to eat dears," said Brufa. "I think I'll try the berry cream cakes myself." She grabbed a large dessert from the carefully arranged platter and took several giant bites. "Oh it's *wonderfully* good!"

Thomas tried to stifle a laugh as she continued talking with a dollop of whip cream on her bulbous nose. Even though her gnomish body matched Noggin's from the round belly to the stubby fingers, her voice did not: in contrast to Noggin's gruff tone, Brufa's was rather high and girly. *'And she keeps calling us 'dear' like she's our grandmother,'* he thought.

Brufa finished the cake and started on a pastry, some of which managed to land in her white hair. "Oh excuse me," she said, finally noticing the whip cream on her nose. She wiped it off with a little laugh then handed each of them a pastry of their own. "Eat first, questions later."

Even Rebecca with her ready list of questions to ask felt compelled to get some nutrition. Although, what they were eating was hardly nutritious. All four of them had completely bypassed the large assortment of meat, bread and cheese, heading straight for the cakes, pastries, puddings and chocolates instead. The Day children eagerly devoured the delicious treats to fill their empty stomachs. Rebecca watched her brother engulf a custard tart in his right hand, then pause only a moment before starting on a chocolate croissant in his left. "'S good!" he enthused.

She herself had eaten three truffles and most of a melt-in-your-mouth lemon Danish. *'I'll have a piece of fruit when I'm done,'* she thought. *'Maybe an app –* '

"Thomas!" she exclaimed "I've lost the apples!"

"What? Where?"

"I don't know! I'm sure I had them in my hand at Jorka's house!"

"Rebecca leave with Jorka before running away," said Jorka with a grin. He rummaged through the sack beside him and produced the familiar plastic bag with its two apples and flashlight.

"Oh wonderful, wonderful!" said Brufa. "Apples from the Tree of Laurea, no doubt? I imagine those will come in very handy!"

"Jorka you're a lifesaver!"

Thomas took the bag and checked inside. "Still haven't spoiled," he announced.

"May I?" Brufa was looking at the bag with interest.

"Um...sure," he said, handing it to her. Truthfully, he was afraid she might eat the apples. Instead she merely removed the red one and began examining it.

"Definitely from the Tree of Laurea," she pronounced. "And what's this?" she continued, taking out the yellow apple. This one Brufa peered at very carefully, turning it round and round in her chubby hands. "An apple from your world, no doubt? Wonderful!" She handed them back. "And now for your questions, dears. Ask away and Jorka and I will try to answer them as best we can."

Thomas kept munching on his pastry and looked at his sister. "Why didn't you tell us Will is the Destroyer?" she blurted out.

"Yeah, everyone told us he was *taken* by the Destroyer," he added.

Jorka gave a confused look. "Will is Destroyer?"

Brufa looked at him and the children sympathetically. "So you did meet him," she said. "Well first of all, I was in no place to tell you anything. But would you have believed it even if you had been told the true relationship between your cousin and what we call the Destroyer?" The children didn't answer right away. "At any rate, Will is the Destroyer *and* he was taken by it – 'it' being the stone. Did he mention the stone to you?"

They both nodded. "He said he found it in a cave in the mountains," offered Thomas.

"That may well be true. Not much is known about it frankly. There were old stories about a stone with the power to destroy Fardoor: one that offered terrible magic to those who wielded it. How a twelve-year-old boy came to possess such a stone in an area that many have passed through is a mystery. Some believe the stone revealed itself to him."

"What do you mean?"

"I mean that some of us believe the stone itself has a purpose and a will, and that it's using your cousin to accomplish its goals."

"What do other people say?"

Brufa looked at them intently. "The others believe that it is the will of the person who wields the stone that determines whether its power is used for good or evil. Those are the people who believe your cousin cannot be saved."

"Like King Irith?" asked Thomas.

"Like King Irith." She placed a hand on each child's shoulder. "All of us here believe your cousin can be saved, but that it must be by someone who knows and loves him. The stone is powerful. Will is now very powerful; it will take great magic to separate him from the stone."

"We'll do it," said Rebecca.

"Yeah," agreed Thomas. "Why all the secrecy, though?"

"The Forest King has made his decree. He believes Will is acting of his own accord, and he is distrustful of you two because of your relationship with him. The King is wary of teaching you magic, as the Destroyer is capable of absorbing power from others."

"Oh I see. Are we to learn magic, then?" inquired Rebecca.

"Yes, I suppose so."

"Something more than how to make a bowl of porridge disappear, I hope," Thomas muttered.

Brufa took a lemon tart and bit into it. "Have you finished eating yet, dears?"

Rebecca was feeling a bit sick from having so much sugar so fast. "I'm done," she said.

"Me too." Thomas was rubbing his stomach.

"Well then do you have any more questions?" Brufa glanced over to where Queen Dalea and the old man were engaged in some sort of healing ritual. "I think we'd better give them a bit more time."

"I have a question," said Thomas. "What's the deal with the Nasrati? They make such a horrible noise that goes right into my head and I can't block it out! Will said only certain young people can hear it."

Brufa nodded knowingly. "That seems to be true. Their presence generally affects about half of those under fifteen, and they are the ones that are targeted first. Of course, their magic can wreak devastation on all creatures."

Thomas shuddered, remembering his encounters with the Nasrati. "What *are* they?" he asked.

Jorka seized this opportunity to respond, having so far been silent throughout the conversation. "Shadows," he announced. "Bad, nasty, Shadows."

The children didn't say anything but waited for Brufa to give a real answer. She noticed their looks and patted Jorka's back. "Actually, he's not that far off. We believe the Nasrati are shadows of a sort. Shadows of beings from another world or possibly another time. No one really knows for sure. They only just appeared when your cousin found the stone."

"He told us the stone helped him call upon the Nasrati," said Rebecca.

"Yes well, they do appear to be under his control, don't they? Although one wonders if it isn't really the other way around."

Again Brufa glanced at the party in the centre of the clearing. "I'll just go over there and see if they're done yet," she announced. She grabbed one more chocolate truffle and popped it in her mouth before heading off towards Queen Dalea.

The children were left with Jorka, whose familiar grin demonstrated how happy he was to see them.

"How have you been Jorka?" Rebecca put a hand on his arm.

"Jorka good. Jorka happy to be with friends Rebecca and Thomas."

"We're happy to see you too. How did it go with King Irith after I left?" She hoped he hadn't gotten in trouble.

Jorka scratched his wrinkly grey head trying to figure out what she meant, before coming to a realization. "Oh – Forest King not there. Noggin took Jorka to safe place and said not worry about children."

"So you didn't know about all this before we met you?"

Jorka shook his head 'no'.

Brufa came hurrying back. "They're ready for you, dears," she said, then eyed the desserts again before apparently deciding there wasn't sufficient time. She stepped behind the children and gave them a little push. "Let's hurry along now."

The Day children took her advice and did a fast walk over to the middle of the clearing. The first thing they noticed was the boy, who was now standing with his eyes closed. The remainder of his armor had been removed, and he looked much less threatening without it. He now wore only a white tunic.

The sprites had spread themselves out on the grass again, and Noggin was conversing with the two gnomes the children hadn't yet met. Both of them sported white beards and pointy red caps like the ones you might see on a plaster garden gnome. *'Obviously someone must have seen a real gnome before fashioning a fake one,'* thought Rebecca.

Queen Dalea was talking to the old man, but stopped when she saw the children approaching. She smiled at them and asked if their questions had been satisfactorily answered. They nodded.

"Well I am sure you will soon have more," she said.

Brufa directed them to a spot across the Queen before rejoining Noggin, who gave her a quick peck on the cheek.

Thomas was once again struck by how regal and serene Queen Dalea looked, and how young. She wore the same robes of green and gold, accentuating the slight greenish tinge of her skin.

"Allow me to introduce the remaining members of our group," said the Queen. "On your right are Cog and Klep," she announced, gesturing to the two gnomes.

"I'm Cog," said one.

"I'm Klep," said the other.

"Pleased to meet you," said both as they tipped their red caps.

"They're brothers," Noggin added.

"This is Hezzoroch," continued the Queen. The old man bowed. "He is one of our few remaining contacts with the humans in Fardoor."

"I'm sorry I couldn't join the rescue," lamented Hezzoroch "but I hear my 'stop powder' was a success." This he directed at Noggin with obvious pride.

"I thank all of you for your help," said the Queen. "And give pause to those who fell." The sprites twittered a bit on the ground as the group gave silent remembrance to the ones who died during the rescue.

Queen Dalea looked up. "Brufa has no doubt told you that we

believe your cousin can be saved, and that it must be by those who know and love him. In fact we believe you two are the only ones that can prevent his total domination of Fardoor and the destruction of Laurea."

"What about King Irith?" asked Rebecca.

"My dear husband is powerful, but not powerful enough I fear. He is distrustful of you and your ability to stop the Destroyer. I must tell you that many share his view. Please do not think ill of my husband. He only wants what is best for Laurea, and has worked tirelessly to defend it."

"Are we all in trouble for meeting here?" asked Thomas.

The Queen didn't flinch. "I admit, King Irith does not know that I have arranged this gathering. However, he will see that we are all trying to save Fardoor."

Thomas noted that she hadn't said 'no' to his question. He had the feeling that all of those present really would be in trouble if the Forest King found out.

Queen Dalea looked at the sprites resting on the ground and gave them a silent instruction. The sprites took off and headed upwards, high above the trees. There they hovered while the children wondered what was going on. They spiralled down again in a beautiful helix to give the Queen their message.

"I'm afraid we haven't much time," she said once the sprites were done. "So I must explain what is to happen next. Rebecca, you carry a crystal with unique properties of its own. I believe it is in your pocket."

"The Native decoration!" exclaimed Rebecca. "I'd forgotten all about it!" She pulled it out and looked at the dull stone with its faint purple color.

"The crystal was a gift of the Uru to the humans that entered Fardoor many centuries ago. At one point it became lost in your world."

"Will found it and gave it to me as a present."

"Interesting," said Velarr.

"Rebecca, you must go with Velarr to the Uru. They will teach you the crystal's secrets."

"What will they teach me?" asked Thomas.

"Thomas you are to go with Hezzoroch and Ochim to the humans."

"You're splitting us up?"

Rebecca began shaking her head. "No way – I'm not leaving him," she said, grabbing his hand.

"I am afraid it is a necessity," responded the Queen. "The Uru live in the sky and have knowledge of its many secrets. The humans possess powerful Earth-magic and are guardians of the stone altars you have seen."

"So? Why can't we both go to one?" asked Thomas. He was hesitant to leave his sister.

As patient as the Queen was, it was clear that the time for discussion was running out. "Knowledge of both will be needed to overcome the Destroyer and save your cousin. When the time comes, *we* will be responsible for getting you past his armies, but *you* must be able to confront him and the Nasrati."

The surrounding crowd was looking at the children with sympathy and anticipation. They knew this was a tremendous burden to bear for two who were so young.

Rebecca looked at her brother, of whom she'd always felt protective. "How long?" she asked. "How long will we be separated for?"

"I don't know," answered the Queen truthfully. "But I do know the humans are being severely tested, Laurea may only last a few months, and the Uru of the sky will be the Destroyer's next target if my husband fails to protect the Forest." She lowered her head. "We may not have as much time as we would like."

In the short time they had, the children were forced to accept her answer. They both knew they couldn't leave Fardoor without trying to save Will first, and this was the only plan presented.

"We'll see each other soon," said Rebecca.

Thomas forced a smile though he'd never felt this nervous in his life. "I'll hold you to that!"

They hugged each other very tight, and Rebecca found a few tears falling down her cheeks.

"I bet you'll learn some neat stuff with the Uru," said Thomas, remembering the ivory bolts Velarr had shot from her hands.

"And *you* better learn some magical way to clean your room. That'll really impress Mom and Dad!"

He laughed a little. "Okay."

Rebecca let go and wiped her eyes. "Ready?"

"Ready."

"Oh wonderful, wonderful!" exclaimed Brufa, throwing her arms around the children.

"Brufa, if I may?"

The jolly gnome stepped back a bit, looking sheepish. "Sorry Your Majesty."

"You are about to embark on a perilous journey," Queen Dalea announced to the children. "I offer you protection." She broke off two of the golden leaves from her crown, then bent down in front of them and pressed the first leaf against Thomas's chest. A golden energy field surrounded him briefly then disappeared.

"Cooool," he said.

The Queen smiled softly and did the same to Rebecca with the second golden leaf. "This will help guard against unwanted influence and control by others," she said ominously, then turning to the rest of the assembled crowd: "My friends, the destruction of Fardoor is not assured. Today we have embarked on a path to save all that we hold dear. The burden we place on Thomas and Rebecca is a heavy one. See to it that they do not bear it alone."

The crowd looked at the Day children and nodded. "And be strong, for many dangers still await us. Bad magic breeds bad magic (more nodding). Cog and Klep, the sprite dust please."

Each gnome produced a large satchel and handed it to Queen Dalea, who began ceremoniously sprinkling it on the members of the group. The children were getting quite used to this. Once done, she handed one satchel to Velarr and the other to Hezzoroch.

Velar came to stand by Rebecca, while the old man motioned for Thomas to come to him. "Ready boy?" he asked. "We'll be guiding Ochim back too. Don't worry – he'll keep up as long as we hold his hands. No need to carry him." This seemed doubtful to Thomas, as

Ochim was still barely opening his eyes. He wondered how the boy was even able to stay standing without toppling over. Hezzoroch noted Thomas's expression and stated "He will not wake up until I cause him to."

Velarr, meanwhile, had just finished explaining the Uru people's city in the sky to Rebecca. "But how do we get there?" she had asked.

"By flying of course. The Destroyer and the Nasrati have made attacks up there on occasion, but fortunately he hasn't yet been able to make his army fly!"

"Then why are you helping?"

Velarr turned serious. "The Destroyer's actions affect all of Fardoor. The Uru have been ignoring him for too long, content up in the clouds. Meanwhile he has grown stronger every day. Soon he will not even need an army to conquer us. One day he will turn his full attention to the Uru and I do not believe we will be able to stop him."

Queen Dalea finished giving instructions to the gnomes. "My friends, we must depart," she announced. "Be safe, and be quick!" Her body became enveloped in a bright light, which receded to reveal a green sprite where the Queen had stood. "Until we meet again!" she said in a tiny voice upon joining the flock of hovering sprites. Together they swirled upwards and out of sight.

"We'd best be off too," announced Noggin. "Thomas and Rebecca, it was a pleasure seeing you again. Remember you've got friends in Laurea," he said with a wink. "Jorka, are you comin' with us?"

He nodded. "Rebecca and Thomas be safe and be quick," he said, repeating the Queen's words. "Remember friend Jorka."

"How could we forget?" said Rebecca, who went over to embrace him. Thomas did the same and an enormous grin broke out on Jorka's face. He let go of the children and joined the four gnomes. Then with a wave the five of them zoomed off in a blur. *'I guess that's what we must look like when we move fast,'* she thought.

"Cooool," said her brother again.

"We must go too," Velarr announced. She put her hand out for

Rebecca.

"Just a second," she said, then gave her brother another big hug for good measure. "Be good and, um, safe and quick I suppose."

Thomas rolled his eyes. "Yes mom."

Rebecca let go of her brother and took hold of the Uru's outstretched hand. "Okay," she said, heart pounding.

Thomas gave her a nervous smile and a 'thumbs up', then watched as the two of them turned and sped into the forest. To his delight he saw a blue speck start climbing in the sky shortly thereafter.

"There they go!" he exclaimed.

"Yes, well, our trip won't be quite that exciting," said Hezzoroch. He grabbed Ochim's left hand and Thomas grabbed the right. "This way," instructed the old man.

CHAPTER TEN

Rebecca held on tight and moved her legs as fast as they would go. Velarr was very quick and she wasn't sure she could keep up if she let go, even taking the sprite dust into account. It was almost as if she was being pulled along. '*I'd say I was being dragged,*' she thought '*except I don't think my feet are touching the ground.*'

Velarr looked back at her. Her graceful features showed very little emotion.

"I guess your leg is all healed," was the first thing Rebecca thought of to say.

"Yes it has, thank you." The corners of her lips moved up in the smallest of smiles (which made Rebecca feel a bit less nervous). "Keep a tight grip Rebecca, we'll be flying shortly."

Her anxiety returned ten-fold. She reached up and held on with both hands. Now she knew she was being dragged: she had stopped making steps all together. The green blur of the forest turned into the blur of open air.

"Please…slow down," she pleaded.

"What was that?"

"Please…sl-"

"Ready? *Here we go!*"

Rebecca yelped as they shot up like a rocket. Very quickly, she could see the forest and the plains below. More and more of Fardoor came into view as they went higher still, and soon even the mountains could be looked down upon. A turquoise ocean glinted at them from far away. It might have been more enjoyable if she wasn't so desperately trying to hang on. Her body started shivering as they broke into the clouds.

"Exciting, isn't it?" said Velarr without turning her head around. "Just...a bit...farther – there!"

Warm sunshine surrounded them as they broke through the cloud cover.

Velarr had clearly enjoyed the trip, but immediately composed herself. She noticed Rebecca's death grip on her hand. "You can let go now," she said.

"I'd rather not," replied Rebecca in a quivering voice. Her face had a look of terror on it. It was impossible to see if the rest of her body was shaking too: whereas Velarr was comfortably standing on the cloud, only Rebecca's head had emerged above it. Although she didn't feel gravity pulling her down (as one might expect), there was still the terrible feeling that letting go of Velarr's hand might result in a freefall.

"H-help, Velarr!" she whispered.

Finally the tall Uru recognized Rebecca's fear. "You're not going to fall," she said matter-of-factly. "It is a simple buoyancy issue. We'll get that fixed as soon as we get to Elori's house." Velarr tried wresting her hand from Rebecca.

"DON'T LET GO!" she exclaimed.

"Oh all right," Velarr relented. "If you must hold on to something, then hold on to my robe, so at least I can stand up straight."

"Okay, if you're sure." Rebecca very carefully grabbed the foot of Velarr's robes, letting go of her hand once she was sure of her grip. Satisfied, Velarr began walking at a decidedly slower pace towards a gleaming city of ivory white. Rebecca glided alongside her.

The Uru city was an elegant construction of marble buildings resting entirely on a cumulus cloud, impossible as that may seem.

Tall spires rose above the surroundings in places, but the city as a whole appeared to be built on an incline. A modest palace stood at the highest point in the centre. Bathed as it was in sunshine, the Uru city reflected so much light that Rebecca found herself looking down to shield her eyes as they got nearer.

"Yes, it can be quite bright here," Velarr observed. "We will get you accommodated to that too."

"Why didn't we just come up inside it?"

"Part of the magic keeping it on the cloud prevents us from breaking through from underneath, but you can travel within the cloud below the city once you've entered it."

"Oh," said Rebecca, calming down. "Well it's very beautiful."

"Nothing compares to it at sunset," said Velarr as they approached the front gate. Two large Uru stood on either side.

"Hello Velarr," said one in a brusque tone. "This is the human girl?"

"It is. Her name is Rebecca."

"Hello," she said, feeling a bit funny at just being a talking head so far down from the standing Uru.

He ignored her greeting and simply stated "The King will see you in three hours."

The large gate swung open and the two of them entered.

"We'll go to Elori's place and I'll explain our situation there," said Velarr, anticipating her question.

"Okay." Rebecca relaxed even further and released one of her hands from the robe. To her relief, she didn't sink any farther into the cloud. Now she could use her free hand to shield her eyes from the glare instead of looking down. She looked up and marvelled at the beautiful marble houses with their delicate stonework.

"Try taking a step," Velarr encouraged.

Rebecca did as she was told and found she moved forward, although there was no sensation of pushing off ground. "That'll take some getting used to," she said.

"Indeed. This way please." Velarr led her young charge through the winding streets on their way to Elori's. Along the way they passed many more Uru with their pale blue skin and white togas. A few looked surprised to see a little girl's head gliding above the clouds. Most, however, gave a quick glance and continued on their way as if they had been expecting her. At any rate it wasn't unusual to see heads poking through the clouds. Sometimes an Uru would do just that, looking around before deciding whether to pull the rest of his body up or go somewhere else. Occasionally they would go the other route, lifting off and floating over a building or two to the adjacent street.

The two of them continued to walk, turning here and there, making their way up the incline. They stopped in front of a non-descript house, still made of marble but smaller than most, and in a bit of disrepair.

"Here we are," said Velarr. She knocked on the door three times, then waited a few moments before knocking again and yelling "Elori!"

No answer.

"Do you have a key?" Rebecca inquired. She quickly felt foolish for asking it, for why would she have knocked?

"I do have a key, in a manner of speaking."

She looked at her quizzically, then realized that Velarr was sinking into the cloud below. "Hold on," she was instructed.

Both of them submerged together. Rebecca's body had grown accustomed to the cold, damp mist, but she didn't like the feeling on her face. Velarr pulled her forward and up so that they re-emerged inside the home on which they had been knocking. The floors of buildings appeared to be cloud as well. *'At least the bottom floors are,'* thought Rebecca. She shivered a bit: her body was still in the cloud and her head was no longer in the sunshine. Lamps on the wall shed a light that was dim by comparison.

"Elori!" yelled Velarr. She walked over to the staircase and stuck her head up it. "Elori!"

A rumble was heard above them. "Coming, coming," came a voice down the stairs. More rumbling, and then an elderly Uru popped his head over the railing.

"Ah Velarr!" he said, bounding downwards. "Oh – and you must be Rebecca. I am Elori - how very nice to meet you!" He bent down and vigourously shook her hand through the cloud. "Having some buoyancy issues are we? Well we can fix that in a jiffy!" He gave her a wink.

Rebecca had been quite unprepared for such an animated person as all the Uru she'd seen so far were much more reserved. She didn't have a chance to respond before he turned his attention to Velarr, eyeing her suspiciously.

"You were hurt," Elori announced.

Velarr didn't flinch. "In the leg, yes, but the Forest Queen and Hezzoroch healed the wound."

Rebecca was surprised Elori could tell as even the blue blood that had previously stained her toga had been magically removed.

"Let's have a look," he said. Velarr pulled the toga over her left thigh aside, allowing him to peer at it closely. He pressed the muscle with his hand and watched for her reaction (there was none). "Yes, well, that is satisfactory," he concluded. "And now for you, young lady. I bet people told you many times to *'Get your head out of the clouds!'* Well that seems to be the only thing you've managed to do this time around!" He laughed at his own joke, but stifled it upon noticing Velarr's impatient look. "Okay," he sighed "Let's get you standing properly, shall we?"

"Please."

He gave Rebecca a startle by leaping into the adjacent room. She was beginning to wonder if he was really elderly at all. She had just assumed it because of his long, white beard that came to a point at waist level. This matched a shaggy mane of white hair that covered his pointy blue ears and fell into his eyes. His face also had a few wrinkles as opposed to Velarr's perfectly smooth blue skin.

"How old is Elori?" she asked in a whisper to Velarr while being pulled into the next room.

"Would you believe I'm two hundred and forty-nine years old?" said Elori, who had clearly overheard her. "Oh no need to be embarrassed," he added on seeing Rebecca's face. "I don't feel a day over a hundred and seventy. I imagine there will be a big party when I turn the big two-five-oh this year, eh Velarr? Don't bother asking her in front of me – she won't admit to anything." He gave Rebecca a big grin and another wink.

"We have less than three hours to prepare before King Arros wants us in his chambers," Velarr announced.

He frowned. "That soon? Then I guess we had better get down to business. First things first – he will want to see more than just your head, I gather. Do me a favour, Rebecca: take a big breath and hold it."

"Like this?" She took in a huge breath so that her cheeks puffed out. Slowly her body rose until her shoulders poked through the cloud.

"Good, good. Now breathe all the way out, as much as you can."

Rebecca did this, and sunk until only the top half of her face was showing. She looked up at Velarr for approval.

"Elori is a master at fixing buoyancy problems," said Velarr.

"It's true," he admitted. "This one shouldn't be too hard." He began rummaging through shelves of variously colored bottles for ingredients. "Rebecca, could you grab me the bottle of blue powder from that bottom cupboard there?"

Without thinking, Rebecca let go of Velarr's robe and walked over to the cupboard. "Oh!" she said upon realizing she was standing in the cloud by herself.

"Did you think you would fall?" asked Elori with a little laugh. "This cloud is magical. We spent years perfecting it so we could build our city on it." He continued rummaging without looking at her. "My advice to you is try not to think about it!"

"I suppose that's good advice." She opened the cupboard to find many glass bottles of various sizes like those on the shelves. Some held plants while others were filled with colored powders and liquids. One held a blue powder, and bore a label in a language she couldn't read. She pulled it out and held it high. "This one?" she asked.

"That's the one." Elori bent down and took it from her. He had now collected three glass bottles and placed them beside what looked like a stove with one element.

"Can I help?" Velarr inquired.

"No need, this won't take long." He placed a pot full of water on the stove then pointed his finger at the element. An ivory bolt like the one Velarr had released when rescuing the children shot out of his finger. This one was much smaller, and served only to heat the element up. Elori then started adding the ingredients: first a pinch of the blue powder Rebecca had handed him, next two silver leaves from another bottle. Finally he poured one spoonful of a purple liquid into the pot and began stirring it.

"My special ingredient," he told her. "It helps hold the mixture together evenly. Go to someone else and you might find they've raised your left leg more than your right arm!"

He gave a little laugh, which Rebecca did not join in: she was too grossed out by the fact that Elori had begun stirring his long, white beard into the pot without realizing it. Thankfully Velarr had also noticed. "Ahem. Elori – your beard," she said.

"What? Oh goodness. Yes that happens sometimes." He pulled out his now-purple beard and strained the liquid out onto the cloud-floor with a laugh. "Okay, let's see what we have got."

Velarr handed him a cup, in which Elori carefully poured a bit of the mixture. This he handed to Rebecca with the instructions to "Just take one sip."

First she checked it for hairs from his beard, and then reluctantly drank. Once again she rose until her shoulders had poked through the clouds, before sinking back down.

"Good, good," said Elori, taking the cup back and pouring the rest back into the pot. "Now let's go the rest of the way." He bent down and scooped up some of the cloud, then placed it in the pot and stirred. This time he was careful to flip his beard over his shoulder and out of the way. "Lighter we go, lighter go," he said in a singsong voice. He put some more cloud in the pot and continued stirring. "That should be enough," he announced, then filled the same cup and handed it to Rebecca.

"Just a sip again?" she asked.

"No, the whole thing this time I should think."

She took a big gulp and marvelled at how light the liquid was. It seemed to barely touch her tongue before continuing on its way down to her stomach. There was a very subtle, pleasant taste. The other two were watching her with anticipation. She too was anxious to see if it would work and quickly drank the rest. As before, her body slowly began to rise out of the cloud. This time there was no stopping at her shoulders though: she continued her vertical ascent and had the curious sensation of floating towards the top of a pool after having been at the bottom. She finally stopped rising when only her feet were left in the cloud, bobbing up and down in position a few times before resting entirely.

"How do you feel?" asked Elori, alarming her.

"Um – I feel fine."

Both he and Velarr visibly relaxed. "Marvellous!" he exclaimed. "Just the right amount, you see. Someone else might be trying to get you off the ceiling right about now. Always best to correct buoyancy indoors of course." He poured the remaining mixture in an empty glass bottle and let her write 'Rebecca' on the label. "Well that is all settled."

"Excuse me sir, but Velarr said you could also give me something so that the light from your cloud-city won't hurt my eyes."

"Paarl, Rebecca. Our city is called Paarl. And I certainly do have something! How could I have forgotten?" He pulled a small golden bottle with a rubber dropper from the shelf and handed it to her.

She held it in her hand and hesitated. "A drop in each eye then?" she asked.

Elori chuckled. "Goodness me, no! One drop on the tongue should do it!" He turned to Velarr while Rebecca measured one drop and swallowed. "Velarr, how much time do we have?"

Velarr looked at a small glass orb on the mantle of the adjacent room. "Just under two hours. Do you think you can finish?"

"I doubt it. But I'll get a good start." He turned to Rebecca, who was still excited about standing on the cloud proper (although she remained over a foot shorter than Velarr). "Rebecca, the crystal you have is very important. I need to prepare it for the upcoming demonstration to King Arros. May I have it, please?"

"Sure." She fished in her pocket and pulled out the Native decoration.

"Oh yes, very promising," Elori mumbled as he took it from her and examined the gem within. "I'll get right to work." He began pulling out more bottles and opened a few large texts that were already on the counter.

"Come on Rebecca," said Velarr "let us eat while Elori works."

She led her into a dining room. Rebecca realized that Velarr hadn't eaten any of the delicious spread that had been wanting for them when they saw Queen Dalea.

"You must be *starving!*"

"Uru do not have to eat as often as humans." She gestured for her to sit down.

This room, like the others, had a slightly worn look about it. Here and there one could see chips in the walls, and the many paintings of sun and sky that hung on them had begun to fade. A purple cloth with tattered edges draped loosely over the dining room table.

Velarr noticed her inspecting the room. "Both of our original homes were destroyed a year ago in a surprise attack, before we had any automated magical defence," she explained. "I would like to do more repairs to this place, but I have been so busy of late. I did manage to procure new furniture for the dining room, though."

"It's nice," said Rebecca.

Like the building itself, the entire dining room set was made of heavy marble and rested still on the cloud as if the ground was solid underneath. Rectangular blocks of stone served as chairs – far too heavy to lift, but she found they would glide quite easily.

Velarr opened the only cupboard in the room. "Will you have something to eat?" she asked.

"Sure. I've really only had dessert so far today – not very filling!"

She pulled out a woven basket and two jars, placing them on the table. Then she got two plates and two knives (all marble). "I think you will like this," said Velarr. "I believe humans call it *'jam and bread'*." She removed a large, doughy crescent from the basket and began smearing it with green 'jam' from one of the jars. "There you go," she said, handing it to Rebecca. "Oh excuse me – I really should have asked if you wanted gramafruit or looraberry."

The other jam was yellow. "Gramafruit is fine, thanks," said Rebecca.

"That's looraberry."

"Um, this one's fine," she repeated. To emphasize the point, she nibbled at one corner. It was surprisingly tasty! The white bread was very airy and the looraberry jam had a nice, tangy flavour. She took a larger bite while Velarr poured each of them a cup of crystal clear water. Rebecca eagerly drank from it.

"How do you get water up here?" she asked.

Velarr began spreading some looraberry jam on her own bread. "We fly our city through a rain cloud and collect the water it holds. We also have clouds for farming food."

Rebecca hadn't considered that the cloud they were on moved across the sky like a regular cloud; she had pictured it and the city to be stationary.

"So this cloud moves?"

"Of course it does! Don't all clouds?"

She felt silly for asking and continued eating. Velarr put down her food and leaned over to the floor. She swirled her hand in the cloud. "Look, I'll show you," she said in a friendly tone.

Where she had swirled a small eddy reached down in the cloud-floor and formed a tunnel through which to view the ground below. A deep blue glinted back up at Rebecca. At first she was confused until realizing that the city was now over the ocean she had seen.

"Neat!" she said. "Can you direct it?"

"If we want. Most often we just let the wind carry our cloud where *it* wants to go." Velarr paused. "I realize this is all very new for you, but there are certain things I must explain to you first: King Arros is the elected ruler of the Uru people. He is fairly knowledgeable in how to govern but not in how to wage war. His magic is limited and he relies heavily on the Uru Magic Council – the *Uraiel* - of which Elori is a member. Are you following thus far?"

Rebecca nodded. "But what about the gem in the Native decoration?"

"Yes – it is known as the Verrakal crystal. That was given as a gift to the humans in the forest hundreds of years ago, before the Uru lived in the sky. The crystal has powers only a human may use but only an Uru may unlock."

"For a brief moment five years ago, the Uraiel sensed its reappearance in Fardoor, after having been missing for centuries. The crystal disappeared again, but the Destroyer soon emerged and began building an army."

"That was me! I had it in my pocket the first time Will and I came here!"

Velarr nodded. "And then its presence in Fardoor was felt again three days ago, following which we heard reports of two human children in the Forest. We knew the Tree of Laurea had been found once more. Most of the Uraiel felt this was a sign – a way to battle the Destroyer. Some disagreed."

Rebecca found it hard to believe there was such a commotion over her and the decoration. She'd also finished her bread and wanted another piece. In her head she debated whether it would be rude to serve herself while Velarr was still speaking.

"More jam and bread?" asked Velarr.

"Please," she replied sheepishly.

"As I was saying, the Forest King is more powerful than King Arros, who does not wish to offend him. At the same time, his own Magic Council has advised him to pursue the crystal."

"So what did he decide?"

"He hasn't decided completely. King Arros has sent a small contingency of Uru fighters to Laurea. But he has also allowed you to come here despite the misgivings of King Irith. He wants to meet you and see the crystal for himself before deciding whether or not to let you stay."

"Really?" Rebecca suddenly didn't feel very good. All this fuss being made over her. All these people going through all this trouble and now she would have to show that it had all been worth it! "Any advice?" she asked hopefully.

"Yes. Bow once to the Magic Council and three times to the King. Address the King as 'Your Majesty' and the Council as 'Your Magistrates'. Give short answers to any questions and answer all questions that are asked of you."

She felt sick to her stomach. "Anything else?"

"Yes. Try not to be so nervous." Velarr gave an encouraging look. "Once the King sees the crystal's power he will realize he has made the right decision in letting you stay."

"But...I don't know how to use it!"

"Do not worry about that. Have some more bread."

At the moment, Rebecca felt more like crying than eating. She wondered if Thomas was under this much stress. Velarr was still watching her, so she took a bite. This seemed to please her and the graceful Uru began eating her own food again.

"It is important to keep up your energy," Velarr instructed as she pulled her golden hair back out of the way. Now she was sounding like their mother.

"Do you have any kids?" Rebecca inquired. She immediately regretted asking, for Velarr suddenly looked very uncomfortable, shifting her gaze and fidgeting with her toga.

"Yes I do - two in fact. I just...have not seen them in a while."

"Oh." She decided not to press further. "So – what's Elori doing, anyway?"

"He is unlocking the Verrakal crystal," said Velarr, obviously happy the subject had been changed. "Remember that the crystal's power can only be unlocked by an Uru. He is attempting this as we speak. It is terribly difficult magic, especially as it has been dormant for a very long time."

"Do you think he'll be done before we have to go?"

"I believe so. He only has to open it enough to show its true nature. He can finish the task later." She noticed Rebecca had stopped eating. "All done then? Why don't you have a rest? I will wake you up in one hour."

This seemed like a great idea to Rebecca. "You don't need my help for anything?"

"Not at the moment. Come, let me show you where you will be sleeping."

She followed Velarr to the staircase. As they walked past the kitchen she peeked in to see Elori looking frazzled as he flipped through the pages of several large books at once. Then it was up the stairs and onto real ground for the first time since she had entered the Uru city in the sky.

"This feels weird," she said. It seemed unusual to hear her footsteps again. "I like walking on a cloud."

"Well then I am sure you will enjoy sleeping on one," said Velarr. She opened the wooden door to Rebecca's bedroom.

"That's my bed?"

At the far end of the cozy, ivory-colored room was a little white cloud that hovered a few inches above the floor. The only other furnishings were a small cabinet and a yellow throw rug. A small window looked out on the street below.

"That is your bed," Velarr confirmed, looking slightly amused. "Please, try it out."

Rebecca jumped on top, fully expecting to crash right through. Instead she found herself lying on the fluffiest, most comfortable bed ever. And there was no feeling of dampness.

"How did you – "

"Magic."

"Mmm it's so comfy!" she said, spreading her arms wide. She paused. "That reminds me – I've been meaning to ask how you get all the sprite dust you need to do magic."

Velarr raised an eyebrow. "Sprite dust certainly is useful, but it is not the only way to do magic."

"Oh."

"Please get some rest." Velarr pulled the curtain over the window and closed the door behind her.

Rebecca instantly fell asleep.

* * * *

A quick knock on the door startled her awake.

"Rebecca, it is time to get up," came Velarr's voice from the other side. The door opened a crack.

"I'm up," she said. "Has it already been an hour?" It felt like she had just closed her eyes. If she'd been dreaming, then she didn't remember it.

The door opened all the way and Velarr walked in. She was wearing a gleaming white toga of finer material and a decorative belt of gold. This matched her golden hair, which had been brushed smooth and straight. Rebecca was struck by her beauty.

"I have brought you something to change into. You have time for a quick rinse." She placed a smaller toga on the cabinet and pulled back the window curtain. "The rain cloud is just at the end of the hall."

Rebecca didn't know how to respond to that last statement. "I'm sorry, what?"

"For your rinse. No, I suppose you have never used a rain cloud before. Come, let me show you."

Velarr continued to talk while Rebecca followed her down the hall: "The humans here use something called a 'bath'. Is that what you use? At any rate, I think you will find a rain cloud to be much more refreshing. Here we go." She opened the door and ushered her into a small room with a plump, dark cloud hovering above the centre. "It's easy," she said. "Say, 'Start' to begin and 'Finish' when you're done. There is soap on the wall, and that door leads to the wind cloud."

Velarr was pointing to another white door only accessible through the current room. Rebecca was about to ask what a wind cloud was for, but guessed it was for drying off. She was handed a small towel and left alone.

Slippery marble lined the entire room. Rebecca took off her old clothes, tiptoed to the middle and looked up at the dark cloud two feet above her head. "Start!" she announced.

The small cloud began churning. More frighteningly, it began to rumble as well. Tiny, distinct flashes could be seen within it. Then all of a sudden a torrential downpour a few feet wide on either side was released upon her. It felt like ten showers at once! *This is unnecessarily strong,'* she thought. *'At least it's warm.'* She quickly grabbed the bar of soap and lathered while the rain cloud continued its deluge. Of course, it only took a few seconds to wash up under those circumstances.

"Finish!" she declared. The rain cloud slowed down and the rumbling stopped. A rainbow formed in the mist that lingered in the air. "How nice," she said, reaching for the towel. "Better see about this 'wind cloud' now." She opened the other door half-expecting to be bowled over by wind of the sort she'd seen in the cave. Instead, she saw a tiny white cloud at the end of a still room similar to the first. On a hunch she yelled, "Start!"

Immediately the cloud began blowing wind. Actually *blowing wind* - as they often do in picture books, where those clouds usually have faces. This one didn't have a face – just a mouth. And it was blowing air at such a high velocity that Rebecca found she was dry in no time. "It sure is quick to get washed and dried around here!" she said to no one in particular.

All cleaned up, Rebecca walked back to her room to get changed. Over the last few days she had been wearing the same t-shirt and shorts from when they'd found the cave (although her clothes had been cleaned by the young sprites in the underground forest lair). She was now thinking how nice it would be to change into something different.

The toga was very comfortable. She already knew how to wear it because her whole class had learned how to put one on when they were studying Greek mythology at school.

Also on the cabinet was a brush that sparkled with a sprinkling of sprite dust. This was fortunate, as the wind cloud had blown her hair into a tangled mess. Once through was all it took for this brush to straighten her hair and make it as smooth as Velarr's.

"Definitely a keeper," she said.

Rebecca was now ready to meet King Arros – a realization that made her very nervous again. Downstairs she could hear Velarr and Elori talking quickly to each other. *'I suppose I should go meet them,'* she thought. Instead she went over to the window in her room, finding it overlooked the street that she and Velarr had used to reach Elori's house. Here and there an Uru walked along the cloud, but mostly it was empty. It was already feeling less strange to see these buildings sitting on a cloud, people carrying about their business on top of it. There was something relaxing in the way it moved underneath them.

The door below her opened and Velarr walked out. Looking up she caught sight of Rebecca at the window and waved her to come down. Rebecca gave a weak smile and waved back. She was as ready as she'd ever be.

"Elori!" shouted Velarr as Rebecca came down the stairs.

The old Uru was still rattling things in the kitchen.

"Hang on, I'm coming," he said, popping out just in time to greet her at the bottom of the staircase. He too had changed clothes, but into a rich, burgundy toga. "That looks good on you," he complimented. "Hmmm. I don't know about the shoes, though." Rebecca had put her hiking shoes back on, not knowing what else to wear. "Didn't Velarr give you a pair of sandals?"

"I certainly did." Velarr had come back inside, presumably to see what the hold up was. Normally so stoic, she was once again fidgeting with her toga. "The sandals are on the floor by the cabinet. Hurry now and change please – we don't want to be late for King Arros and the Uraiel."

"Sorry," said Rebecca as she scooted back up. Both of them were outside when she came back down wearing a small pair of golden sandals.

"Oh yes, much better," said Elori, smiling happily at her. She noticed the small brown package he held tight in his hands.

"All right, this way."

Velarr began walking at a brisk pace towards the palace. Elori was able to keep up but Rebecca was forced to do a little trot, her legs being much shorter than either of theirs.

"Why don't we just fly?" she suggested. "I see other people doing it."

"Velarr would find it difficult to carry both of us, I imagine," said Elori.

"You don't fly?"

"No, I'm much too old for that. At my age you learn to trust your legs a lot more than your flying ability."

"So you're stuck on this cloud?"

She hadn't meant to say it like that, but Elori didn't seem to mind.

"I hardly consider it being *stuck*," he laughed. "Plus every now and then I get one of the younger Uru to fly me down below."

"He makes it sound like he's an invalid," said Velarr without slowing down. "Really he is a highly respected and extremely talented member of the Magic Council – probably the only thing he doesn't boast about."

Rebecca wondered why his house seemed to be less nice than the others if he was part of such a prestigious group. She pushed this thought aside and concentrated on trying to keep up. It really was unfair for them to walk so fast when they knew she couldn't!

"Can we please walk a bit slower?" she asked.

"Nonsense," said Velarr. "Give me your hand."

This she did and for the second time that day Rebecca was pulled by Velarr. This time she stood up straight and glided on the surface of the cloud behind the tall Uru as if she were on roller skates. She imagined the three of them made an odd sight as they hurried towards the palace. If that were true, however, then the other Uru on the street either didn't notice or didn't care. This seemed to be a common trait of theirs. As far as Rebecca could tell, she was the only non-Uru in the city. She suspected they would care more if they knew what Elori was carrying. Both he and Velarr had attached much importance to the crystal, and Elori held onto the brown package as though it contained a great treasure inside.

Gliding up the cloud-street was actually a lot of fun. "Wheee!" exclaimed Rebecca as Velarr pulled her along. This spontaneous act was greeted with quizzical looks from several of the Uru, including Velarr and Elori. "Sorry," she said.

"No...harm...done," said Elori. Even he was now struggling to keep up with Velarr. She ploughed ahead anyway.

"Remember both the King and the Uraiel will be judging you very carefully," she said. "Do you recall how to address them?"

"Yes."

The last turn they took had brought the marble palace into full view. From outside the city all she could see of this palace was that it loomed large over the surroundings from its perch on top of the cloud-hill. Up closer she could see the elegant stonework that transformed this giant square building into a work of art. Holding up the roof on all sides were pillars carved into the shape of standing Uru, their eyes looking out onto the city below, faces all frozen in solemn looks. Some of the Uru pillars rested their hands on swords that touched the ground. Others had been carved wearing an outfit similar to Elori's. Golden doors several times the size of a normal person marked the palace entrance.

Velarr stopped about thirty metres away from the gates.

"Thank...Heavens!" said Elori as he caught his breath.

She adjusted her toga, then fixed both of theirs as well.

"It's beautiful," Rebecca remarked, gazing at the palace.

"It is, isn't it!" said Elori. "The King is particularly proud of the cloud sculptures, which I helped to create. See?"

Rebecca did see – behind the gates were several large figures that sprung from the clouds below. These depicted various scenes involving Uru, and were totally formed from cloud.

"That's pretty neat," she agreed.

"I should say so!"

Velarr raised an eyebrow. "If you're done bragging, the King is expecting us."

"Yes of course." Elori clutched the package a bit tighter.

The three of them walked at a regular pace up to the gates, which were opened by two Uru guards. They were now in the courtyard with its cloud sculptures of Uru conversing, consulting texts, or looking solemnly at passers-by. Up close, Rebecca could see that the sculptures kept their shape even though the clouds within them moved. *'How interesting,'* she thought.

Elori noticed her admiring his work and gave her a wink. Velarr continued her serious look.

Two further Uru stood aside the giant golden doors, dwarfed by them and the surrounding pillars. She nodded at the guards to permit them entry while they waited at the threshold. A loud, low rumble was given off by the terrific doors as they slowly opened. Stony silence greeted them from inside.

Rebecca held her breath as they entered an immense hall. More pillars. More marble, this time polished to a shimmering sheen. In between each pillar that lined the sides of the hall was an Uru dressed in the same burgundy toga as Elori, about twenty in all. Most of them were elderly, with a few younger ones. A single spot was left empty, which she presumed to be Elori's. At the far end of the hall, King Arros sat atop his throne dressed in a rich gold toga, gold crown, gold rings and a gold sceptre. He looked uncomfortable in his gaudy attire.

Velarr and Elori gave three small bows to the king, and one to each side of the Magic Council. Rebecca copied their movements, and was surprised when they remained at the edge of the entrance. They seemed to be waiting for the King to speak. Only he wasn't speaking, just staring - as were the members of the council. After what seemed like minutes, King Arros finally said something.

"Velarr, Elori, and…?"

Rebecca looked at them but they didn't speak. Elori gave her a little nudge.

"My name is Rebecca, Your Majesty."

"Rebecca, Rebecca. An interesting name. You are human, I presume?"

"Yes Your Majesty."

"Interesting, interesting."

"*Most* interesting," agreed the elderly Uru closest to the King. He had a long, white beard similar to Elori's, but his unfriendly look told her he wasn't quite as jolly. In fact, none of the Magic Council gave her any encouragement. Most continued to look at her with seemingly no emotion. This particular member's face was the least heartening.

"Your Majesty, if I may?" he inquired. King Arros nodded. "Thank you, Your Majesty."

The Uru turned to Rebecca, whose palms had become very sweaty. She wondered why Velarr and Elori hadn't said anything.

"Rebecca did you use the Tree of Laurea to enter Fardoor?"

"Yes, um…" Rebecca tried to remember what she was supposed to call members of the Magic Council. Velarr and Elori began breathing faster on either side of her. *She knew it was similar to*

'Majesty'! "…Your Magistrate!" Their breathing calmed.

The Uru continued. "Did you do so five years ago?"

"Five of your years, yes Your Magistrate."

"Did you bring the Verrakal crystal with you?"

"Yes, Your Magistrate."

"Did you bring the Destroyer with you?"

"No, Your Magistrate." The Uraiel whispered to each other. *'That got their attention,'* she thought. King Arros motioned for them to stop.

Rebecca didn't wait for the next question. "I brought my cousin Will – or rather, he brought me. Back then he wasn't the Destroyer. He wasn't even a teenager!"

"But he *is* the Destroyer now," said the King.

"And you *did* leave him here," said the same elderly Uru. "That part is undeniable."

Rebecca felt a pang of guilt. "Too true," said the King as he rubbed his chin. "Elori?"

Elori jumped at the opportunity to speak. "Thank you, Your Majesty. Yes the boy has become the Destroyer. But that is not Rebecca's fault. And now we have the means to defeat him!"

The Uru beside King Arros scoffed. "By giving her the power of the Verrakal crystal, so that she may turn around and give it to him? Your Majesty, I do not need to tell you that this is exactly what the Forest King was afraid of!"

"I will make my own decisions, Rukell," said King Arros.

He didn't say it very firmly. In fact, despite the show of veneration towards the King, Rebecca was beginning to think the real people behind each of his decisions were the members of the Uru Magic Council. *'The Uraiel – that's what Velarr called them.'*

"We know how *you* feel Rukell," said Elori. "However, the Magic Council voted on this and the majority of us feel that the Verrakal crystal is the best way to counter the Destroyer. It holds tremendous power – as far as we know, it has never been fully unlocked."

Another Uraiel interjected: "Because we could never trust a human with that much power! Sorry, Your Majesty."

Rukell was nodding vigourously in agreement. This was turning into a full-scale argument and King Arros was looking out of his element. "Elori?" he asked again.

Elori was happy to leap into the fray. "Why does the Verrakal crystal exist? Why is there a crystal of such power that can only be unlocked by an Uru, and only wielded by a human? We certainly did not create it, and neither did they. It represents a trust between our two people and it exists to serve a purpose. This is that purpose."

"There are plenty of other humans in Fardoor!" said Rukell. "Let us give the crystal to one we *can* trust!"

Although he said it, Rebecca got the impression Rukell didn't trust any humans.

"You know that the best chance of defeating the Destroyer is by getting past the influence the stone has on him. That will require someone who knew and loved him as he was before." A female Council member much older than Velarr but just as statuesque spoke this. She looked at Rebecca without smiling.

"I *don't* know that." Rukell retorted. "You assume the stone holds sway over the boy and not the other way around. Not all of us have come to that conclusion. I for one believe the Forest King is right in withholding power from that girl. Furthermore, Uru magic has progressed much in the last few hundred years. We may be at a point where we *can* wield the Verrakal stone ourselves. We should be using it to protect the Uru!"

Rukell then did something strange: he closed his eyes and pointed an open hand at Rebecca. Immediately she began glowing yellow and he gave a look like he was struggling. Quickly Elori raised his own hand and a ripple shot through the air at Rukell, knocking him down. Rebecca stopped glowing (to her relief). The Uraiel began whispering again. Velarr was looking pleased.

"What were you doing?" exclaimed Elori.

"Yes, what *were* you doing?" asked the King.

"I was merely seeing if she could be trusted," said Rukell as he got to his feet. He looked angry.

"Your Majesty?" Velarr had finally spoken.

"Yes, Velarr."

"Thank you Your Majesty, Your Magistrates. Whatever Rukell was trying to do, it could not penetrate the protective magic Queen Dalea has given Rebecca."

"I see. Rukell, I hope you won't try something like that again. And I will remind you that this very issue was already voted on by the Magic Council: the majority of you felt it unlikely an Uru could wield the Verrakal stone. The human before us should be trained to use it against the Destroyer. That is my opinion as well."

"Yes, Your Majesty," he responded in what sounded like mock reverence.

The King looked uncomfortable, but soldiered on. "Since both Rebecca and the Verrakal crystal are with us presently, I think we should at least see what the crystal is capable of." He looked around and was pleased to see many of the Council members nodding in agreement. "Elori – have you been successful in unlocking it?"

"I have Your Majesty – partially. I will need more time to fully unlock the crystal's power."

"Very well then, proceed."

Elori unwrapped the brown package, producing a violet gem. Rebecca recognized it as the one from the Native decoration, but its color was more vibrant, and it had been brightly polished. He bent low in front of her with the crystal in his hand.

"What am I supposed to do with it?" Rebecca murmured under her breath.

"Just hold on to it," he said. "You'll see." He handed her the crystal.

Surprisingly, it felt warm in her palm. Less surprisingly, nothing happened. She was nervously aware of everyone in the room watching her so she closed her eyes and cupped the crystal tight in both hands. She thought of Will as he was back home – so bossy, so much fun. She thought of Thomas and hoped he was okay, realizing how much she missed them both. She hoped something would happen soon so everyone could stop staring at her.

Rebecca opened her eyes and blinked a few times. Everything around her had turned purple. *'I'm glowing again!'* she thought. More accurately, the Verrakal crystal was glowing – a rich purple hue that surrounded her and rapidly increased in intensity within seconds.

"What's happening?" she exclaimed, now realizing that her feet were several inches off the floor. Instinctively she raised the crystal above her head and a beam of violet light shot from her body straight up through the palace ceiling. In shock her hands let go of the crystal and it dropped to the ground. The glow ceased, and Rebecca fell too.

"Sorry about your roof," she said.

No one was paying attention to the large hole she had made. All eyes were focused on this young girl, amazed at the incredible display of power she had shown without even trying. Rebecca was afraid to pick the crystal up off the soft cloud on which it had landed. Elori claimed it instead and brought it to the King. The Uraiel continued to stare at Rebecca, who grabbed Velarr's hand and held it tight. Even Rukell looked dumbstruck.

"What's going – "

"Shhh," said Velarr softly.

King Arros accepted the crystal for inspection, rolling it between his fingers and holding it close to his eyes. "I don't think any of us expected something quite so dramatic. You say you've only partially unlocked it Elori?"

"Yes, Your Majesty. I believe the crystal holds considerably more power still."

"Will the girl be able to control it?"

"She will need training, of course. Velarr and I will help her, and several of the other Council members have volunteered as well."

A male Uraiel, young enough to still have golden hair, turned his attention from Rebecca to the King. "Your Majesty?"

"Yes, Korall."

"Your Majesty, there is still the question of whether it will be enough."

King Arros looked to Elori for an answer.

"It probably won't be enough – at least not by itself. At this moment Rebecca's brother is with the humans learning their Earth magic."

Rukell reasserted himself. "Their magic is useless against the

Destroyer!"

"They know the secrets of the stone altars, Rukell – that is knowledge we do not possess," he replied.

"The humans lost that knowledge generations ago!" Rukell was getting angry again. "If they still knew the altars' secrets we would have seen them use it against the Destroyer already!"

Velarr stepped forward. "I have spoken with one of their elders, Your Majesty. The knowledge still exists. I have seen it and so has Queen Dalea."

King Arros nodded. "Yes, and we know they have now managed to hide their cities with magic. Let us hope they know more than just that." He handed the Verrakal crystal back to Elori and scanned the palace to see if any more members of the Magic Council wished to speak. Most were still fixated on Rebecca, which made her very uncomfortable. Even Rukell had decided to remain quiet, although he was clearly thinking things over in his head.

"I believe that will be all for now, then," said the King. "I suppose her training will begin right away. Elori, Velarr, Rebecca, thank you. Please keep us apprised of any developments."

"Thank you, Your Majesty," said Elori and Velarr in unison.

"And Elori - if you do come across a way an Uru could wield the stone, please inform me," the King added as an afterthought.

"Yes, Your Majesty."

They bowed to the King and the Magic Council, and Rebecca followed their lead. With great relief she then followed them out of the palace.

As the giant doors closed behind them, a breathtaking sight was laid out in front: the setting sun bringing the Uru city alive with color. The normally staid, white marble buildings were awash in rich hues of red, pink, and orange. The city itself had become a magnificent painting, and the best view was right where they were standing at the top of the cloud-hill.

"It's so beautiful," said Rebecca, momentarily forgetting her worries.

Elori sighed. "It is worth waiting for every evening."

Velarr took both their hands. "Well I would say today has been very productive. Come along, I'll fly both of you over – it won't be a problem."

Up they went and downwards they headed to Elori's home. He and Velarr walked her up to her room as soon as they arrived.

She climbed wearily into the cloud-bed. "Elori, *can* the Verrakal crystal be used by an Uru?" she asked.

"No," he said softly. "That is not its nature, although Rukell and some others would have us believe it so."

"Oh." Rebecca was kind of hoping it *was* possible, so that all of this responsibility wouldn't be on her shoulders.

They left her to sleep after saying goodnight. But despite feeling exhausted, she got up and stood at her window to watch the remaining sunset. Some uneasiness returned when she remembered the power the crystal had released while in her hand, and the fierce attack by Rukell. She reasoned there were probably many others that did not want her here.

At that moment, Rebecca desperately missed her family and wished she could see them again. Mostly she missed Thomas; they had started this adventure together and were now separated by it.

'I wonder if he's having as rough a go as I am,' she thought.

CHAPTER ELEVEN

"It isn't fair," announced Thomas. He was peering out the tent flaps at a gorgeous sunset that played its multicolored light against the bottoms of numerous fluffy clouds in the sky. "Rebecca's up there playing in one of those clouds while I'm stuck here on the ground in some ratty old tent!" He kicked the ground for emphasis.

Hezzoroch shuffled over to Thomas and looked out at the sky. "She's not up in one of *those* clouds," he said.

"What – you mean you can recognize which one the Uru live on?"

He nodded. "Oh yes – it's very distinctive. There are actually more than one, you know." The old man frowned. "And I don't think this tent is all that bad."

Truth be told, it wasn't really 'ratty' at all. To begin with, the tent was quite large. A comfy rug covered the spacious floor and a pile of heated rocks kept the air at a nice temperature. More importantly, this same air was filled with the delicious aroma of food that had been laid out in one corner. Several beds had been neatly made, and the boy lay asleep on one of them.

"It's still a tent," said Thomas. "Why are we waiting here again?"

"We must wait for Ochim's family to arrive," said Hezzoroch patiently. "He has been under the influence of the Destroyer. We must ensure that he is no longer under this influence before we take him to our city, or the Destroyer will surely learn its location." The old man shuffled back to one of the beds and sat down. He patted the teenage boy in a grandfatherly manner. It had been quite a shock to see Hezzoroch move so spryly when they had run here with the aid of some sprite dust. In the dim light of the tent he was back to looking frail and aged.

The three of them had been waiting for almost a day now, after having crossed a very large distance to get there. The mountains were behind them – Thomas remembered running past an ocean to get around the range. At first he hadn't even seen the tent, owing to the fact that it was invisible. Once they were on the other side of the mountains however, Hezzoroch had pulled out a small, three-pronged instrument and begun lining it up against geographical landmarks. Every so often he would pull it out and make a measurement, then they would run a bit more (the sprite dust had not yet worn off). After a few stops, the old man apparently found what he was looking for; Thomas could see each prong lined up perfectly with a different mountain peak. This time, Hezzoroch chanted something under his breath and the tent magically appeared before them, flapping in the wind. Inside was a young woman who had been waiting for their arrival. She looked at Ochim and Thomas with excitement. *'Bring his family here,'* Hezzoroch had instructed. And now the three of them were left behind to wait while the girl rode off on a horse tied out back.

Thomas had already eaten and taken a nap. There wasn't anything left to do but watch the old man and the boy; he wasn't allowed to go outside. He absentmindedly began fumbling with the polished stones in his pocket.

"You are nervous," observed Hezzoroch.

"Yes."

"I think it is time for your first lesson."

He grabbed two pillows and placed them on the rug, then gestured for Thomas to sit down.

"Show me the stones, Thomas."

"Alright." The smooth, brown stones were removed from his

pocket and handed to Hezzoroch.

The old man turned them over repeatedly and traced the symbols on each with his finger. "Do you know what these symbols mean?" he asked. Thomas shook his head. "I'm sorry to say that I don't either. Now don't look so surprised! This language hasn't been spoken for centuries. I need a language key to decipher it." He gave one of the stones back to Thomas and kept one for himself. "I'll tell you what I *do* know, however: this is the same type of stone that makes up the altars you've seen – in which case, it did not come from Fardoor."

"What do you mean?"

"I mean, the altars were made of stone that came from *your* world."

"But that makes no sense," said Thomas. "The stones altars are *magical!*"

"Make no mistake: it does come from your world." Hezzoroch crossed his hands and sighed. "Not all information has been lost. We know that the stone first appeared in Fardoor over two thousand years ago – that is also when the Eechawey first used the Tree of Laurea to cross into this world."

"You came from the Eechawey!" exclaimed Thomas. "I knew it!" He looked at Hezzoroch and Ochim. "But you don't look like Natives I've seen." This was something he had noticed a while ago: the features and complexion of Hezzoroch, Ochim, and the young woman suggested a mixed ancestry.

"Let me explain," he continued. "The Eechawey appeared in Fardoor and brought the brown stone with them. They settled in the Forest of Laurea and for a time coexisted with its other inhabitants. The Eechawey discovered the brown stone could act as a powerful conduit for magic in this world. They set up many altars and attempted to learn the stone's secrets. During that time, they continued to travel back and forth between the two worlds. There was a different Forest King then, and he agreed to share the forest with them as long as they abided by his rules."

Hezzoroch's eyes twinkled. He could see that Thomas was captivated by his story.

"And did they?"

"They did. In time, however, they learned about the existence of other humans in Fardoor on the other side of the mountains. Although these humans were of a different origin: their skin was pale."

"But how is that possible?" interrupted Thomas. "They couldn't have used the Tree of Laurea before the Eechawey! Where I come from there were only the Native people until a few hundred years ago."

"We too believe they did not use the Tree of Laurea. At least, there is no record of it."

Thomas pondered the conundrum for a moment before coming to a realization. "So then there's another portal between my world and Fardoor!"

"Perhaps. Its location, however, has been lost over the ages."

"It must be somewhere in Europe," mumbled Thomas.

This clearly had no meaning to Hezzoroch, who persisted with his story: "About eight hundred years ago the land the Eechawey lived on in your world became consumed in fighting, and they came to stay in Fardoor permanently. Irith had recently become the new Forest King. The Eechawey had shared some of what they learned with the old King, and even gave him a stone altar as a gift. However, the young King Irith was jealous of the magic the humans possessed and the connection they seemed to have made with Laurea. He looked upon them as unwelcome guests in the forest and insisted they leave. By then, contact had been made with the other humans in Fardoor. The Eechawey went to live among them, and their children intermarried. We are the descendants of both, and traditions have been preserved from both sides."

"Amazing," said Thomas. "But what about the stone altars?"

"The other humans had been mostly living without magic. When the Eechawey joined them, it was thought that the knowledge of the stone altars was forgotten."

"But it wasn't, was it?"

"No. The Eechawey language was lost, but their knowledge was written down in fifteen books. In the last few years there has been a determined effort to regain this knowledge by studying and translating the ancient texts with a language key that was found several decades ago. It is the only way we have been able to protect ourselves against the Destroyer; as he grew stronger, so did we."

The boy stirred and gave a great yawn. Hezzoroch looked at him with sympathy.

"He's waking up," said Thomas.

"No, not yet. I am keeping him asleep."

"Why? Don't you want to talk to him, to see what he knows?"

"If he becomes conscious while still under the Destroyer's power, then the Destroyer will be led right to us! That is why we take all these precautions. We've managed to keep the locations of our three cities a secret after we fled to foothills of the Jagged Mountains over a year ago."

"Oh." There was so much that he didn't understand yet!

Fortunately, Hezzoroch was a patient teacher. "Let me explain," he said.

"The Destroyer – your cousin – first began attacking us three years ago. He'd spent the previous two becoming consumed by the Destroyer stone in relative isolation. He'd learned to summon the Nasrati and communicate with them. No one knew where he was, although we all knew of his existence; we could feel it. And then one day, he attacked. Back then he wasn't so powerful and he had no army – just the Nasrati. Of course, we also had very little in the way of magical defence. Your cousin moved from village to village before ending in our capital, Kadeon. Along the way he devastated homes while the Nasrati took the young boys and girls within them. Hundreds of children were taken that first time, all between the ages of ten and fourteen. These were the ones who were old enough to be of use but young enough to easily subjugate with his mind."

"So his army is made up of kidnapped kids?"

"Yes, all of whom he controls." The old man's eyes welled up. Thomas felt awkward, as he wasn't used to seeing adults cry. Fortunately Hezzoroch composed himself before going on, causing Thomas to feel guilty relief instead.

"The Destroyer disappeared for several months before returning

– this time with his army. By then we had relearned some of the Eechawey's secrets – but what could we do? We knew it was our children behind the armor! He came back several more times, each time more powerful and with a larger army. Ultimately the texts revealed how to shield our cities from view altogether, so we fled to our current locations and did just that. We've managed to stay hidden ever since."

Thomas looked at the teenage boy sleeping softly in the corner. It was hard to imagine him as dangerous, although he'd seen it himself. "So I guess it's a pretty big deal when one of them gets rescued, huh?"

Hezzoroch smiled. "It *is* a big deal. But risky too – we have had close calls where a rescued child remains under the Destroyer's control and our location is almost revealed. Removing his influence can be hard indeed." He gave a sideways pump of his fist. "But worth every effort! Ochim's family will be extremely happy – he was one of the first taken."

Now Thomas smiled. "Well then I don't mind waiting in this tent."

"I'm glad for that. And now I believe it really is time for your first lesson, wouldn't you say?" Hezzoroch rolled back the sleeves if his beige robe and grabbed one of the stones. His bushy grey eyebrows furrowed in concentration.

"What should I – "

"Patience Thomas." His face went more relaxed but the eyes remained closed. "Ah, there we go."

Thomas looked on amazed as soft light began streaming through the cracks of the old man's clenched fist. "Cooool!" he said.

"The Eechawey called these small stones *wachaoum*. Please take the other one in your hand as I have done," instructed Hezzoroch.

He did as he was told.

"Are your eyes closed?"

He closed them. "Yes."

"Good. Now, the brown stone acts as a conduit to the essence of Life itself – what we call the *Gaia* force. Feel *through* it."

"You got it," said Thomas. "Feel through the stone. Um – how do I do that, exactly?"

"Patience," the old man repeated.

He waited, holding the stone in his closed hand. *'It would be easier to feel through the stone if I knew what that meant!'* he thought. But then something clicked. For a moment he was aware of something much larger than himself – and then it was gone.

"That's right – you had it," said Hezzoroch. "Try again."

Thomas didn't say anything, but concentrated on making that same connection. *'The stone is a conduit...'* he thought to himself. *'Such a small stone. But* Life itself *– that's got to be big I'm sure!'*

It started near him. He felt the boy and the old man, the dry bush around the tent and the insects among the bush. A bird flying overhead. Suddenly this feeling began racing outward in all directions. Up through the sky and down, down through the earth below. Out across the Eastern Plains to the Jagged Mountains where Thomas could feel thousands of people and knew their city must be there. More than that, he *felt* the mountains themselves!

Life was enormous. It wasn't just the animals and plants he was connected to – the planet itself was alive! Thomas felt as though everything was humming at the same frequency and he had just tuned in to the correct station. He opened his eyes and wasn't surprised to see light pouring out between his own fingers.

Neither, apparently was Hezzoroch. "Hold on," he said.

He tried to hold on but the experience was overwhelming. He was a tiny little corner of a vast web that his brain was trying to wrap itself around. He knew he was losing his grip. In an instant the connection withdrew like the snapping back of a stretched elastic band. Thomas was left panting.

"Well done," said Hezzoroch. "You have true talent, as the Eechawey must have. I suspected as much since you have grown up amongst the brown stone as they did."

"I've...never...seen it." He was still trying to catch his breath.

"Nonetheless, it is there." The old man got up and poured Thomas a glass of water. "Have a drink. It won't be quite as dramatic next time. I must confess I helped you further along than you would have gone on your own – just to see if you could get there. Quite remarkable. Your power will exceed all of ours quite handily, I'm sure of it."

Thomas's eyebrows were raised as high as they would go.

"You're not there yet, of course," he added. "Everyone has to start somewhere though, don't they? Here you go."

He eagerly gulped down the water while Hezzoroch watched, searching his face before coming to some unknown conclusion in his mind.

"All right, take a few minutes then try to make the link again. I'm going to have a nap myself, so you'll be on your own this time." He shuffled off to one of the beds.

"Wait, I have a question!" said Thomas.

Hezzoroch was already pulling up the covers. "Yes?"

"Did it take you three years to learn all you know?"

"Dear me boy, no! (Thomas felt a wave of relief.) It actually took much longer. There are some of us who made a point of reading the ancient texts long before the Destroyer arrived. I've been studying them for the latter half of my life. Of course, reading is one thing. The texts are written in code and verse and open to interpretation. Having a good teacher – which I never had – makes things much easier on the practical side of things." He saw the concerned look on Thomas's face. "Don't worry – I will be your teacher, and others of course. We've made great strides in understanding the ancient texts over the last few years, with so many more of us studying them." He gave a great yawn. "Now this old man is going to sleep while you keep practicing."

"Okay."

Hezzoroch shut his eyes and began snoring softly after only a minute. Thomas picked up the same *wachaoum* and felt its smooth edges. He grabbed the other one and compared the two. *'I wonder what these symbols mean?'* he thought.

He kept the stone he had originally used in his hand, placing the other one back on the rug. He held it in a closed fist as before and concentrated - unsure if he was ready for the same tremendous experience of connection with the life around him, but excited about it all the same.

This turned out to be a moot point: he found he wasn't able to make any sort of connection the second time around. "Just how much *did* Hezzoroch help me anyway?" he said under his breath after about ten minutes of intense concentration. Thomas traded the stone he held for the one on the rug. Nothing. This one lay lifeless as the first: an ordinary brown rock in an ordinary boy's hand.

Still, he did not give up. He held the wachaoum, repeating a continuous mantra of *'Feel through the stone'* in his head. Without noticing it, his breathing changed considerably into a slow and steady rhythm. Intense concentration became meditation. Thomas imagined the stone for what Hezzoroch had called it: a conduit. And then he began to actually feel through it. This was very different than his initial experience – although he had been racing outwards with his connection to Life all around, it was so fast and overwhelming that it almost felt as if everything was rushing in on *him*. This time he was much more in control. He had 'tuned in' to the same station, but the volume was way down.

He probed outward through the stone. As before, he felt his immediate surroundings first: the boy and the old man, the ground beneath him. He went farther. The wind picked up outside the tent (*'Did I do that?'* he wondered). He heard its howling while *feeling* its strength at the same time. He was in more control, yes, but it was also much harder to expand outwards. He wouldn't be able to zoom out with his connection even he wanted to. After a few minutes the strain wore on him and he released the stone.

"I'm really doing it!" he exclaimed. He looked to see if Hezzoroch had noticed, but the old man was still asleep. After another short rest, he tried again. This time he made the connection sooner and expanded outwards further.

And so it went that Thomas kept practicing for over two hours, each time making some progress. Twice while he was deep in the link he thought he heard someone whispering to him and looked up to see if Hezzoroch was out of bed. He wasn't, and Thomas decided it must have been exhaustion. Indeed, the length of time he could hold the connection was decreasing rapidly. When he was no longer able to hold it for more than a few seconds, he crawled into one of the beds and fell fast asleep.

* * * *

It was a strange dream. Thomas was back at his home in Muskoka having dinner with the family. Hezzoroch and Ochim were also at the table, and Thomas's mom busied herself serving them her famous chicken casserole before sitting down. Rebecca was talking about an upcoming sleepover at her friend Jenny's house. Their dad wanted to know if boys would be attending. Hezzoroch was trying to tell Thomas about the time he'd crashed his jeep during the war, but Thomas was thinking that Grandpa had already told him that story. Ochim was looking down at his plate, eating the casserole without speaking. Something wasn't right.

"Where's Will?" Thomas asked.

"Oh, he won't be able to come tonight," said his mom.

Ochim looked up and smiled. Thomas looked back at his mom.

"You know the Destroyer is very busy, honey," she said.

He looked back at Ochim. The boy winked.

"Eat your casserole, dear. The Destroyer will be very angry unless you eat every last bit!"

Hezzoroch (Grandpa?) patted Ochim on the head, who continued to look at Thomas, eating and smiling. Suddenly a blue light filled the dining room.

"Mom, the light!"

"What light dear?"

The sound of the Nasrati approaching.

"There's no noise," his mom volunteered.

He clasped his ears in pain as the sound intensified. No one else seemed to notice! Falling off his chair onto the hardwood floor, he tried to scream but couldn't.

Thomas woke up with a startle and gasped. The boy was no longer sleeping. He was lying in his bed, staring at Thomas. Hezzoroch's soft snoring filled the background.

He hesitated a moment after the initial fright, then whispered "Ochim?"

The boy blinked but said nothing.

"Ochim?" Thomas whispered again. No movement this time. *'Should I wake Hezzoroch to tell him Ochim's no longer asleep?'* he wondered.

Perhaps not asleep, but not really awake either. The boy's vacuous eyes stared straight ahead, with nothing behind them. Another blink.

He sat up to see if the boy would track him with his eyes. He didn't, and Thomas decided not to wake Hezzoroch after all, as the boy clearly was not awake himself. In fact, he closed his eyes after another minute.

Of course, there was no way Thomas could go back to sleep. He had already forgotten the dream, but the idea that Ochim may or may not be staring at him was disconcerting. Instead he got up and tiptoed to the food.

'Can't bite into any fruit,' he thought *'too loud. Better stick to the pastry!'* He sunk his teeth into a jam-filled sugar bun and opened one of the tent flaps a crack, permitting a thin shaft of sunlight to poke through to the floor. "It's day!" he whispered excitedly. "I must have slept for hours!" He opened the flap a bit more and scrunched his eyes against the bright sun. Outside a light wind stirred the bush but nothing more. He could see for miles.

Thomas decided to get a little practicing in with the stone before Ochim's family showed up. Happily, he found he could pick up right where he left off. And now that he wasn't tired he could hold the connection for much longer, probing ever farther through the stone in increments he could handle. He sensed a party on horseback approaching the tent, about two miles away. And then he sensed something much closer.

"You're awake, Hezzoroch – I can feel it."

"Or perhaps you just noticed the snoring stopped."

The old man shuffled over and Thomas opened his eyes. "No, don't stop on my account. Hold onto it. Feel through the stone. Now let me see where you are."

Thomas closed his eyes again as Hezzoroch picked up the other wachaoum.

"Ah, very good. That's Ochim's family on the way as I'm sure you've guessed." He let go of the stone and Thomas followed suit. "Invigorating, isn't it?"

"Yeah," he agreed "I think I'm getting the hang of it!"

The old man chuckled. "I should say so! Thomas, I believe I've still underestimated you after last night. The progress you've made already, the control – well it's nothing short of extraordinary!"

Thomas thought of something. "When Rebecca and I found the tree in the cave in our world there were sprites in it. They said I *'have the power'* – me specifically. But they said I wasn't ready; they wanted Rebecca to come along."

"Thomas, you're a natural. The sprites sensed it and King Irith must have too."

A hand poked through the front of the tent and opened it. It was the young woman and she had brought Ochim's parents. "Ochim!" they cried as they rushed over to his bed. He was still asleep.

Hezzoroch joined them at his side. "Before I wake your son, it is important that we establish he is no longer under the influence of the Destroyer," he said.

The parents didn't seem to be listening. Tears of joy were running down their cheeks as the boy's father held his hand and his mother stroked his face.

"Only you can do that," said Hezzoroch more forcefully. "Do you understand?"

His mother nodded. "Yes, what do we do?"

"Hold one of his hands, each of you. I will bridge you to his thoughts. You must search to see if anything does not feel right. Look for something that does not belong."

"Alright Hezzoroch."

The old man reached into his pocket and pulled out a brown stone of his own. This was placed on the sleeping boy along with a sprinkle of white powder on all three family members. Thomas hadn't moved from his spot on the rug and the young woman stood a respectable distance back from the family. They both watched as Hezzoroch began a barely audible incantation. With a wave of his hand the parents closed their eyes and an orange field of energy went up around them and the boy. Flashes of people and places began appearing in the field, like watching clips of home videos without the sound. Here and there the smiling faces of Ochim's parents were recognizable, often looking much younger. Playing with other children, eating a meal, sitting in what looked like a classroom – they were all watching Ochim's childhood memories! Hezzoroch gave him a look as if to say 'Impressed?' Thomas just smiled back and continued to watch in amazement.

A few more minutes and the old man flicked his hand again. The field stopped and Ochim's parents opened their eyes, accepting the glasses of water provided them by the young woman.

"Well?" said Hezzoroch. He was studying their faces for a reaction. The mother squeezed Ochim's hand. "He's our son."

"Yes, but did you sense anything wrong?" he pressed. "Any part of Ochim's thoughts that did not fit or belong there?"

"No, nothing. He is untainted by the Destroyer."

The father looked confused. "Hezzoroch, it seemed as though nothing from our boy's last three years was there."

"His last three years were spent under the Destroyer's power. The ceremony performed by Queen Dalea and myself has removed any and all influences of the Destroyer, including those memories. I will wake Ochim now. To him, the last three years never happened; he will believe he went to bed yesterday an eleven year-old boy." Hezzoroch sighed. "This will take a lot of explaining. You must be patient with him."

"Yes of course," said the mother. "Whatever it takes."

Hezzoroch indicated for everyone to stand back. The brown stone was brought out again and held on his open palm. The old man gazed at the peacefully resting boy. "Awake," he commanded.

Ochim slowly opened his eyes and yawned. He blinked a few times while taking in the unfamiliar surroundings, before latching on to the faces of his parents. "Mom? Dad? Where am I?"

"Oh Ochim!" exclaimed his mother. Both parents rushed forward to embrace their son. Tears streamed down their faces.

"We thought we'd never see you again!" said his father.

Ochim looked to be in shock. "Dad what's going on?" he asked.

"You were taken by the –"

Hezzoroch shook his head and mouthed 'No'.

"What?" asked Ochim.

"What matters is we're all here together," said his mother.

Ochim appeared very confused. He looked at the other people watching him in the tent. "I know you," he said to Hezzoroch. "You're the librarian."

"He's much more than that, son," said his father. "His name is Hezzoroch."

"Pleased to meet you."

"Hello young man. A pleasure indeed. Let me introduce you to everyone else and then we must be leaving. Your parents will fill you in along the way."

Hezzoroch introduced Thomas as a friend from a distant part of Fardoor. Ochim's parents seemed to know the truth, however. The young woman turned out to be the boy's cousin Nojanna. ("Impossible!" Ochim exclaimed. "Nojanna's only fourteen!")

The five of them left the tent and headed back towards the mountains by horseback. Thomas rode on Hezzoroch's horse while Ochim's cousin shared hers with him. Initially impressed by the magic that hid the tent from view, Ochim became even more shocked upon recognizing that his body had changed: he now stood several inches taller than his mother whereas before he had looked up to her. His parents immediately began telling him that he had fallen under a powerful spell that kept him asleep for the last three years. He was also informed of the ongoing war that had caused them to flee their old city and build a new one that was shielded like the tent. They neglected to tell him who the enemy was, and Ochim didn't ask. Instead he wondered where his people had learned such magic. "From the Uru or the inhabitants of Laurea?" he inquired.

Hezzoroch then joined the conversation, telling Ochim that the magic had been learned by studying their people's own ancient texts. Ochim found this amazing, saying that he too would like to read them.

Thus far Thomas had remained totally silent. He had never ridden a horse before and was using most of his energy making sure he didn't fall off the steed he shared with Hezzoroch. This despite the fact they were currently at more of a trot than a gallop. "Don't let me fall," he said to the old man.

"Don't worry, I've got you." He offered Thomas the reins as a joke but was politely refused. "No? Then just try to relax – it's easier and more comfortable riding a horse when one is not so rigid."

Thomas did try to loosen, and eventually found how to share the horse's rhythm.

"There you go," Hezzoroch congratulated him, and then to everyone else: "I suggest we move a bit faster."

A little kick to the side and each of the horses sped up. Instead of tensing, Thomas found the horse's new rhythm. Riding in the open like this was exhilarating! He breathed in the fresh air and smiled under the warm midday sun. Everyone else concentrated on riding their horses, except Ochim (who sat behind Nojanna); he was busy taking in their surroundings.

'He seems to have accepted his parent's explanation pretty quickly,' thought Thomas. *'I don't know if I would have handled it as well.'*

He decided to also check out this new environment. Looking around he could see that this side of the mountains was not as flat as the expansive plain he and Rebecca had seen on the other side. Rolling hills dotted the landscape, becoming steeper and more frequent as they approached the range itself. "The mountain's foothills," he mumbled. "That's where I felt the human city."

Wild green grass covered the ground, with prickly shrubs and squat trees making an appearance here and there. A glittering blue ocean could barely be seen to his left in the distance. This was definitely something Thomas hadn't noticed when traversing the plain on the other side of the mountains, although he wondered if perhaps he'd just been too far away from it.

He looked up at the sky. Yesterday Hezzoroch had said none of the clouds up there carried the Uru city. *'I wonder if I could find it using the brown stone,'* he thought, realizing he had a better way of exploring their environment at his fingertips. Hezzoroch was directing their horse, and Thomas was doing a good job of keeping steady on it at their current speed. He reasoned there was nothing else for him to do, so why not get some practice in? Slipping his hand in his pocket, he felt the stone's familiar smooth edges. This would require keeping his eyes open while trying to make a connection – something he had never done.

It wasn't hard: after only a moment's concentration he got it. The world around him responded with an intensification of its color – something he had missed when his eyes were closed. He also found he could look in one direction while feeling outwards in all others. Instantly he was already searching at the foothills of the Jagged Mountains and knew exactly where the human city was.

'Will must not have this power,' he thought *'or he'd have found it already.'*

Thomas was proud of himself for this accomplishment. Without looking, he focused on the people around him. Each individual offered a different feeling – a fingerprint with which to identify him or her. Somehow, though, Ochim felt 'less there' than the others. It was the same muted feeling he had received from both Ochim and Hezzoroch when they were sleeping last night.

'I hope he isn't sleeping,' thought Thomas *'or he'll slip off the back of the horse!'*

He glanced over at Ochim. He wasn't sleeping. In fact, he was staring at Thomas. Or rather, he was staring at Thomas's pocket where a distinct glow could be seen. In panic he released the stone, ending the glow and the connection. In his peripheral vision he could see Ochim look up from the pocket to his face. He pretended not to notice while the boy's big, brown eyes peered at him in wonder. He allowed another quick look in Ochim's direction; the boy did not look away. Thomas turned instead, feeling very uncomfortable. *'I wish he'd stop staring,'* he thought. *'Maybe he's never seen the brown stone do magic before. Maybe he'll want to learn too, and then at least I'll have a friend.'* Thinking of this made him miss Rebecca, and wonder if she had made some friends already. He glanced back at Ochim and was happy to see he'd stopped staring. He pulled himself up closer to Hezzoroch's ear.

"We're almost there," the old man said before it could be asked.

"I just wanted to say good job with the riding. I already know where the city is; I felt it."

"Is that so? Good for you."

"Ochim saw me do it though."

"Did he now?" Hezzoroch chuckled. "Well I suppose everyone will find out soon enough. There will be many eager to share with you what they know already. Don't worry yourself about that now, though."

"Okay."

He sat back and enjoyed the view. The land was beginning to rise and fall in ever-increasing inclines. Verdant hills dotted with evergreens were just up ahead; twenty minutes more and they were navigating between the foothills themselves. A small river carved a convenient path for their group to follow. The riders slowed their horses back down to a trot and let Hezzoroch lead the way along the red-brown riverbank, stopping when they reached a point where five hills surrounded them on all sides.

"All right Thomas," said Hezzoroch "which one is it?"

"I need to use the stone," he whispered back, feeling embarrassed; they were all looking at him.

"By all means Thomas, use the stone."

"Okay." Reluctantly he reached into his pocket and grabbed the brown stone without taking it out. "That one," he said, pointing to a hill just to the right.

Everyone's jaw dropped. Even Hezzoroch was surprised with the speed of his determination. "Well done Thomas! Let's hope the Destroyer never figures it out!"

"That was really impressive," said Nojanna as they rode towards the hill. "How old are you?"

Thomas blushed. "I'm ten."

"Well I'd say that's pretty good for a ten year-old! Where did you say you're from again? No wait, you don't have to answer that. I'm sure my Dad will want to talk to you – he's nuts about the ancient texts and stuff."

"All right," he said, unsure if that was an invitation or not.

Hezzoroch looked back at him. "Well young man, here we are.

Brace yourself."

With that, he rode their horse *through* the hill. Thomas had been expecting Hezzoroch to reveal the city after some sort of incantation – much as he had done with the tent. Instead they walked through seemingly solid ground as if it were water. They emerged on the other side to find a rambling city nestled in the steep valley between two real hills. A giant, fluid barrier surrounded them on all sides, and sunlight poured down through it from above.

"Welcome to New Kadeon, Thomas."

"Cool!" He looked back to see the others coming through. On the other side of the barrier he could see the valley from which they had come, only it was like looking through a shallow pool. The rest of the group came through the field, causing ripples to spread out from where they entered.

"That's really neat, Hezzoroch. But does it mean anyone or anything can just walk through it?"

The old man pointed to two thin towers. "No. The watchers up there permit entry."

One adult stood on the flat roof of each tower. No sooner had he pointed them out than Thomas saw the watchers raise their hands and mouth something he couldn't hear. An orange shimmer raced across the barrier and was gone. The group stayed on their horses and trotted down the central street.

"See? Now anyone or anything that comes across our city will walk right over it without ever knowing it's there - including the Destroyer!"

"What – he's walked over your city?" Thomas said with alarm.

"No of course not. But he has sent the Nasrati looking through all the foothills. They've been very close by without finding us."

"The Nasrati were also looking for Jorka's home!" Just mentioning their name made him shudder. "First there was this creepy blue light and then they came bursting through the door. His house was hidden too." Then in a much quieter tone: "They only found it 'cause I opened the door the night before."

Hezzoroch looked at him sympathetically. "Yes, most unfortunate. The blue light you saw was the Destroyer's magic guiding the Nasrati. They only come searching at night, which is precisely why we don't allow anyone to go in or out of the city between sunset and sunrise. Nojanna didn't bring Ochim's parents to the tent until this morning for that reason."

"Oh." He had stopped paying attention to Hezzoroch and started noticing the people they passed on the street. Many of them waved at the old man and looked at Thomas with curiosity. Some of the adults seemed to recognize Ochim, and most of these had tears in their eyes. Their own small children tugged at their parents' clothes, wanting to know why they were crying. Ochim's parents rode proudly beside their son, faces beaming. "It's Ochim!" they yelled to some people they knew. "Our son is back!"

Thomas couldn't help but feel proud too. Ochim, for his part, couldn't look more bewildered or embarrassed by the attention. *'Glad it's not me,'* thought Thomas.

Shortly they arrived in what seemed to be the main square, where many more people were waiting for them. The square occupied the flattest part between the two hills, and the city seemed to grow outwards from it. Most of the buildings were square themselves – from the large, impressive structures that bordered the immediate area, to the smaller houses that spread up the hill. And all of them were smoothed over with the same red clay that lined the streets and the riverbank.

Hezzoroch stopped his horse in front of a large group of official-looking people. A young man wearing a smart blue vest helped him and Thomas off the horse.

"Some of you may remember Ochim," the old man said upon dismounting.

The boy's parents watched proudly as the officials lined up to shake his hand in turn. Ochim gave a puzzled half-smile as each of them introduced him or herself, saying things like "So nice to see you again!" and "Welcome back!" A tall, fortyish man with jet-black hair and a trim beard shook Ochim's hand the most vigorously and introduced himself as the mayor. Thomas correctly guessed that the rest were councillors.

"Can we go home now?" Ochim whispered to his parents.

"Please, don't let us keep you," said the mayor. "You should be spending this time together as a family. We're all happy to see you though, Ochim."

The boy's parents thanked the council and then let the young man in the blue vest lead them away. All attention turned to Thomas.

Hezzoroch put his arm around him protectively. "I'd like to introduce you all to young Thomas here," he said. "He has travelled a considerable distance to be with us, and has accepted the challenge of facing the Destroyer. His sister has also accepted this challenge and is with the Uru as we speak learning the magic of the Verrakal crystal."

A murmur passed through the crowd - something along the lines of thinking that the Verrakal crystal was a myth and if it wasn't then why hadn't the Uru offered it to them already?

"The crystal was in the children's world," he explained. "Our ancestors left it there hundreds of years ago, and it only re-entered Fardoor with the children."

Murmurs of understanding moved through the group, followed by silence. Most of them looked at Thomas with apprehension, but a wizened old lady that matched his height exactly stepped forward to greet him.

"Hello Thomas," she said warmly. "I hope my husband hasn't been giving you a hard time!" She gave him a peck on the cheek and then did the same to Hezzoroch.

The old man embraced her and returned the kiss. "My wife Zire, Thomas."

"Nice to meet you. He wasn't giving me a hard time – he was showing me how to use the brown stone."

"Yes, the stone," said Hezzoroch, addressing the councillors. "Thomas and his sister brought two of them from their world as well. They have been living amongst it, and Thomas has shown himself to be extremely adept at using the brown stone after less than a day of practice."

"So then you think he has a chance?" asked one of the councillors.

"Absolutely."

"I'd like to arrange a demonstration," said the mayor.

"Yes of course."

"Not until he settles in," interrupted Zire. "He's travelled a very long distance as my husband pointed out, and I'm sure he'd like a hot meal and a change of clothes. That goes for you too Hezzoroch."

"I'm fine, and there is much that needs to be discussed with the council. And that goes for you too Zire," he said jokingly. "I do agree that Thomas should get settled in, though. Let me call for someone to take him up to our home."

"Nonsense," Zire admonished. "I will take young Thomas to our home myself. You can fill me in later."

"That's fine," said the mayor.

Hezzoroch sighed. "All right." He turned Thomas around and pointed to a large red clay building a short distance up the hill. "You'll be staying with us Thomas. That building is the library, where all the ancient texts are housed. We live just in back of it."

"You live in the library?"

"I'm the librarian, Thomas. Didn't I tell you that? Go with Zire and I'll see you in a few hours."

The matter settled, Hezzoroch and the councillors turned one way and entered the City Hall. Zire led Thomas in the other direction, across the square and towards the library.

"I hope you're hungry," she said. "I have a great meal planned!"

"I sure am!" he enthused.

Zire looped her arm around his and patted him on the hand. "Well Thomas, Hezzoroch sees a lot of potential in you – I can tell. But you know what I see? A young boy without his family. You must miss them terribly. Well you can tell me all about them while we eat, how's that?"

"Okay," said Thomas. He had taken an immediate liking to this old woman. And while he did miss his family, he also couldn't help feel excited about learning how to use the brown stone. He breathed in the fresh air and warmed at the sun beaming down on what may be the last day of summer. He was sure there was a big adventure still to come.

CHAPTER TWELVE

It had been another hard day of training. Exhausted, Rebecca collapsed on her bed and stewed over the day's events.

'Why am I having so much trouble controlling the crystal's power?' she wondered. Over two weeks now of nearly continuous practice, and she still found the smallest attempts at magic could easily go awry. After that first day when she'd blown a hole through the roof of the palace, Elori had backtracked and 'dialled down' the crystal's power as he put it. Since then he had unlocked it in small increments each day.

'Maybe that's the problem,' she reasoned: *'Just when I get the hang of it one day, he goes and unlocks more of its power the next!'*

Elori insisted it was necessary, as the crystal's full power would be needed when facing the Destroyer. Rebecca was still having a hard time reconciling the fact that her cousin was now this terrible person that she and Thomas would have to confront and somehow defeat. But she had to face that reality when he unexpectedly appeared over Paarl several nights ago.

The loud sound of energy fire outside her bedroom window had awakened her. It was the city's magical defences responding to Will's presence, unleashing a tremendous barrage upon him. She looked out the window and saw him hovering calmly overhead, surrounded in a blue force field. Elori ran up the stairs and burst into her room.

"Stay here!" he ordered. *"He doesn't know you're in Paarl!"* He turned on her light and ran out as quickly as he had come.

Will hadn't yet figured out how to bring his army up to the cloud cities, which carried a spell so that the knights would fall right through if they tried to stand on them. Her understanding was that he periodically showed up to test the Uru, and have the Nasrati take some of their children. The Uru had developed magic that could defend against the Nasrati but could not defeat them. It was a form of light that caused them great discomfort, and she had been told to keep her blinds open in the case of an attack.

That night Rebecca stood in front of the window, watching Will. He didn't move. In the corner of her eye she saw a shape take form in shadows of her room, and turned around in fear to see a Nasratum approaching. It was coal black and moved like a billowing sheet.

The room began to fill with a soft light from the window behind Rebecca before the creature reached her. The light was like a mist, and it slowly moved as if it had substance. The Nasratum reached out and emanated dark energy from its shadowy hand. The Uru light stopped advancing but did not retreat. Rebecca stared at the creature and imagined that if it had eyes, then they were staring right back. *'He might not have known I was in Paarl before, but he'll definitely know now,'* she thought at the time.

The Nasratum moved further back into the shadows and disappeared. Rebecca risked turning around and looking out the window, where the entire city was filled with the same light. She saw Will disappear too.

Each time the Nasrati appeared, the Uru were able to cast the spell earlier. However, Rebecca later learned that four Uru children had still been taken that night. There was no getting around what Will had become. But she continued to hold hope that the next time they saw him he would be open to reason. Maybe if she could get the crystal under control...

Each day she practiced for several hours with different members of the Magic Council. Half the time she wasn't even sure what she was doing – things just happened. Yesterday she was trying to focus the crystal's energy into a shield and she'd released a puff of purple smoke that put her instructor to sleep instantly. Two days ago she'd tried the same thing and most of her body went invisible for three hours!

Still, her instructors remained diligent and calm, telling her they were pleased with her progress. They continued to teach her their methods for learning magic, explaining how to direct energy beams, for example, and how to use her mind in adjusting its power level. The problem was, Rebecca was beginning to realize that using the Verrakal crystal was not the same as using Uru magic. Uru are born with the ability to release energy bolts and learn how to control it as they grow up. Her situation was different, and only Velarr and Elori seemed to understand. Elori encouraged her to try and adapt the Uru techniques as best as possible. "Do what you can," he would say kind-heartedly.

When Velarr was around she would usually stay with Rebecca during her lessons. But Velarr was often away, acting as a liaison between the Uru and Laurea, bringing reports to King Arros and the Uraiel. Twice the King himself had dropped by to check on her progress. Rebecca felt sorry for him. At first she had thought he looked ridiculous all decked out in gold as he was. It was clear that he didn't enjoy it either, though.

The Uru had apparently laid down a law that a Uraiel could not run for King. The Magic Council had always been made up of the most magically talented Uru, and in the past such rulers were less likely to listen to the advice of others since they possessed so much power already. Rebecca could imagine how Rukell might tend towards tyranny if he was King.

Electing a ruler from the masses to serve a ten-year term was probably a better idea, but King Arros was effectively a puppet of the Magic Council and he knew it. He followed the decisions of the majority, and fortunately the majority of the Council were willing to give Rebecca a chance. Ten Uraiel even volunteered their help in her training. Several of the others continued to be outspoken in deriding her, and these were led by Rukell.

"I'll show them Elori is not wasting his time with me," she said with a yawn. "Tomorrow I'm gonna work harder than ever!" Then with another yawn, Rebecca pulled up the covers and closed her eyes.

After a short while of lying there she became aware of a faint noise - like static on a radio. It kept her awake, moving in and out in an annoying fashion. She had actually heard it the last two nights as well for about thirty seconds, and had wondered if it had something to do with the Verrakal crystal. Tonight it continued for several minutes.

"Uhhh! What is that noise?" she said, pushing the pillow over her ears to no effect.

"Rebecca? Can you hear me? Rebecca!" A voice barely cut through the static.

She bolted up straight and strained her ears. "Thomas?"

"Rebecca? Can you hear me?" the voice repeated, a bit louder this time.

"Is that you Thomas?" she whispered. "Where are you?"

A fuzzy image began forming in the middle of her room. It flickered a bit before resolving into a clear picture of her brother, although he was wearing some strange clothes.

"Thomas I can see you!" she exclaimed. Actually, she could see through him.

The static receded and her brother's voice came through clear as a bell. "Hey Rebecca! I thought I was never gonna get this right!"

Rebecca was ecstatic to see his familiar face. "How are you doing this?" she asked.

Thomas was beaming. "Oh it's really cool," he said. "You know those brown stones we found and how the stone altars are also made up of it?"

"Uh-huh."

"Oh neat!" he said suddenly. "You get to sleep on a cloud!"

Rebecca patted her bed. "Yeah it's pretty comfortable. Now finish your story!"

"Okay, well it turns out the brown stone is from *our* world. The Eechawey brought it to Fardoor and it acts as a magical conduit."

"Meaning what?"

"Meaning you can use it to connect to some – I don't know – 'Life force' I guess you could call it. What's really neat is that when I make that connection and really listen hard, I can hear the Life force *talking* to me, telling me its secrets. That's how the Eechawey found all these spells that the people here have kept in some ancient texts." He was really excited now. "They're still decoding it, but in the last two weeks I've already done things that they didn't know about!"

Rebecca was getting more excited now too. "Like what?"

"For example when one of the wells went dry I made a new source of water burst up through the ground! Yesterday I made the earth push up into a cliff and then I blasted it with this orange bolt of energy that just came out of my hand! And now I'm talking to you. I just searched until I found your presence, and then it took me three days to figure out how to communicate!"

"Wow Thomas, that's really amazing."

"Thanks! But what about you? Hezzoroch told me about the Verrakal crystal - have you learned anything cool yet?"

Her heart sunk a bit when she recalled her own failures with magic as compared to Thomas's experience. "Well, I've started being able to fly," she said. This was no lie. What she neglected to tell him was that each time she tried flying she could only control it for a minute before flinging herself into a wall or a ceiling. Her head was still bruised from the last attempt.

"That's awesome!" he exclaimed. "I hope I'm able to learn how to fly too!" The image of Thomas flickered a bit with his excitement.

Rebecca decided to change the subject. "Where are you right now?" she asked.

"Same as you - in my room. I'm actually sitting cross-legged with my eyes closed if you can believe it."

Her brother's image was standing and looking directly at her. But right about now Rebecca thought she could believe anything.

"Are you staying with Velarr?" he asked. "I'm staying with Hezzoroch and his wife. She's a really great cook. I think she likes having a kid around!"

"Where is He-He-"

"Hezzoroch." Thomas paused in thought. "He's two rooms over."

"Wow Thomas, I guess no one can sneak up on you!" She thought of something. "Can you sense Will?"

He shook his head. "I've tried, even though Hezzoroch doesn't want me to. He seems to think it might be dangerous. Anyway, I can sense his army. A lot of them are in Laurea and more seem to be appearing out of one part of the mountains. I think that's where we were headed before we were rescued."

"But what about Will?"

Thomas bit his lip. "I don't know. Sometimes I get this glimpse of a big...darkness. But I can't say that it's Will for sure. If it is..." he trailed off.

"What?"

"Come on Rebecca – what do you want me to say? If it is Will, then maybe there really isn't anything left of our cousin!"

This isn't what she wanted to hear. "Don't say that Thomas! You heard Queen Dalea and the others: it's the Destroyer stone that has taken over. That's what you're sensing! It's up to us to bring Will back!"

"I know," he said ashamedly.

An awkward silence followed, which Rebecca used to change the subject again. "You said you sensed the army in Laurea? Well Velarr's been going back and forth between here and the forest. She said that half of it is controlled by them but pretty soon the entire forest will be overrun."

"They weren't even *in* the forest when we arrived! Can't the inhabitants of Laurea fight back?"

"They do what they can during the day, but at night the Nasrati come out and no one knows how to defeat them. Plus, we're talking about mostly gnomes and sprites here against an army of a thousand knights!"

"What about King Irith? And Jorka? And Queen Dalea?"

"They're all in hiding. Velarr says King Irith wants to face Will but Queen Dalea won't let him because she says Will is too strong.

He now knows what we're doing and has reluctantly agreed to wait until we're ready. I don't know why he didn't just help us in the first place!"

Her brother was incredulous. "And in the meantime we're just supposed to let the army take over Laurea?"

"It's funny," said Rebecca. "The image of you gets fainter when you're mad. I would've thought it gets brighter."

"It's 'cause I'm losing focus." He took a long, deep breath and the image brightened again. "There. Where's Velarr now?"

"She's away. And so is Elori. He's the old man – er, Uru – that *I* live with. You've got Hezzoroch and I've got Elori," she said happily.

"*Anyway*, what about the fact that Will's army is taking over the forest?"

"Velarr says that as long as the Forest King's lair stays secret then there's not much the army can do. Will wants to find the Tree of Laurea and King Irith. He can't do either without finding the lair first." She paused.

"What?"

"I was just thinking. It's kind of like *all* of Fardoor is in hiding. The inhabitants of Laurea are in the Forest King's lair. The Uru are up in the clouds…"

"And the human cities are shielded so they can't be found!"

"Exactly. Everyone is hiding and just…waiting."

"They're waiting for us," said Thomas.

"I know – it's scary."

"They're not just waiting though – they're also preparing for some sort of battle. Hezzoroch hasn't told me the details, but he has told me that much."

Rebecca nodded in agreement. "Elori's told me the same thing. The Uru Magic Council is trying to find ways of attacking the Nasrati and not just defending against them. All they have now is defensive magic," she clarified.

"I don't know what the people here are working on," said Thomas "but basically I think the plan is to hold off the army and get us to Will. I don't see why that's such a big deal: his army only has a couple thousand troops. If you combine the Uru, the humans, and the inhabitants of Laurea, they must be outnumbered a hundred to one!"

"You forgot the Nasrati – there's no way of fighting them yet."

"Yeah, but you said the Uru are working on it."

"Well how about the fact that these 'troops' are basically children. And not just human children – Uru too. I think Velarr's kids were taken."

"She told you that?"

"No - I sort of guessed." Every time the Destroyer's army had been brought up Velarr had looked very uncomfortable and changed the subject quickly. "So they can't just go and kill those in the army. Plus, everyone here acts as though Will holds all the cards at the moment. I think he must have some pretty powerful magic at his disposal."

"So we all just wait then," sighed Thomas.

"Yeah."

"And if he finds the Tree of Laurea?"

"I don't know Thomas." This was not a prospect she liked to consider. In his current state, if Will managed to find the Tree of Laurea he might try to destroy it. They would be stuck in Fardoor forever. "Anyway, Velarr and Elori seem pretty confident that only the Forest King has the ability to reveal the Tree, so he'll have to go through King Irith first. And we'd know if that happened – there'd be a battle."

"Well I guess the sooner we get a handle on this magic thing, the better. I should probably get some sleep then."

"Me too," Rebecca agreed. She yawned and pulled up the covers. "Thomas?"

"Yeah?"

"Thanks for finding me. I was getting pretty lonely up here."

He broke out into a big grin. "No problem! To tell you the truth I'm pretty lonely down here too. I mean, Hezzoroch and Zire are great and so are the others, but…well, you know what I mean."

She nodded. "Hey – is there any way I can call you so you'll know to contact me?" she asked hopefully.

"I don't think so. But I'll try to get in touch with you every night, deal?"

"Deal. Goodnight Thomas."

"'Night."

His image receded as he waved goodbye. Rebecca waved goodbye too. The unexpected visit by her brother had lifted her spirits, and she felt truly happy for the first time since arriving in Paarl. In fact she was even looking forward to training tomorrow! *'Got to show him I can keep up,'* she thought before closing her eyes and drifting towards sleep.

Only a few minutes had passed when the sound of her bedroom door slamming open shook her awake again. Four Uru glided into the room.

"Wha-"

Three of them pointed an open palm at Rebecca and she was struck by a force that kept her in place. Immediately the golden energy field sprung up around her. The fourth intruder set about searching her room, while the other three struggled against Queen Dalea's protective force field – though not nearly as much as when Rukell had attempted the same thing by himself two weeks ago in the Palace.

Rebecca's heart was pounding with fright. She couldn't move or speak, but she tried to at least identify the intruders. Unfortunately the room was too dark to make out any of their features, the golden energy field providing only enough light to see the fourth intruder rifling through her cabinet. She had a feeling one of them was Rukell.

"The crystal!" exclaimed the fourth in a triumphant voice that she did not recognize. He had found the small box she kept it in.

"Unnnh!" Rebecca struggled to get free, frantic they would leave with the Verrakal crystal. But the Uru were too strong.

He showed his prize to the other three.

"UNNNH!" She grunted, staring at the crystal. To her surprise (and the Uru's as well) it leapt out of his hand and into hers. She had never done that before.

A burst of violet-colored energy from the crystal shook the room, releasing her from their grip. It raced towards the Uru, and only one of them managed to put up his own force field and reflect it. The other three were knocked down.

Rebecca went invisible. She was acting on instinct now – it was almost as if the Verrakal crystal itself was somehow guiding her.

"Where'd she go?" exclaimed one of the intruders in a female voice. The three knocked down were getting back up.

"I don't know," said another. They all shot bolts of energy at her bed but she had already moved. Next they aimed in different directions and this time one of them struck her. She wasn't hurt, but briefly they could see where she was standing. Rebecca aimed an energy bolt of her own at all four, hitting two and knocking them back down again. They didn't get up.

"We must go!" hissed one intruder. The voice was unmistakably that of Rukell.

The two left standing picked their partners up from the floor and flew out of her room. Rebecca stood frozen, heart racing, body shaking, not only terrified that they would return, but also frightened at what she herself had done.

Slowly she became visible again. After two minutes of standing still she walked over to the window. A beautiful, starry night greeted her, and the pale glow of two moons illuminated the empty streets. The intruders were gone.

Rebecca began to cry.

* * * *

The static noise came back.

"Rebecca?"

An image of Thomas began to form in her room again.

"Rebecca, I forgot to tell you that..." He noticed his sister standing at the window. "Hey – why aren't you in bed?" he asked before hearing her soft sobs. "Rebecca what happened?!"

She wiped her tears but they kept coming anyhow. "Oh Thomas, I'm so glad you're here!" she exclaimed.

"What happened?" he repeated.

"I don't know – I was attacked! Four people just barged into my room and tried to steal the crystal. They used magic on me – I couldn't move!"

"Are you okay?"

"I - I think so." She checked herself. "They didn't get it. The crystal flew into my hand and then I went invisible, and then – oh no, first the crystal released this burst of energy and then I could move and then I went invisible and they shot energy bolts at me but I shot back and –"

She was rambling hysterically. "Rebecca," Thomas interrupted "are you saying you fought them off?"

She stopped talking and thought for a moment. "Um, I guess so."

"That's amazing!" he declared. "Did you see who they were?"

Her sobbing slowed down. "No, but I recognized one of the voices. I think they were all members of the Uru Magic Council; some of them don't want me here."

Thomas wished he could give his sister a hug. Instead he offered some encouragement. "Well whoever they were," he said "they'll think twice about coming back!"

Rebecca gave a weak smile. "I hope so."

"I'm sure of it. Hang on, I'm gonna try and find Velarr to let her know what happened. Do you know where she is?"

"She went to Karrum. That's another cloud city, and there's a person there that has something she can use to talk to Queen Dalea. Velarr says going to Laurea has become too dangerous, and she needs whatever this person has if they're to keep communicating with each other."

Thomas gave a thumbs-up. "Alright, I'll search the sky." His image began to fade.

"Wait!" said Rebecca. His image returned. "What about Elori? He's just at a meeting here in Paarl. Why don't you find him?"

"Because I've never met him, so I wouldn't know it was Elori even if I did find him."

"Oh."

"Don't go anywhere – I'll try to be quick." Thomas's image disappeared and Rebecca was left alone.

Something was hurting her hand. Looking down she realized her fist was still tightly clenched around the Verrakal crystal, her skin stretched taut over white knuckles. It had been like that since the intruders fled. Now she slowly opened her stiff fingers, allowing color to return to the hand. Deep impressions had been made in her palm by the crystal's sharp edges, and trickles of red blood began to seep through the lines where her skin had been broken. Rebecca watched in amazement as the crystal absorbed the blood from her palm. It glowed softly for a moment. The cuts healed and the pain in her hand ceased. "What was that?" she wondered aloud. She continued staring at the crystal.

"Rebecca?"

Startled, she looked up to see the image of Thomas in front of her once more. This time she hadn't even heard the preceding static noise.

"You're getting better at that Thomas. I didn't have a warning this time."

"Yeah, well you seemed to be pretty wrapped up with whatever it is you're holding. Is that the Verrakal crystal?"

She held it up so he could have a better look. "Yup. And you'll never guess what just happened: it just absorbed the blood from a cut in my hand!"

"Ew! That's gross!"

"Well now the cut is healed!" She showed him her palm. "Anyway, that didn't take you long. Did you find Velarr?"

"Yeah, she was already on her way back. She said she'd be here in twenty minutes." He laughed a bit. "I think she was surprised to see me floating next to her!"

"I'll bet!" giggled Rebecca.

"I'm gonna stay here until she shows up."

"Thanks, Thomas."

An awkward silence followed next. Rebecca was still shaking a bit from what had happened. Sensing this, and eager to get her mind on to something else, Thomas asked his sister for a flying demonstration.

She hesitated, remembering her previous difficulties. Her brother looked very eager though, so she decided to give it a try. *'I'll stop if*

I feel any wobbliness,' she thought. Feeling wobbly was often a prelude to losing all control and flinging herself into a wall.

"Okay," she announced "but I'm just going to hover for a bit – nothing fancy."

"That's fine," he agreed.

"Alright, here I go."

With the crystal cupped in her hands, Rebecca closed her eyes and concentrated on raising herself a few inches off the floor.

"Oh cool," said Thomas "you're doing it."

She opened her eyes and checked the ground. Sure enough she was floating several inches above it. "Great, now let's see how long I can hold it for." She steadied herself and prepared for the inevitable wobbling that usually started within a minute. Except this time it never came. Rebecca never lost control.

"Wow Rebecca you're really good at this!" exclaimed her brother at the two-minute mark.

"You're right – I am!" she agreed in a surprised tone.

"Why don't you try moving or something?"

"Okay."

She tentatively began flying to one side of the room, half-expecting to lose control at any moment and either fall to the floor or put her head through the wall. Instead she did a graceful glide to the far side and gently touched the wall with her fingertip.

Amazed and excited, she continued flying while Thomas encouraged her to try more and more manoeuvres. "Do a somersault!" he would say, then "Now do a log roll up the wall!"

When Velarr walked in her bedroom and interrupted them twenty minutes later, she not only got the shock of seeing Thomas again, but was also very surprised to witness Rebecca doing cartwheels across the ceiling.

Thomas said a quick goodbye to both and let his sister know he would contact her the next day.

"That's some impressive flying," said Velarr once he'd left. Rebecca floated gently down onto her bed. "Yeah, all of a sudden I can do it properly!"

"Do you think it may have something to do with what happened tonight?"

She shrugged. "I'm not sure. Did Elori lessen the crystal's power?"

"Not to my knowledge."

"Then I think it probably *does* have something to do with tonight," she decided.

Velarr sat down beside her. "Your brother was able to relate to me some of what occurred. He said you weren't hurt." Rebecca nodded. "That's quite the skill he possesses, by the way. I'm glad he was able to reach me." She lowered her voice. "Now, I would like you to tell me exactly what happened."

Already the night's events seemed much less frightening. Rebecca was able to give the whole story without difficulty, and even spoke of chasing away the intruders with pride.

Velarr's blue eyes flashed with anger when she heard that one of the intruders' voices belonged to Rukell. "Are you certain it was him?" she asked. "You didn't see his face?"

"No. But I'm sure it was him."

The normally well-composed Velarr stood up and paced angrily back and forth. Rebecca had never seen her like this.

"The fool!" she said. "Did he think we wouldn't find out? No, I suppose he didn't care. He still believes you will hand the crystal's power over to the Destroyer."

"So he was going to give the crystal to another human after stealing it?"

She stopped pacing and thought for a moment. "Knowing Rukell, he probably would have kept it in the hopes of finding a way to harness its power himself."

"Elori doesn't think that's possible," said Rebecca.

"No. It is clear the Verrakal crystal can only be wielded by a human. But Rukell would have still held onto it in a futile attempt to exploit the crystal, at the expense of everyone else."

"So what happens now?" she asked, followed by a giant yawn.

Velarr looked at her carefully. "What happens now is you get some rest. I'll inform Elori when he returns."

Rebecca was too tired to argue. She said goodnight to Velarr and fell fast asleep as soon as her door was closed.

CHAPTER THIRTEEN

The next morning Rebecca threw on some clothes and raced downstairs for breakfast. After last night's events she was more keen than ever to train with the crystal.

Elori was already waiting for her at the table with the usual breakfast spread of bread and looraberry jam (her new favorite).

"Ah! There you are," said Elori as he flipped his long beard over his shoulder and started serving her. "Velarr has explained the whole situation to me, and I am so proud of you!" Velarr walked in from the kitchen and flashed him a look of concern. "And, ah, of course I am also shocked and dismayed by the actions of several of my colleagues," he hastily added.

She smiled. "Thanks Elori. So you think the other three were members of the Magic Council?"

"Most likely. And I'm fairly certain of their identities as well."

"So what's gonna happen with Rukell and them?" Rebecca wondered if the Uru people had a jail.

"Don't you worry about that," interjected Velarr. "Just eat your breakfast."

Elori huffed. "Nonsense, Velarr. She has a right to know."

"Know what?"

The elderly Uru looked right at her and spoke in soft tones. "The truth is, not much will happen. Rukell and the others will deny any involvement, and we haven't much proof."

"But I *heard* him!" she exclaimed.

"*We* believe you Rebecca," said Velarr.

"Yes," he agreed. "We believe you, but many on the Council may not. Even some of those who are helping in your training would find it hard to believe Rukell would resort to such a measure." He noticed her downcast expression. "I don't want to discourage you entirely. Rest assured that I will bring the matter up before Council, and many of us will be keeping a much closer eye on the actions of Rukell."

"There will also never be another night when both Elori and I are away at the same time," added Velarr.

"Okay," she conceded.

"I also understand that you've found a new mastery of the crystal's powers," he said with a wink and a nudge.

Rebecca got all excited again. "You should've seen me flying last night, Elori. It was fantastic! I feel like I've bonded with the crystal or something."

"Or something indeed," said Velarr. "And the ability of your brother to project himself like that!"

"Yes. Quite remarkable on both counts."

"If I had that ability I would not have needed to get *this*." Velarr pulled a funny shaped mirror out of her robe – an octagon with uneven sides.

"What is it?" asked Rebecca.

"It's a communiglass. I can use it to talk with the Forest King and Queen. With the Destroyer's army covering much of Laurea, I can't risk going there anymore, and they cannot risk exiting their lair!"

Elori was stroking his beard. "Hmmm, perhaps I should increase its power today," he said absentmindedly.

"If you're talking about the crystal, please let me enjoy the feeling of being in control – at least for today!" Rebecca was really looking forward to the day's lesson, without having to worry about what would go wrong.

"Oh, all right," he relented. "But tonight I will see how much farther the crystal can go. I believe we may have crossed a threshold here."

"I sure hope so," she muttered.

A knock on the door told them her instructor had arrived.

"Come in" said Elori without moving.

A few seconds later the head of an elderly female Uru poked up through the cloud entrance of his home.

"No wonder Rukell and them were able to get in so easily," said Rebecca under her breath.

"It only works if one is invited in." Velarr whispered.

"Eh, what's that?" said the woman. Rather than bring herself totally up and then walk to the dining room table, her body gradually rose through the cloud as she glided over.

Rebecca couldn't help but wonder if she had been one of the intruders last night, and eyed her suspiciously. Elori, however, appeared quite comfortable. *'And he seemed to have a good idea who the other intruders were,'* she reasoned.

"Good morning Mirall," he greeted her while Velarr fetched another plate.

"Hello Elori. Velarr. Rebecca." Each name was accompanied with a slight nod of her head.

"Hi," said Rebecca. This was actually the fourth time Mirall had instructed her, and she had always been quite pleasant as far as Uru go. In fact, Rebecca felt a bit foolish for thinking she might have been one of the intruders.

Mirall accepted the plate and began serving herself. "Thank you Velarr. Now tell me, Elori: did you increase the crystal's power today?"

"No."

"Good. Because I was planning on conducting today's lesson in the park, and I would hate for a mishap to occur in public." She gave Rebecca an understanding look.

"I did not increase it Mirall, but our young pupil may just surprise you with her level of control today." He winked at her.

Mirall already looked surprised. "Really?"

"Well, I'm not so sure I'm ready to practice out in public," Rebecca said nervously.

"There will be lots of people practicing magic in the park," said Mirall. "That's what it's there for."

"You are planning on teaching her the power of words today?"

"That is correct."

He smiled at Rebecca. "You are in for a treat. Words can amplify almost any magic. Best you go outside though to save my furniture."

"All right, please get the Verrakal crystal and follow me," Mirall ordered. She had barely touched the food on her plate, and Rebecca had been planning to have a second piece of bread herself. But her instructor was already heading for the exit. The crystal was in her pocket, so she said a quick goodbye to Velarr and Elori then followed Mirall, watching as she descended into the cloud again. Rebecca decided to use the door instead, exiting Elori's home in time to see her come up through the cloud on the other side.

"Give me your hand, please," she instructed. "We will be flying there."

"Actually, I think I'll be able to fly there on my own today," said Rebecca with some excitement.

"Oh! Is this the surprise?" she asked. "You've been practicing flying, have you? Splendid."

With that, Rebecca began to raise herself off the ground.

"Tut, tut," chided Mirall, who reached up and pulled her back down. "Flying indoors is one thing. Flying *outside* is quite another. I'd hate for you to lose your orientation and go shooting off in some unknown direction. I may not be able to catch you."

Rebecca hadn't thought of that. Still, she felt fairly certain she could handle it. "But I-" she started to say.

"No 'buts'; I insist on holding your hand. I won't pull you, however – you'll be flying on your own power."

That seemed a reasonable compromise. Rebecca gave Mirall her hand and the two of them lifted off together. The old lady directed them towards the park.

They flew over glistening white buildings and narrow streets, passing the occasional Uru in the air as well. The rare times Rebecca had ventured outside in the past she'd noticed that the other Uru seemed to tolerate her, even if they didn't always acknowledge her presence. Today was no different. Mirall would only give slight nods to the Uru they passed, choosing to focus her attention on Rebecca instead.

"Well done," she complimented. "Your flying has indeed improved remarkably."

"Thank you. Look Mirall – I can also do this!" Rebecca instantly went invisible.

"Oh! Dear me!" she said, visibly shaken. Her own arm that held Rebecca had disappeared up to the shoulder.

Rebecca had to stifle a laugh before popping back into view. "Sorry," she offered.

Mirall gave a weak smile and touched her arm to make sure it was really there. "That is quite all right," she said. "Just…unexpected. Well, you seem to be in good control today. Perhaps Elori could have increased the crystal's power after all."

Shortly they set down in a large open space she had never seen before.

"Here we are," Mirall announced. "This park has been enchanted so that no errant spells can escape its boundaries. It is the perfect place to practice magic."

Looking around, Rebecca could see there was already a young couple teaching their small child, the little Uru delighting at the tiny zaps and sparks that came out of his finger. He watched as his father shot his own ivory energy bolt. It travelled to the edge of the park where it was promptly absorbed by an unseen barrier.

"This does seem like a great place to practice," she observed. "Why haven't I been here before?"

"Well, of course it wasn't really *necessary*," said Mirall matter-of-factly. "At least not initially; the magic you were doing was so small."

She looked at the little child practicing and wondered if Mirall's explanation was more of an excuse. Maybe she hadn't been here before because they weren't sure how the other Uru would have received her. The young couple didn't seem to mind. She sighed and sat down cross-legged as Mirall had done.

"Now take out the crystal, please."

Rebecca removed it from the pocket of her robe and held it up. It shone bright violet in the morning sun.

Mirall admired it without touching. "Unlike the Destroyer stone that has your cousin, the Verrakal crystal needs guidance and direction from the person who wields it," she said.

Rebecca wasn't sure she understood but nodded anyway.

"History has told us that the crystal responds to the power of words. By saying the appropriate words – and meaning them – you should be able to increase the spell's power."

"All right, but what words are the 'appropriate' ones?"

She patted Rebecca's knee. "That is what we will have to find out! Here, let me give you an example."

Mirall adjusted her toga and began rubbing her hands together. With one graceful movement she scooped up a piece of cloud and released it into the air. Still pointing at it, the cloud broke apart into several pieces, which then formed bird shapes and languidly flapped their wings to the park's boundary before disappearing.

"Neat!" said Rebecca.

"Yes, but now watch." She swept up more cloud and threw it into the air. "Birds of the sky, fly away!"

The cloud burst into a dozen real, small white birds. Rebecca watched them fly straight ahead before once again disappearing at the edge of the park.

"See? Much more impressive the second time around, don't you agree? Now it is your turn. Hmmm." Mirall tapped her chin. "Let us begin with a spell you can already control well."

"How about the invisibility thing?"

She continued tapping her chin. "Yes…that seemed to be *reasonably* well controlled. Am I correct in saying you are currently only able to make yourself invisible?"

"Well, that and your arm apparently."

The old lady gave a chuckle despite herself. "And my arm, of course. But you were holding onto my arm. Let us have you try it again."

"Okay." Rebecca went invisible. She didn't even have to think about it anymore.

"Splendid." A small divot in the cloud told her where Rebecca was sitting.

"Do you want me to become visible again?" she asked.

"Yes, there we go. Now we're going to do it again, but this time you will use words to invoke the crystal's power. Ready? Now say *'Make me invisible!'"*

"Make me invisible!" she repeated. She did disappear, but no more than before.

"You have to mean it," said Mirall.

"I did mean it!" she exclaimed while reappearing. "Here let me try this: *Invisibility now!"*

Once again Rebecca disappeared, but nothing else happened. Next she tried "Invisibility power!" and "Crystal invisibility power!" to the same effect. She even tried coming up with a rhyme, since the spells she'd seen on television always did. Mirall said it wasn't necessary though, and anyway the only word she could rhyme with 'invisible' was 'visible'.

In the background the little Uru squealed as a small energy bolt escaped his finger and traveled two feet before dissipating. "Pay attention," her instructor scolded.

"I am, but maybe it's not in the power of the Verrakal crystal to respond to words after all."

Mirall's eyes widened. "The power of the Verrakal crystal," she repeated.

Rebecca gave her a quizzical look. "What?"

"When you said *'The power of the Verrakal crystal'* just now, the crystal glowed. When I said it nothing happened."

"Yeah, I've seen it do that before."

Mirall clapped her hands. "Well, *those* are the appropriate words dear girl! Now say it again."

"The power of the Verrakal crystal."

It glowed for a moment then stopped. Mirall was shaking her head. "No, no, no. Again, but really mean it!"

"The power of the Verrakal crystal!"

A light from within the stone glowed bright, even against the full sun.

"Now!" she instructed. "Your spell!"

Without thinking Rebecca yelled "Invisible!"

Everything within twenty feet of her disappeared, including her elderly instructor. "Well done!" said Mirall's disembodied voice.

The nearby family couldn't help but notice the forty-foot crater that had opened up in the cloud. They moved further off.

"Well," said Mirall when they had reappeared "shall we try it with some different spells?"

* * * *

Over the next few hours the large park filled up with more people, most of them families with young children. They all kept a wide berth from Rebecca, who kept busy experimenting with her spells. Among other things she found that by invoking the crystal she could create walls of energy and levitate other objects instead of just herself. Mirall always congratulated her, but she was actually hoping for some recognition from the people in the park. Each time she would do something impressive she would look around in the hopes someone had noticed. Often they had, but as soon as they saw her looking their way they would turn quickly.

After creating a particularly impressive whirlwind (that caused most of the Uru to move even farther away) Rebecca began noticing there were a couple older Uru whose looks seemed to linger much longer. Something about them was unnerving. Two more Uru flew overhead and one of them was Rukell. In panic, she realized that Mirall hadn't been told about last night's events.

"Rukell attacked me last night with three other people!" she quickly blurted.

Mirall was clearly taken aback. "What was that? Rukell may have some disagreements with –"

"We have to leave!" Rebecca cried. "Now!"

"– never resort to such a tactic," she finished.

"Please!"

Other people were beginning to notice the commotion. The two she'd caught staring walked towards her. The two above continued hovering.

Suddenly one of them yelled *"That girl is an agent of the Destroyer!"*

People began panicking. Parents picked up their children and either ran or flew in various directions.

"Rebecca is no such thing," Mirall tried to calmly reassure everyone. She looked up and saw the two Uru hovering overhead. "Rukell what is this all about?"

"Stay out of this Mirall!" he said.

Rebecca wasted no time and went invisible. This time they were prepared for her though. One of them blew a powder from his hand into the air. It turned into a thin fog that filled the park. Her outline could be seen. Rukell and the Uru beside him aimed a massive blast of energy her way, which Mirall managed to partially shield. Both of them were still struck down. She and Rebecca aimed bolts of their own up at those two but the energy was absorbed just before striking them.

"They're flying just outside the park's barrier!" Rebecca exclaimed.

Neither of them were paying attention to the two Uru already in the park, and didn't see the energy bolts they had shot until too late. Rebecca was hit in the leg and Mirall took one full on in the chest.

"Remember your training!" she whispered before collapsing.

"Mirall!" She put up a shield as more energy fire raced towards them. Her leg was bleeding badly and she couldn't get up. Mirall wasn't moving.

Even through the thin fog she could see that the park had emptied, but countless people were watching from the periphery. *'Why don't they help?'* she thought desperately.

"The power of the crystal!" she cried. "Wind!"

Several swirling tornadoes formed in the park and swept up all the fog. The two Uru in the park momentarily stopped advancing on her and tried to stop them, but the magic was too strong.

"Lokarr!" yelled one as she was swept up by a tornado.

"I'm trying!" said the other one. All he could do was duck out of the way of the other tornadoes and watch as the one carrying his partner took her around the park before dissipating at its boundary. She fell to the ground unhurt.

Rebecca meanwhile had been trying to escape. With the fog gone she was invisible again. She now extended the field to also include Mirall. Her leg was so badly hurt she couldn't walk, and the wind she had created was so powerful that flying wasn't possible either. Instead she tried dragging herself and Mirall out of the park. The tornadoes stayed out of her way, perhaps because she had created them. Still, the park edge was about a hundred feet away. It might as well have been a hundred miles away at her current speed and mobility. "Help me!" Rebecca yelled at the people watching. It was hard to see them with her hair blowing across her face.

One by one the tornadoes disappeared as they tried crossing the park's boundary. She was still seventy feet away from it. "Fly!" she yelled at Lokarr and the female Uru who was just standing up. They were both lifted off the ground and thrown back against the park's invisible barrier, but not before aiming energy bolts in Rebecca's general direction. They missed. She decided the tornadoes had worked well. "Wind!" she yelled again. Several more tornadoes formed but disappeared before gaining any strength. Rebecca should have been watching Rukell and his partner, for all the while she'd been trying to escape, they had been repeating the same unheard incantation, their hands just inside the park barrier and pointed right at her. Now she watched as the Verrakal crystal flew out of her pocket surrounded in a sphere of blue energy - a dampening field.

She let go of Mirall and tried to catch it. She missed.

Without realizing it she had become visible again. The crystal flew towards Rukell as Lokarr and the others shifted focus and tried once more to restrain her. The golden force field sprung up around Rebecca as she felt the familiar, frightening feeling of paralysis.

All of a sudden the Uru beside Rukell stopped hovering and tumbled down into the park! He had been hit with a bolt of energy by one of several Uru flying towards them. Five more entered the park from below and began attacking Lokarr and the female.

"Elori!" Rebecca exclaimed when she saw who one of them was. "Rukell's got the crystal!"

Elori rushed over to her. "He's being apprehended - look!"

Up above Rukell was making an attempt at flying away, but several Uru were in close pursuit and shooting energy bolts at him, while he shot back wildly at them.

"We'll catch him," he assured. "You're hurt."

"It's just my leg." She winced as the pain from her wound began to register. "I...I think Mirall is dead!" she exclaimed. "And it's all my fault!"

One of the other rescuers was checking on her elderly instructor. "She isn't dead," he announced "just stunned." A wave of relief washed over her.

"There you go," said Elori "a bit of good news. And this isn't your fault, Rebecca." He produced a jar of green goo from his pocket and began rubbing it into her leg wound. The whole area started to tingle and some of the pain went away. "If anything I blame myself," he continued. "I told you we would be keeping a closer eye on Rukell but I should have also been watching you. In truth, even I never believed they would resort to so desperate a measure as attacking you in a public place!"

She gave him a hug. "Better late than never!"

All four attackers had been caught. Two lay unconscious, including Rukell (from flying into a wall while looking back at his pursuers). The Verrakal crystal was removed from him and raced over to Elori. "I believe this belongs to you," he said, handing the crystal to Rebecca.

By this time King Arros had arrived along with the remaining Uraiel not involved in the attack on Rebecca and Mirall, or the subsequent rescue. The King was enraged. "An attack in a public area?!" he yelled. "By members of the Magic Council no less?!"

"That girl is the enemy!" spat Lokarr. "She is an agent of the Destroyer!"

"*You* are the enemy!" he shot back. "That girl is working to save our people and the rest of Fardoor. I will not wait for the Magic Council to deliberate on this matter. *You four are hereby banished from Paarl!"*

Clearly this was an affront to the Council, who were used to making decisions for the King. But many of the spectators actually began clapping.

"None of those people helped when Mirall and I were under attack!" said Rebecca.

"Forgive them Rebecca – they were scared. Their magic is not very strong." Elori shook his head. "But some of them knew to come and get me, which they did right away. And look how they support you now!"

It was true. The applause had grown as Rukell and the others were carted away. Many of the Uru assembled outside the park were looking right at her and actually smiling! She smiled back, a bit embarrassed.

Elori signalled for one of the other rescuers to come over.

"I'm sorry I'm not able to fly you back myself, Rebecca. And you should keep off your leg for a bit."

She looked down and was surprised to see the bleeding had stopped. Whatever it was Elori had used, it had congealed into a protective layer over the damaged skin. "Are you coming back too?" she asked.

"Oh yes. I just hope someone was able to get in touch with Velarr!"

A stately Uru with just a smattering of white in his hair arrived to take Rebecca. It was Kojirros, one of her instructors.

"Take her back to my place, would you?" said Elori.

Kojirros nodded. "And you?"

"I'll be walking."

He shook his head. "I'll call for someone else to get you."

"That's quite all right Kojirros - I don't want to be a bother."

"You should not speak that way Elori. Come now, my brother will fly you back."

Elori relented and a second Uru (not wearing the robes of an Uraiel) came to pick him up.

They headed back to Elori's home. While flying, Kojirros had time to compliment Rebecca on the tornadoes she had created

(which he'd seen when approaching the park.)

"I was working on that this morning with Mirall," she said. "She's a good teacher."

Kojirros sniffed. "Yes, well perhaps *I'll* teach you how to direct their motion at our next lesson," he said.

They touched down and dropped Elori and Rebecca off at his front door. Velarr was inside waiting for them

"Oh! You're back!" she said rushing to meet them. "I heard everything. How awful! I'd like to teach Rukell a lesson of my own! Now who else was involved?"

"Lokarr, Jurell, and Anjarri. King Arros has banished all four of them from Paarl."

She looked impressed. "So soon? Without the Council deliberating? Well it was the correct decision at any rate."

"Agreed. Now let us help young Rebecca over to a chair, please. She has been hit in the leg."

"I'll be all right." She hobbled over to the table. "Whatever you put on it is like magic!"

"It *is* magic," he corrected. "But it still needs time to work, so you must stay off your feet for a couple days I'm afraid."

Velarr left for a moment and came back with two bowls of soup. "In the meantime, there is someone who would like to speak with you. If you're feeling up for it, that is."

Rebecca wondered who it could be and asked Velarr as much.

"Just a minute," she responded before leaving the room again. When she returned it was with the communiglass in her hand. "Here you go," she said, handing it to Rebecca.

"Good friend Rebecca?" a muffled voice inquired.

She turned the glass over. "Jorka?"

A blurred face could be seen moving on the other side of the glass, like viewing your reflection on a bathroom mirror that's all fogged up.

Elori looked over her shoulder. "I can fix that," he declared. He flipped his beard over his own shoulder and headed to the kitchen, where all his magical ingredients were stored.

"It was working fine before," said Velarr. "Sometimes all it needs is a good shake. May I?"

Rebecca handed her the glass and Velarr began shaking it vigorously. Jorka continued talking in the background: "...Jorka stay hidden...army not find...Brufa make special cake..."

"There you go," she said, handing it back.

Now Jorka's wrinkled, grey face could clearly be seen in the foreground while the background remained foggy.

Elori re-entered the room carrying three bottles and an ornate feather. "Oh! It has been fixed," he said, disappointed. He went back into the kitchen.

"Good friend Rebecca!" said Jorka excitedly. "Jorka very happy to see you!"

She smiled, but it was nothing compared to the wide grin he was displaying. "I'm happy to see you too, Jorka."

"Good friend Thomas still with humans?"

"Yes, Thomas is still with the humans. He's becoming very good at magic."

"And so is Rebecca!" Elori piped up from the next room.

"He can't hear you unless you face the glass," said Velarr. "You know that!"

"Where are you Jorka?" she asked. In the swirling fog behind him she could make out several moving shapes.

"Jorka in Forest King lair. Jorka must go soon. Forest King has *special task* for Jorka." He said this proudly, but didn't elaborate any further.

"Well I don't want to keep you," she said. "It was really nice seeing you again."

Jorka said his goodbye as well, then the fog swirled around him and dissolved until it once again became a simple mirror. Rebecca was left looking at her own reflection. She looked awful! Her hair was sweaty, tangled, and plastered to her forehead. Blood from her leg had somehow become streaked across her face in two places. Surprisingly, she didn't feel that bad on the inside. Knowing that Rukell and the others wouldn't be bothering her anymore was very uplifting.

She handed the communiglass back to Velarr. "I think I need a shower."

"Soup first, shower second," said Velarr.

Rebecca took several big spoonfuls under her watchful eye.

"Good, now let me have a look at your leg." She bent down low and inspected her leg without removing the green mass congealed over the wound.

"Is that stuff waterproof?" asked Rebecca.

"Yes. Does it hurt?"

"Not that much anymore."

Velarr was thinking. "Still, Elori is right in saying that you shouldn't walk on it for at least a couple of days. Now how are you to get around?"

She shrugged. "Crutches?"

"I don't know what that is, but perhaps Elori could fashion something." Velarr got up and continued thinking.

"I know!" said Rebecca. "I can just fly!"

Velarr was about to ask if she thought that wise considering how recently she had been slamming into walls and ceilings. Rebecca pre-empted her by lifting off the chair, then flying out of the room and up the stairs. She same back down. "See?"

"See what?" asked Elori as he strolled into the dining room. "Oh you'll be flying around? Marvellous." He handed her a small jar of the same green goo. "Here's more ointment. Use it tonight and again tomorrow morning, and then that should be enough to heal your leg."

"Thanks Elori. And thanks for the soup Velarr! I'm gonna go have a shower now." She turned around and flew up the stairs.

"And then get some rest!" Velarr called up after her. She sat down and started eating her own soup. "What terrible events Rebecca has had to endure over the last day!" she said in a low voice. "At least now she won't have to worry about attacks from Rukell and his group!"

"Yes. Unfortunately this may also mean a delay in the completion of our Nasrati attack."

She looked at him quizzically.

"As despicable as they were toward Rebecca," Elori explained

"Lokarr and Anjarri were instrumental in helping develop offensive magic against the Nasrati. Currently the Destroyer is focusing on Laurea. But I fear it won't be long before he returns to Paarl." He looked very grave. "Even without his army the Destroyer can wreak havoc with the aid of those terrible creatures he controls!" Elori sighed. "But we must not tell Rebecca any of this. She has held up remarkably well through all of the recent turbulence!"

"Agreed," said Velarr. "This gives me hope that she will be able to face the Destroyer. What do you think?"

Elori stroked his beard. "She will be ready – eventually. I hope her brother is making considerable progress though, because the day when both children must face their cousin is sooner than we think."

CHAPTER FOURTEEN

"Thomas! Your dinner is ready!"

"I'm almost done Hezzoroch!" Thomas called back. "Just a few more minutes!"

The old man was calling him for dinner. That usually meant he had made it himself. And while Hezzoroch had many good qualities, his culinary skills were not one of them. Zire, on the other hand, was a fantastic cook who loved making Thomas whatever he wanted. His current favorite was Roasted Gralk, a bird the humans here raised that tasted just like chicken.

"Five minutes Thomas! I made your favorite – Roasted Gralk!"

He grimaced. Last time Hezzoroch had made it he'd forgotten to remove the gizzard. "Okay, five minutes!" He turned his attention back to the ancient text in front of him.

Everyone was surprised when Thomas discovered he could read the texts, himself included. Apples from the Tree of Laurea enable one to understand any language being spoken. The inhabitants of Fardoor seemed to already have that ability, suggesting that the magic of the fruit lasts for generations. Reading another language was something altogether different, however, and initially the ancient texts looked like nothing more than gobbledegook to Thomas. That changed a week ago, when he discovered that every book retains an imprint of the person who wrote it. By using the stone he found he could connect with the lasting imprint and feel what the author was thinking at the time of writing. It was almost as if he could *hear* the words being spoken to him.

Since the ancient texts were written in code and verse, they not only needed to be translated, but deciphered too. What Thomas was doing was so much more than reading, though, and he had been making significant progress in the last week. A book that would take several people four months to interpret, Thomas could do in four days. He spent most of his free time studying the texts and learning their secrets, even neglecting to contact Rebecca for the last few nights.

'I've got to remember to get in touch with her tonight,' Thomas reminded himself. He held his hand up, closed his eyes and thought of a forest. *"Kallae buuloos, kella,"* he said, then opened his eyes to see the forest he had pictured in front of him. Another wave of his hand and the illusion disappeared. "Got it!" he shouted. "Hezzoroch come and see this!"

The old man could be heard shuffling down the hall. "Dinner is still waiting you know," said Hezzoroch as he entered the room.

"I know," said Thomas, craning his neck backwards to see the old man's kind face behind him. "Last thing, I promise."

He turned back the other way and raised his hand as before. *"Kallae buuloos, kella,"* he repeated, without closing his eyes this time. A gentle forest reappeared, complete with chirping birds and the smell of trees.

"Very good," congratulated Hezzoroch. "It took ten of us and a stone altar to create the illusion that hides our city." He waved his hand but nothing happened. "*Very* good. But now kindly return my library and come to the dinner table please."

Thomas waved his hand and the forest was replaced with rows of bookshelves. "Aren't we waiting for Zire?" he asked innocently.

Hezzoroch raised one of his bushy eyebrows. "No, her city council meeting will be going late tonight."

It was worth a try. In the past when he had messed their dinner Zire had often whipped up something quick.

Hezzoroch started down the hall and Thomas followed. "Kallae buuloos, *kella*," the old man muttered, shaking his head.

"Isn't that what you chanted when creating the illusion?" asked Thomas.

"Not quite. No wonder it took ten of us."

"And a stone altar!"

The altars, Thomas had learned, were used to perform difficult magic requiring more than one person. The people involved would stand in a circle around the altar with their palms on it, and recite the incantation. The words for these incantations all came from the ancient texts. But since these texts had to first be translated and interpreted, they didn't always get the words exactly right. It was much easier for Thomas, since he didn't really have to translate at all. Still, he had no idea what 'Kallae buuloos, kella' or any of the other words in the incantations actually meant – he just knew to say them. The words didn't come from the Eechawey language, but from something much more profound: they were words from the language of magic: of Life itself. They were the same words Thomas alone sometimes heard being spoken to him if he listened very carefully while meditating with the brown stone. The Eechawey must have heard them too and then written them down so the information could be shared and passed on.

There was more Thomas had learned about the stone altars: he discovered that within a certain radius of one of them he didn't even need a wachaoum to do magic. Each human city had one altar, with New Kadeon's being in the City Hall. Currently the distance he could be from it and still utilize its power was about fifteen hundred feet, but that distance was growing every day. He reasoned this must be why the Eechawey spread several of the altars over the Forest of Laurea.

Hezzoroch began carving the Gralk, putting some meat and green vegetables on two plates. "I removed the gizzard this time," he said after seeing Thomas's look of apprehension. "Go on, have a bite!"

He relented. It was nice of Hezzoroch to cook dinner, after all. They didn't make Thomas do any cooking or cleaning, preferring to let him spend more time on his magical training. He bit into the white meat and encountered an unusual, chalky taste. "Much better," he lied.

Hezzoroch tried some himself and gave a little cough. They both poured large amounts of sauce over their meals.

"I'd like you to spend more time with Ochim," said the old man out of the blue.

"Why?" asked Thomas.

His hopes for a friendship had been dashed when it became clear that Ochim was not adjusting well. Thomas had only seen him a few times over the last month, always with his parents. Each instance was a chance encounter while walking through the city, and he only stopped to talk to the family if Zire or Hezzoroch were walking with him. Ochim always carried a blank look and would say very little, and only if spoken to directly. His parents, however, would carry on as if everything was perfect and back to normal.

"I'm sure you've noticed how withdrawn Ochim continues to be. None of the other children rescued had so difficult a time integrating back among us once their memories of the Destroyer were gone. Ochim is different somehow." Hezzoroch paused to choose his next words carefully. "You have unique abilities Thomas. When linking through the brown stone, you can look and feel deeper than anyone else. I need you to do this with Ochim to see if we have missed anything."

"Like what?"

"I'm not sure." Another pause. "I plan on inviting the boy and his parents for dinner tomorrow. But you are not to tell them what you are doing. It is clear they have convinced themselves that nothing is wrong."

His insistence on secrecy worried Thomas. What was the old man expecting to find? Of course, there was that time they were all riding to New Kadeon and he had used the stone to make a connection with those around him. Then, Ochim had felt as if he was still sleeping even though he was awake. He was about to relate this to Hezzoroch when Zire walked in the front entrance and interrupted their conversation.

"Still no word on the Destroyer's activity!" she announced loudly after closing the door.

Hezzoroch stood up and gave his wife a peck on the cheek. "How was the council meeting, dear?" he asked.

"Oh fine, fine. We've got ample crop this year to carry us through winter." She sat down at the dinner table and eyed the meal suspiciously.

"No gizzard this time," confirmed Hezzoroch as he too sat down. "However, I do suggest using a lot of pepper sauce nonetheless." Thomas nodded in agreement.

"Thank you dear for making dinner." Zire took small amounts of meat and vegetables, and drowned them both in sauce as per his suggestion. "So continuing with the meeting, it was determined that we have food enough for winter. That's the good news. The bad news is that we haven't received any reports on the Destroyer's activity for the last three weeks! The fact that Laurea hasn't been able to send a messenger is very worrying."

"Last time I spoke with Rebecca, she said that Velarr told her the whole Forest of Laurea was completely overrun with Will – er, the Destroyer's - army," offered Thomas, adding "All the inhabitants are hiding in the Forest King's lair."

"Yes, now remind me how Velarr is getting this information?" asked Hezzoroch.

"She's using something called a *communiglass* to speak with Queen Dalea."

"If only we had such a device," sighed Zire. "And you are not able to communicate with Queen Dalea the same way you communicate with your sister?"

"I advised against it," said Hezzoroch. "I am concerned that the Destroyer may sense Thomas's connection with the forest and be able to use it to locate him. You haven't been trying, have you Thomas?"

"No. But I think I sensed him again anyway two days ago when I was meditating with the brown stone – just not in the forest."

"Well where, then?"

Thomas had been waiting to bring this up. "I like making a connection with the stone and then feeling outwards, connecting with Life and really listening hard," he explained. "Two days ago I was searching the ocean at the end of the Jagged Mountains. I sensed an incredible darkness in an area far out, miles from shore."

He remembered the feeling well – like a cold hand squeezing him, a dark shadow clouding his mind and an intense blue light at the same time. It was the same feeling he'd encountered before when searching Laurea (before Hezzoroch had told him not to). He had quickly let go of the stone to break the connection.

"What in the name of Fardoor would the Destroyer be over the ocean for?" wondered Zire aloud. Both she and her husband looked to Thomas for an answer.

"I wasn't sure either," he said "so today I connected with the ocean again and found something."

"What?" they both asked.

He hesitated. "I'm still not sure. But it was something filled with incredible magic. A tree."

"A tree?"

"Another portal between our worlds," said Hezzoroch knowingly.

"I think so."

Zire was incredulous. "Another portal?"

"Yes," said Hezzoroch. "We know that humans weren't always in Fardoor, dear. The Eechawey arrived using the Tree of Laurea, but our other ancestors were around before the Eechawey. One suggestion is that they arrived not by the Tree of Laurea, but by another portal that has long since been lost to us. If it *is* under the ocean, then that would explain why."

"Oh my!" said Zire. "Are you sure that's what you felt Thomas?"

"I said I *wasn't* sure. But I also have a strong feeling it could be another portal."

"And now the Destroyer has found it," said Hezzoroch.

"No," he disagreed "if that was Will I sensed, then he wasn't anywhere near the portal. But it does probably mean he's looking for it."

"The council must know about this!" Zire exclaimed.

"It won't change anything," said her husband dejectedly. "There is nothing we can do to protect the portal: we've become prisoners within our own cities."

"Hopefully it's already protected," Thomas offered.

"Yes, hopefully that is the case."

That ended their discussion on the possibility of another portal. The rest of dinner was spent talking about Zire's meeting and what Thomas had learned from the texts that day. He repeated his forest illusion for her while she cut the remaining slices of a sweet berry pie from yesterday's dinner.

After their meal, the elderly couple commenced their usual evening routine: Zire began planning her work for the next day, while Hezzoroch retired to the small living room and worked on translating one of the ancient texts. He did this every night, hunched low over a table by the fireplace with the book on one side, his pen, paper and an elaborate language key on the other.

It was tedious work, but he continued it despite the fact it was now apparent how much faster Thomas could do the same task. He reasoned that even if Thomas were to translate one of the fifteen ancient texts every couple weeks, it would still take him many months to finish.

Lately Thomas had been joining him in the living room to work on a text of his own, only helping the old man if asked. Tonight, however, he was feeling extra tired and decided to go to bed early. He fell asleep quickly, once again forgetting to contact his sister.

* * * *

"We have to do something!" said Rebecca frantically.

Three days ago Queen Dalea had given Velarr some terrible news: in probing the mind of a rescued knight, they had learned the Destroyer was close to determining the location of one of the hidden human cities. The Queen believed an attack was imminent.

Velarr remained calm. "Thomas still has not contacted you?"

"No! It's been a week since I talked to him last! What if the attack has already happened?"

Elori shook his head. "We would know if an attack had occurred;

we keep watch below us."

Rebecca began pacing angrily. "Then there's still time to warn them!"

"They *are* being warned," said Velarr. "The Forest King and Queen have sent two sprites to their main city, New Kadeon."

"But Queen Dalea also told you she wasn't sure if a sprite could make such a long journey," Rebecca answered back, still pacing. "They should've sent someone bigger!"

"We have been over this," said Elori. "Someone bigger could indeed make the trip with the magic of sprite dust to help them move fast."

"Which is what they used to do to communicate with the human cities," Velarr interjected.

"Yes – *before* Laurea became completely overrun with the Destroyer's army. Now the only thing small enough to escape the Forest *is* a sprite, and even that is risky."

The lines on Elori's face became more pronounced. He looked worried. "I must confess I am concerned the sprites may not make it even if they do get out of Laurea. It is a *very* long way for them to journey. Remember: a sprite's speed must come from the beating of its tiny little wings."

Elori's explanation certainly didn't make her feel any better. "That's why *we* have to warn them!" she exclaimed.

Velarr put her hand on Rebecca in an effort to calm her. "There are three human cities," she said softly "and each of them is hidden. All we know is that they are somewhere on the Eastern side of the Jagged Mountains. Queen Dalea uses the stone altar in the Forest King's lair to guide their messengers to the human cities. We do not have that ability."

"Then that's it! They're done for!"

Rebecca collapsed to the ground sobbing. She was exhausted. She had barely slept a wink since hearing the grim news, partly out of worry and partly because she didn't want to miss Thomas if he did try to contact her. *'Why hadn't he contacted her yet?'* she wondered.

Both Velarr and Elori helped her up off the ground and into a chair. "We *are* trying, Rebecca," said Elori. "At the very least, we are keeping Paarl stationary, watching the area where we think the cities might be. As soon as we see any evidence of attack we will be sending help."

"Why not send it down there already?" she asked between sobs.

"It is a very large area, Rebecca: thousands of square miles. From up here we can see it all, but down on the ground we would have no clue." He lifted her chin and wiped some tears from her damp cheeks. "With any luck, someone will notice that our cloud is staying stationary over them and realize there is something wrong."

"I hope so," she sniffed. It was going to be another sleepless night.

CHAPTER FIFTEEN

Thomas woke up late in the morning. The sun had already made good headway across the partly cloudy sky by the time he showed for breakfast. Zire was all dressed and about to head out the door.

"Look who's up!" she said cheerfully. "My you must have really needed sleep. He's working too hard, Hezzoroch."

"I'm fine," Thomas assured them. "I think it just caught up with me last night."

It looked like Zire didn't know whether to believe him. At any rate, she put on a light jacket and opened the door to leave. "Well I'm off," she said. "I baked some cookies, Thomas - they're in the yellow tin. Hezzoroch has already had three and isn't to have any more today."

The old man threw up his hands. "You have nothing to worry about Zire; three cookies are all I wanted." This she clearly did not believe.

"Wait – where are you going?" Thomas asked.

"First step: I'll be asking Ochim and his parents to dinner, which was Hezzoroch's lovely idea. I'm not sure if he told you yet. Their darling niece Nojanna can come as well if she'd like. Second stop is City Hall where I'll be telling the mayor that you may have confirmed the existence of a second portal." She went halfway outside but then popped her head back in. "If you find out anything more regarding this portal, please tell me or Hezzoroch right away!"

"Okay," he promised.

Zire shut the door completely. Hezzoroch waited a few moments to make sure she was gone before opening the yellow tin. "Just one more cookie, Thomas."

"All right," he said "but if I didn't know any better, I'd say it seems like Zire doesn't know your real reason for inviting Ochim's family to dinner."

The old man gave a guilty look and busied himself wiping crumbs from the counter. "She doesn't. And I doubt she would agree to such a plan, so this must be kept between us." He stopped cleaning the counter and looked at Thomas directly. "Do you think you can search Ochim through the brown stone without other people knowing?"

Thomas had never known the elderly couple to keep secrets from each other. He did know he could trust Hezzoroch, though. "I can do it," he said. "But you have to promise me you won't have any more cookies today."

"Er – of course." He put down the one he'd started eating and closed the yellow tin.

"I thought I'd search for the tree in the ocean again," said Thomas, changing the subject.

"A good idea. But first Zochirrem is coming to work on offensive magic with you. He already dropped by this morning but I told him to come back later because you were still sleeping."

"Will you be working with us too?"

"No, I will be searching for all references to a second portal."

"You mean in the ancient texts."

He shook his head. "The ancient texts were written by the Eechawey. It was our other ancestors that may have arrived by the second portal you sensed. We have books and documents from before they met the Eechawey, but they are not very well preserved, and from what I have seen magic is only infrequently mentioned. I must admit: I have spent most of my life studying the Eechawey texts and neglecting the rest." He paused in thought. "Of course, it is possible the Eechawey sensed the same thing you did in the ocean. I myself have not come across any reference to it in their texts."

A firm knock on the door interrupted their conversation. The handle was tested and the door opened a crack. A wiry-looking man of about sixty poked his head in. "Is the boy up yet?"

"Come in Zochirrem, he's up." Hezzoroch went to close the door behind their guest but saw several more people approaching.

"Will you be opening the library today?" asked one of them.

"Oh silly me," he said. "I neglected to open the library. You two go ahead and get started while I help these people. I won't be joining you today Zochirrem."

"All right then." The wiry man sat down in a chair while Hezzoroch led the group of people to the library portion of the building. "Don't mind me, Thomas," he said. "Finish eating - I'm just going to brush up on some of these spells." Zochirrem took out a small, weathered book. In it were translated passages and incantations from the Eechawey texts – the result of years of work.

"I'm almost done," said Thomas.

He smiled and opened the book anyway. Then Zochirrem began mumbling incantations, saying each one repeatedly to get it right and committed to memory: *"Arraiu, kella storr,"* then *"burrosow caleerae"*.

"I think it's pronounced cal-AH-rae," Thomas corrected.

"Is it?" asked Zochirrem. "Cal-AH-rae, cal-AH-rae," he repeated while taking out a pen and making a correction to the book.

Thomas was used to this now. In many ways his knowledge was starting to exceed those who were helping him train; his abilities already surpassed theirs individually. Still, it was very helpful having someone to train with. A sort of coach, really: someone who's magical ability may not come close to Thomas's but who could provide constructive criticism and encourage him to do better. And there still were some parts of the Eechawey texts that had already been translated but Thomas had yet to learn. (There were many more parts that had yet to be translated or learned by anyone.)

When he finished eating and getting ready, the two of them walked to a large open enclosure that was outside the city, but still within New Kadeon's barrier. Nestled in the same valley as the city, the enclosure was much longer than it was wide. Unlike the cloud park Rebecca had visited, there was no protective field to prevent errant spells from striking the city buildings, though New Kadeon's barrier did provide some insurance against magic escaping into the open proper.

They spent four hours practicing offensive magic, Zochirrem creating illusory targets for Thomas to attack in various ways. For example, he could control the earth, making it rise and fall or even causing giant rock-hands to spring up and crush whatever they grabbed. And when Zochirrem made some of the rubble fly into the air as moving targets, Thomas was able to pulverize them with orange-colored blasts of energy (although his aim did need some work).

At that point Zochirrem reminded him that if he faced any knights from the Destroyer's army, he was to only use the minimum force necessary to subdue them. Perhaps he was alarmed at the image of Thomas blasting rocks into clouds of dust.

"That's all fine," said Thomas in response "but I doubt if any of this will be useful against the Nasrati."

"I share your concern," he said. The wiry old man took the weathered book out again and flipped through its pages. "Unfortunately, we have yet to come across a passage in the ancient texts that explores a way we might deal with them."

"The Eechawey probably didn't even know about the Nasrati," Thomas suggested. "I was told they didn't appear until Will found the Destroyer stone."

Zochirrem rubbed his bald head (something he often did absentmindedly). "While that is true, we were hoping to find something useful anyhow. The key must be with light..." he said, trailing off at the end.

"With light?"

"Yes. That is the one thing we know they can't stand. After all, they only come out in the dark. Everything we've tried so far has been easily overcome by the Destroyer. We need to create a light that will at the very least impede the Nasrati if not kill them." He looked wistful. "You haven't seen anything new like that in your reading, have you?"

Thomas shook his head. The only spell he knew that could create light had been taught to him by Hezzoroch.

Zochirrem's look turned to one of disappointment. "I didn't think so," he said. "Still, as long as we remain hidden we have more time to try and find such a spell."

'While Laurea gets trampled,' thought Thomas.

They ended the day's practice with the old man trying one of the incantations he had had trouble with earlier *('Burrosow cal-AH-rae')*.

It was a magical binding spell - meant to hold a person in place - but it met with limited success. Each time he attempted the spell, Queen Dalea's protective field sprung up around Thomas, surrounding him in a bright golden shimmer. He tried not to laugh as Zochirrem scrunched up his skinny face in concentration, trying to hold on to it for more than a few seconds.

"Burrosow cal-AH-rae! Burrosow cal-AH-rae!" The old man's face scrunched even tighter. *"Burrosow cal-AH-rae!* Are you sure I'm saying it right?" he asked as the spell was repelled for the fifth time.

"Yeah, that's how you say it." He went over and patted the much older but only slightly taller man on his back. "It's just the force field Queen Dalea gave me and Rebecca. No offence, but if you could beat it, I don't think it would stand a chance against Will!"

Zochirrem gave a weak smile and began collecting their stuff from the ground. "Yes, I suppose you're right. Help me gather our things, won't you? This old man needs a rest."

Thomas looked up in the sky and guessed there was about an hour of sunlight left to be had. "If it's all right with you," he said "I think I'm gonna stay and meditate with the brown stone for a bit. Unless you need me to carry something back, that is." He didn't tell him that the reason he was staying was to see if he could find another portal between their two worlds that may be lying in the ocean somewhere.

"No, no – stay for a bit," said Zochirrem. "It certainly is a beautiful day. The trees are in their fall glory, and soon there won't be many leaves left in their branches."

He helped Zochirrem pick up their things – mostly food they had brought. He also made sure the old man could carry it all in one basket, and then watched him walk back to the city. Thomas was left alone.

Zochirrem was right – it was a beautiful day. He and Rebecca had arrived in Fardoor when summer was just winding down. Now the trees scattering the adjacent hills were rich with leaves of red, gold, and orange. A valley wind shook a few more of them loose each time it made a pass.

Fall was one of Thomas's favorite times of the year – not only because the trees were so colorful, but also for the cool, crisp air that seemed so invigorating. On a sunny, fall day like today, you could play outside for hours without getting too hot, but it wasn't so cold that you had to bundle up either.

He sat down on a mossy rock. This valley was a great place to commune with the brown stone, and he often came here to do just that. These days he liked practicing magic without a wachaoum in his hand. With the city's altar nearby he felt like he was always connected: no longer was there a turning 'on' or 'off'. Still, listening to the Gaia force (as Hezzoroch called it) required him to stay focused without distraction. He liked to call it meditation, and wondered if it was anything like the weekly yoga classes his mom attended.

Thomas cleared his mind and focused. His breathing slowed. Then, the familiar rush of spreading outwards and linking with Life all around. (Or was it rushing in on him? He was never sure.) He passed New Kadeon and continued along the Jagged Mountains toward the water, past another human city he'd never visited. (New Gerron or New Shale?) He was at the ocean again, searching its vast, deep expanse.

The incredible magic he'd sensed yesterday had come from a spot miles offshore. It was on the ocean floor, with another mile of water above it. He remembered the strong feeling that it was a tree, and that it was alive.

'If it is another portal,' he wondered *'how could anyone get from where it is, to land?'*

The ocean was so big that Thomas was having trouble remembering where he'd even sensed the tree, filled with magic though it may be. He started listening, hoping the Gaia force in the ocean would guide him there. He heard whispering, but nothing intelligible; this was still very difficult for him.

"Is that you Thomas?" asked a girl behind him. "What are you doing?"

Her familiar voice startled him and he lost the connection. Turning around, he saw Ochim's cousin Nojanna standing a few feet away.

"Sorry for surprising you," she said. "Were you sleeping or something?"

"N-no," he stammered "I was meditating."

"Really?" She looked intrigued.

He stood up and swept the seat of his pants. "Yeah, but I was almost done anyway," he lied. "What are you doing out here?"

Nojanna brushed the light brown hair out of her face, but a gentle breeze kept blowing it back across her eyes. "Just going for a walk," she said. "This is about the only place within the barrier that you can really feel like you're *outside*."

"I know what you mean. I'm surprised more people don't use it." He put his hands on his hips. "I haven't seen you here before."

"Well I've seen you several times," she admitted. "Practicing magic. That's really amazing what you can do! I can't believe you're only ten!"

He blushed. "Thanks - I think."

"I'm seventeen and I can only do a little bit of magic. I think I'd know more if I had my own wachaoum, but they're kind of in short supply. My dad has one that he shares sometimes. He's on the city council, you know. He likes reading the Eechawey translations. Says we should all be getting prepared."

"Well I have one here – did you want to show me?" He fished in his pocket and pulled out one of the stones Will had found in the cave.

Nojanna hadn't been expecting to give a demonstration. "Um, you've already seen me reveal the invisible tent on the Eastern plains," she said, fidgeting. "*That* I can do for sure. Oh I know! I'll try a spell I just learned last week and maybe you can help me with it!"

She grabbed the stone out of Thomas's hand and stared hard at it. Next was a deep breath in and out, and then she chanted *"Araiu stella, eram orr!"*

The stone glowed orange momentarily, before shooting out of her hand to the far side of the enclosure.

"Oh sorry!" she exclaimed. "That was supposed to give a signal in the air for locating."

"That's all right," said Thomas. He got up to go find the stone and Nojanna followed to help.

"I think it landed somewhere over there," she said as they walked to the general vicinity in which it had flown.

He looked where she was pointing. "Oh!"

"You see it?"

"No," he said, then mumbling "but I see something else."

Thomas strained his eyes. He knew where the barrier was, Hezzoroch having showed it to him much earlier. About ten feet outside it was a curious flower he thought he recognized.

"I found your wachaoum, Thomas." Nojanna stood up with it in her hand, taking a moment to register where he was headed. "You shouldn't go any farther," she announced. "The barrier ends a few feet from you."

He said a quick spell and a portion of the force field in front of him wavered a bit. "There, now I'll be able to get back in again."

She protested further.

"I don't see anyone out there, do you?" he asked.

If there was someone watching from outside, they were about to witness Thomas emerging from the inside of a hill.

"What is it? What do you see?" asked Nojanna, hesitating a moment before deciding to follow him.

"It's that flower," he said. "Have you ever seen one like it?"

He knelt down and Nojanna saw what he was talking about: a

single yellow flower with streaks of pink and ginger, small so that it barely rose above the surrounding grass.

"It's pretty," she said, joining him. "No, I've never seen one like it."

"I have. I saw many of them when Rebecca and I were being rescued." He touched the tender petals and examined it more closely. "A flower like this springs up in the place where a sprite has died."

"Where a sprite has died?" she repeated. "Why would a sprite be this far from Laurea?"

"That's a good question." He looked around to see if there were any others. "Look Nojanna – there's another one!" he said excitedly.

"Another flower?"

He shook his head. "Another *sprite*."

A further ten feet from where they were sitting a pair of butterfly wings flapped furiously for a few beats, raising a tiny head above the grass blades for less than a second before collapsing to the ground again.

"It's hurt," said Nojanna.

They approached the sprite cautiously, watching as it tried to raise its tiny body up once more. Its look was one of considerable determination, but its eyes opened wide when it saw Thomas and Nojanna coming. Again it collapsed.

They found the sprite lying very still on its side, two beautiful red and silver wings making slow movements back and forth. It was clearly exhausted.

"I think it's trying to say something," said Nojanna.

The sprite's mouth was indeed moving, but no sound could be heard. It began to cry softly.

"The poor thing! What can we do, Thomas?"

"Hang on," he said. He gently cupped his hands under the sprite and carefully raised it to his ear.

Unlike the previous times he'd had a sprite so close, this one's voice was barely audible. "The Destroyer," it whispered. "He knows where the human city is hiding. He's…coming!"

Thomas's heart suddenly began racing. The sprites had come all the way from Laurea to warn them of an attack!

"Where?" he asked frantically. "Which city?"

The sprite did not respond. He took it away from his ear and looked at the poor creature still cupped in his hand. Its eyes were now closed and its wings even slower. It shed one more tear before the delicate wings stopped moving altogether. He placed it on the ground where it promptly faded into the soil. A small flower sprung up and bloomed in its place; like the first one they'd found, but with red and silver petals instead.

Nojanna had been alarmed by Thomas's reaction. "What did the sprite tell you?" she asked. Instead of answering, he sat there frozen and staring at the flower.

"What did it tell you Thomas?" she repeated, shaking him.

He snapped out of his momentary shock, a terrible realization taking its place.

"It said the Destroyer is coming."

CHAPTER SIXTEEN

Nojanna was hysterical. "The Destroyer is coming to New Kadeon?" she asked wildly.

"I...I don't know!" said Thomas. "The sprite just said he knew where the human city is hiding. It didn't say which one!"

She pulled him up. "*Come on*, Thomas! We have to warn everyone!"

They started running back to the city. Nojanna being much taller was also much faster; she raced on ahead without waiting for him. Thomas just knew he had to warn Hezzoroch.

If he was thinking clearly, he probably would have realized it would be faster to contact the old man through the brown stone instead of running home. However, Thomas was not thinking clearly. In addition to wanting to get to Hezzoroch, other thoughts were running through his head, such as how Will had found out, and was he himself somehow to blame?

Nojanna was yelling something back at him that he couldn't quite hear. She kept running, and so did he. *Almost at the city! 'What if the attack had already happened?'* he thought. *'What if he and Nojanna were so far out they hadn't heard it?' 'Just keep running,'* said a voice inside him. He slipped and fell on the grass instead. It was a hard fall but he got up quickly (practically leapt up!) and kept moving. Nojanna had reached the city and gone straight along the first road. She was heading for the main square. Thomas reached the city thirty seconds later and made a sharp turn to the right, heading straight for the library. He just hoped Hezzoroch was there.

A turn here, a turn there; these streets had become second nature to him. Many people stopped what they were doing and watched him whiz by. *'I should be warning them,'* he thought, but for some strange reason kept his mouth closed. Perhaps he was concerned it would slow him down somehow. *'Find Hezzoroch,'* said the voice.

Thomas was almost at the library where he'd spent the last five weeks living with the elderly couple. He rounded one more corner and nearly wept with relief when he saw the old man standing outside.

He seemed to be staring at the sky, and didn't see Thomas approaching right away.

"He-Hezzoroch!" he exclaimed, not as loud as he would've liked as he was nearly out of breath from running.

"Ah Thomas!" said Hezzoroch quickly. "Just who I'm looking for. Ochim's family is already here, but first I've been meaning to show you something."

He pointed to a large cumulus cloud quite unlike the wispy ones that dotted the rest of the bright sky. "That is Paarl," he announced "one of the Uru cloud cities I've been meaning to show you. I've noticed it in the same place overhead for at least the last three days, which is somewhat unusual. See?"

He did see.

Another terrible realization swept over Thomas as he reached the old man. "They…were trying…to warn us!" he panted. *Why hadn't he contacted Rebecca for the last week? How could he be so stupid?*

Hezzoroch turned his attention from Paarl to Thomas, taking in his ragged appearance and the look of true fear on his face. "Warn us of what Thomas?"

Thomas saw the same fear spread across Hezzoroch's own face. The old man knew what he was about to say.

"The – the Destroyer knows where we are and is coming!" he stammered, recognizing he hadn't even called him 'Will' this time.

"Nojanna and I saw a sprite just outside New Kadeon's barrier. It came all the way from Laurea to warn us. It was almost dead but it managed to tell me the Destroyer had found where the city was hidden and was coming to attack!"

"*Which* city Thomas? *Which city?*"

"I – I don't know!" he cried. "It died before it could tell me!" He started shaking.

"Laurea's messengers always come to New Kadeon," said Hezzoroch "then we give word to New Gerron and New Shale. They must be warned as well!"

"I think Nojanna's gone to City Hall," said Thomas.

No sooner had it been mentioned than the loud bells of City Hall began ringing – a warning to the inhabitants of New Kadeon. People all around gave frightened looks, some running into their homes, others exiting them to see what the commotion was.

Zire came outside in her apron, followed by Ochim and his parents. "What's going on Hezzoroch? Is this a drill of sorts? It's still light out."

Thomas was continuing to try and catch his breath.

"Dear me! You're a wreck!" she said, taking in his grass and mud-stained clothes.

"This is not a test Zire," the old man informed her. "Thomas and Nojanna have received warning that the Destroyer has located of at least one of our cities and an attack is imminent."

"If it hasn't already happened in New Gerron or New Shale!" added Thomas.

"I spoke to representatives of both cities only an hour ago!" said Zire. "Who told you this?"

"We must prepare," Hezzoroch interjected. "I will go to the stone altar. I think you should join me Thomas."

"It's too late!" he said. "Look!"

A dark figure had just materialized in the air outside New Kadeon's barrier. Three rows of ten knights each appeared below him. They all watched in terror as Will approached the city.

From where Thomas was standing he could see the two slender towers that kept watch on the city's entrance. The guards of both were outside with their arms held high, no doubt chanting. A ripple raced across the force field. *They're trying to strengthen it,* he realized.

Will continued gliding towards New Kadeon, standing upright yet floating fifty feet off the ground. His knights marched below. All of those watching the scene unfold stood frozen, unable to turn away from the sight. The knights stopped in front of the barrier; a forested hillside would appear to lie just ahead of them.

Nobody breathed as Will came closer still. Thomas recognized his blonde hair and the same dark armor he'd worn on the plains, but he remained too far away to make out his face. He shivered some more, unable to reconcile what had become of his cousin.

Will's hand touched the barrier but did not go through. In response the energy field strengthened at that spot, emitting an orange glow. The guards on the tower platform continued their manic chanting, now joined by several more guards on the ground.

He withdrew his hand and did something even more frightening: he laughed. It couldn't be heard on this side of the barrier, but the sight was thoroughly chilling to all who witnessed it.

"It still may hold," whispered Hezzoroch, breaking the silence. Thomas squeezed his arm tight. He didn't feel ready for a confrontation with his cousin yet.

A fist was jammed into the barrier. Cold, blue energy emanated from it, spreading out in a slow wave, fighting against the barrier's own orange light. He took his other fist and did the same thing.

It was if someone had flipped a switch. The silence was shattered by a loud, chaotic din that rose up in its stead. People were screaming, babies crying, bells ringing *(had they ever stopped?)*. Everyone ran towards the main square, parents desperately clinging to small children in tow.

New Kadeon had a contingency plan: in the event of an attack, a link had been made to magically transport its citizens to the other human cities. The link was in City Hall, and it could only transport small groups at a time. There was also the problem of knowing when to close it at the other end so that they couldn't be followed.

Hezzoroch raced inside his home, re-emerging seconds later with three small books – his translations. The Eechawey texts would have to be left behind. "Everybody follow me!" he ordered.

Unfortunately neither he nor Zire could run very fast. People all around zipped past their group towards the main square where City Hall was located. There also seemed to be a problem with Ochim. His parents were desperately pulling on his arms to get him to move, but he did so with reluctance.

"Please, Ochim!" his mother cried. "We must move quickly!"

Thomas stayed with Zire and Hezzoroch. He looked behind him and saw the blue energy Will was emitting had spread much farther. With the sound of a small explosion, it intensified greatly and caused an energy wave to race outwards. Screams became louder and people tried to run faster, many falling as they headed downhill. Zire tumbled onto her side.

"It won't hold much longer!" exclaimed Thomas as they helped her back up. He came to a decision: ready or not he would have to confront his cousin today. "Hezzoroch, I have to face him!" he shouted over the noise.

"It's too soon – you aren't ready yet!" the old man shouted back. "You must escape to New Shale!" They started moving again.

Closer to the city entrance, a hundred New Kadeons trained in magic had assembled on either side of the valley. Many others were likely gathered around the stone altar preparing spells; this was Hezzoroch's destination.

They were a meagre defence against the army, meant only to slow its progression so that more people could escape.

"If I don't help, no one's gonna make it to New Shale!" Thomas yelled. He didn't wait for Hezzoroch's reply.

During the past week Thomas had learned how to travel through the earth. This he did now, disappearing into the ground and racing towards the city centre at an incredible speed. He burst up through the middle of New Kadeon's main square in a shower of red rock and clay. Those who saw it paused only a moment before continuing to City Hall. Thomas paid them no attention, focusing on Will instead.

He could feel the stone altar behind him and drew power from it

– or through it, rather. This was it. The blue energy from Will had nearly engulfed New Kadeon's barrier and it was doubtful if it would hold for more than thirty seconds. People continued streaming past Thomas to their supposed salvation behind him. Another hundred citizens young and old had assembled in various positions near the entrance getting ready for battle. Even from this distance he could see their frightened expressions.

Thomas was calm now. Connected with Life. Focused. *Listening.* The blue energy intensified further, creating another explosion that collapsed the barrier altogether. The city was visible. Three rows of knights marched forward, still only thirty in number altogether. Will had no doubt left the rest in Laurea, confident in his ability to destroy New Kadeon with just thirty knights…and the Nasrati. Thomas saw with horror that his cousin was recreating the black dome he'd seen him form previously, only this time it was much larger. He hadn't noticed Thomas.

The knights began their attack. Heavy clubs struck the ground, sending powerful blue arcs hurtling towards buildings and people alike. Those with maces spun them in the air to the same effect. The volunteers at the front used their limited knowledge of magic to throw up shields and occasionally aim energy bolts of their own at the knights (which mostly did a harmless glance off their armor). They stayed far clear of the knights themselves.

Will concentrated on forming the black dome and ignored the melee below. Thomas hadn't made a move yet. Before he could, a giant cloud of orange smoke swirled out from the roof of City Hall behind him and zoomed towards the knights. Since they had now scattered somewhat in their advance, it only struck three full on. They stopped moving, and several more nearby slowed down considerably – like watching a film at half speed.

This got Will's attention. He stopped forming the dome and aimed a powerful blast at City Hall. Thomas seized this opportunity to throw up a massive shield in its path that absorbed the blast entirely.

Will didn't skip a beat. "Thomas!" he exclaimed, magically amplifying his voice and coming a bit closer. "I hoped you would be here!"

Another cloud of smoke swirled out of City Hall and headed towards the knights. With a wave of his hand, Will reversed its direction so it struck the hall instead. "That should hold them for a bit!" he said cheerfully.

"Will! You don't have to do this!" shouted Thomas. Rather than wait for a reply, he mustered a large energy bolt of his own and sent it hurtling at his cousin.

"You're going to have to do better than that," he said, blocking it.

He returned to the task at hand with arms outstretched. Inky darkness spread like oil from where Will was floating and a chill wind filled the air. The volunteers at the front had dwindled in number, and those remaining couldn't stop the knights from spreading out into the city. Thomas had to choose whether to help them or continue an attack on Will. He pounded the ground and hundreds of metres away a giant wall of earth raised up, blocking the knights' progression.

Will aimed a blast at the wall, partially destroying it. A second blast was aimed at Thomas which knocked him off his feet despite being mostly deflected.

"Not good enough!" roared Will. The black dome was nearly complete, covering the city with darkness.

"Marae ilaeros!" said Thomas as he got up. This was the spell for creating light that Hezzoroch had showed him. A glowing orb shot from his hand straight up above him where it exploded into hundreds of smaller orbs that bathed the city in soft light.

Will chuckled then gave a quick blow as if putting out a candle. The orbs disappeared, and any lights from within houses went out as well.

"Aren't you curious how I found New Kadeon," he asked casually, as if carrying on a normal conversation.

"You used me!" shouted Thomas, full of guilt and anger. Hezzoroch was right: he never should have tried to seek out Will through the brown stone.

"Don't flatter yourself," he scoffed. "I did sense you looking for me, but Ochim is the real star here. I knew those taken from my army were having their memories of me erased, my control removed. With Ochim I found a way to keep my control there, buried deep where it wouldn't be noticed by that Forest Wretch or the humans." He sighed as he blocked another of Thomas's energy bolts. "It worked too well, though. It was so deep that it took some time for me to find and reassert my power so he would lead me here. Ah well – better late than never!"

"So you used me and Rebecca to make sure Ochim was rescued!" shouted Thomas.

He smirked. "Well yes, that part is true."

The dome was complete, the city made dimly visible only by a cold blue light that seemed to come from nowhere.

With a sickening feeling in his stomach Thomas watched as a suit of armor materialized beside Will, then went flying towards the hillside where Ochim could be seen standing still. His parents were still trying to get him to move, Zire was pulling on the parents and Hezzoroch was pulling on Zire. They were so far away.

The armor attached itself to Ochim, an unfeeling helmet covering his face. He raised a terrible club and smashed the ground. Boom! All those around him fell. Thomas's aim wasn't good enough to hit Ochim with an energy bolt from such a distance; his parents might be hit by mistake. He cast a shield separating Ochim from Hezzoroch and the others instead. Boom! An arc of blue light reduced an adjacent building to rubble, but the shield had protected them.

The knights at the front were streaming through the ruined portion of Thomas's wall, the volunteers now in retreat. He recognized Zochirrem and several of his other teachers among those running, watching helpless as Zochirrem was suddenly struck down by an errant blue arc from one of the knights.

Hezzoroch and Zire were back on their feet but Ochim's father lay motionless, his wife kneeling beside him. The old man levitated some rubble and aimed it at Ochim to slow him down - easily taken care of with one swipe of his club. The shield was still in place *(how long it would last?)*. People continued running past him to get to City Hall.

So much was happening at once, Thomas didn't know where to look or how to act. Things were about to get worse. He looked up at Will, who gave him an evil grin in return.

A noise. A horrible, familiar noise began filling Thomas's head. The Nasrati were coming. All around him children of varying age collapsed to the ground. Shadowy figures emerged from the darkness and headed for these children first. Screams grew louder and pandemonium ensued.

Something curious happened with Thomas, though: he didn't collapse. The sound of the Nasrati remained distant, muted somehow. Through the brown stone he was able to block them out.

Will was laughing maniacally. "Managing to hold on this time, Thomas?" he asked. "Well good luck trying to save everyone else!"

Thomas didn't respond. Nasrati were descending everywhere, creating walls of fire between children and their desperate parents. He shot an energy bolt at a nearby Nasratum, which traveled right through it without doing any damage. A young boy below the dark figure was going into a fit. The Nasratum reached down and covered him with its shadowy cloak. They both disappeared. Will continued laughing. "There's nothing you can do!" he said.

But there *was* something he could do. There had to be. Zochirrem had said the key to defeating these creatures was with light. He had already tried one illuminating spell to little effect. He knew what to do: he had to find the spell that would work. It existed – he just had to *listen*.

Thomas encased himself in a powerful force field. He closed his eyes and grabbed the wachaoum in his pocket fiercely. He blocked out everything happening around him. He listened.

An unseen hand could be felt guiding him towards the answer almost immediately. Three words appeared in his head. Though his eyes were closed he could see them forming. He could hear them being spoken, chanted. The Gaia force was telling him what he needed to know. He saw what the magic would do.

Will was watching him carefully. Thomas removed the force field and stared him in the eye. *"Dragus maerrabi etheros!"* he yelled.

The ground rumbled. An enormous, dragon-shaped animal emerged from the earth below, gently swaying its impressive tail. The ethereal creature seemed to be composed totally of light, and its glow was great to behold. This was the incredible magic Thomas had seen and heard in his mind.

Will looked mildly impressed. "That's a neat trick," he started "but I don't think –"

"LIGHT!" yelled Thomas.

The creature roared, rearing its great head and thrashing its tail before exploding into hundreds of powerful white beams that shot in every direction. They struck the Nasrati, who reacted as if in pain. It was a mortal wound to each one. They did not just disappear: they *disintegrated.*

"NO!" yelled Will. *"WHAT HAVE YOU DONE?"* He pointed at Thomas, who was taken aback by the tremendous force that suddenly struck him. Queen Dalea's golden shield materialized, blocking the dark tentacles of thought that pounded just outside his head. Something…Will…was trying to enter his mind.

He wanted to scream, to run, but was frozen in place. He couldn't even turn his eyes away from his cousin's face. He could see that Will was shocked, angry, surprised at being rebuffed. His efforts redoubled and the golden shield momentarily grew brighter in response before starting to flicker. The tentacles began intruding into Thomas's head, wrapping themselves around his brain. He started seeing things from his cousin's point of view.

Meanwhile, the beams of light from Thomas's spell had also poked straight through the dome of darkness covering New Kadeon. It too disintegrated and evening sunlight filled the city. With great joy, the citizens of New Kadeon looked up to see hundreds of Uru descending upon them from above. They began aiming their ivory bolts at the knights below and Will himself. From behind Thomas, a massive energy blast burst out of City Hall and struck Will, indicating their release from the stop spell. Knocked loose from his cousin's grip, Thomas wheezed as though he had just escaped suffocation. Will was visibly shaken despite being unharmed. The Nasrati were gone and he had only brought thirty knights with him, confident they would succeed. Between the humans, the Uru and Thomas, even he was unmatched at the moment.

"This isn't over!" he spat angrily. With a wave of his hand, he and the knights disappeared. Ochim was gone as well.

A loud cheer erupted in New Kadeon and joyous commotion ensued. Thomas was rapidly surrounded by people much taller than him, clapping him on the back and shaking his hand. Parents came up to thank him. And though he did enjoy the attention, he also wished they would move so that he could go see Hezzoroch and Zire.

"Make way, make way!" said a firm voice.

The crowd parted and admitted entry to the mayor. "Well done Thomas!" he enthused while pumping his hand vigorously. "*Most* impressive! Well folks we have finally found a weapon against the Nasrati, thanks to young Thomas here!" He addressed this last part to the assembled crowd, who erupted in another cheer.

"And let's not forget our friends from the sky!" he continued grandly. "The Uru!"

All over Uru were descending and being greeted warmly. Thomas used this momentary diversion to slip into the ground and travel to the area where he had last seen his elderly caregivers. He burst up through one of the hillside roads, about fifty feet from the two of them.

The first thing Thomas saw was Zire sobbing, abruptly shaking him out of the reverie he'd been enjoying until then. All of a sudden he noticed there were cries of anguish along with the cries of joy throughout the city. Many people had been killed, many more hurt. Those with wounds were being tended to by both Uru and human healers.

Hezzoroch lay on the ground and Zire was crying next to him. Further still were the unmoving bodies of Ochim's parents. A young male Uru knelt beside the old man, hands moving gracefully over his body without quite touching it.

Thomas ran up to them, a well of tears building up inside. Hezzoroch wasn't moving and his eyes were closed. Falling rubble had battered the old man's body, bruising him badly and leaving his clothes in tatters.

"Is he alive?" asked Thomas, fearing he already knew the answer.

"I'm sorry," said the Uru "there was nothing I could do; his injuries were too great."

He knelt beside Hezzoroch and looked hard into his tired face. Desperately he wished the old man would open his eyes again, if only so he could say goodbye. Inside him the well sprung loose and tears began to fall.

This only made Zire's crying greater. "He was *such* a good man," she exclaimed. "He would have been *so* proud of what you did."

It was clear from the way she said it that he had died before witnessing Thomas vanquish the Nasrati. He had died unsure if the people of New Kadeon would survive.

Zire saw the look on Thomas's face. "He may not have seen it happen," she said "but I'm sure he now knows what you accomplished." She looked up, as if expecting to see him watching them from above.

"I'm sorry Zire," he said with downcast eyes. "I wasn't fast enough. I could've saved more people. I could've saved Hezzoroch!" More tears. The old man had begun to feel like his own grandfather, and it hurt to lose him this way.

She gave him a hug. He couldn't even look her in the eye, but she pulled up his chin and began cleaning his face with a handkerchief. Her own eyes were red from crying, and still she tried to cheer him up.

"There, there," she said. "No one blames you, Thomas - *I* certainly don't. Look at all the people you did save!" She forced him to look down on the city. It seemed the entire population of New Kadeon was outside, but all Thomas took notice of were the hurt, the dead and the grieving. He still felt guilty.

The young Uru who tended to Hezzoroch tried to attend to Zire's leg but she brushed him off, choosing instead to lay by her husband's side, stroking his hair and kissing his cheek.

A hand on Thomas's shoulder startled him. He turned around to see Velarr, the Uru who had helped rescue him and Rebecca so long ago.

"Hello Thomas," she said gently. "I am sorry for your loss, and yours Zire. Hezzoroch was well-respected and I very much enjoyed the opportunities I had to meet him." Zire gave a small smile and nod.

The sight of Velarr made him cry even more. "Is Rebecca here?" he asked hopefully.

She shook her head. "Rebecca is in Paarl."

"You knew there was going to be an attack, didn't you? That's why you were floating over New Kadeon. I should've contacted Rebecca days ago! *Why* didn't I contact her?" He looked to Velarr for an answer.

"Yes, that was unfortunate," she said. "But a great tragedy was avoided here nonetheless. I was told you were responsible for defeating the Nasrati. No one has done that before: not the humans, not the Uru, not even the Forest King. The Magic Council will be very interested to know how you accomplished such a feat."

Velarr continued talking but he was only half-listening to her while staring at Hezzoroch. "What was that?" he asked.

"I said it is time for us to leave now Thomas."

"Us?"

"Yes, you will be accompanying me to Paarl. You and your sister have been separated for too long."

"But – they need me here in New Kadeon! What if Will comes back?"

"The humans are not staying in New Kadeon either, Thomas. Look down there."

She stood him up so he could see better. He followed her gaze to the streets below, where thousands of people were once again streaming towards City Hall, hands full of what little they could carry.

"I don't understand," he said. "Why are they still leaving New Kadeon?"

"That the Destroyer will return is a certainty. When he does it will be with far more knights than just now. If he brings his entire army it would take all the Uru, the humans and all of Laurea to defend this city. That is why it must still be abandoned."

Thomas didn't say anything. Hezzoroch was gone, and now the city he'd grown accustomed to would be gone as well.

"They'll be safe in New Shale and New Gerron," said Velarr. "We don't believe the Destroyer knows their locations."

That was probably true, since Ochim never visited those cities.

"But...what about Hezzoroch? I'll miss his funeral! And what about my training?"

"I understand you have been using the humans' ancient texts. There are copies in the other cities, and the mayor has agreed to let you take these ones with you to Paarl."

"And Hezzoroch? If I go now will I be able to come back to see him buried? Will I be able to visit Zire?"

She was now accepting help to lift his body off the ground, but the tears had yet to stop.

"We don't know where the other cities are, and travel will be too dangerous for the time being. I'm sorry Thomas; you will have to say your goodbyes now."

The old man had been placed on a makeshift platform beside Ochim's parents. Despite his shield they'd died as well. Thomas left Velarr and went to stand beside Zire.

"The poor people," she said. "They didn't know their own son. I suppose none of us knew there was anything wrong."

"Hezzoroch suspected it," he revealed. "That's why he invited them to dinner. I was supposed to search Ochim using the brown stone."

"Oh!" she said, unsure how to take this new information. "I guess he didn't tell me because he thought I'd oppose such a plan. He was probably right," she sniffed.

He held her hand. "Velarr says I have to go to Paarl now."

"I know dear."

"I'll stay if you want me to."

She looked at him with warm eyes. "No, no - Hezzoroch was your teacher. What you are doing is more important than hanging around an old fuddy-duddy like me. I have friends I can stay with – don't worry. But...perhaps you could visit me sometime – you know, the way you did with your sister using the brown stone? I'm not sure how it works."

"I promise to keep in touch," he said, then gave her a big hug. She squeezed him back so hard he thought she might not let go. He didn't mind one bit.

Next Thomas looked upon Hezzoroch one last time, giving him a hug as well. "Thanks for everything," he whispered.

Velarr gave Zire a rather awkward embrace and promised to take good care of Thomas. She took his hand and led him a few steps away.

"Say hi to your sister for me!" Zire called out.

"I will!"

"And don't forget to contact me!"

"I won't!"

"You'll probably want to hold on with both hands," advised Velarr.

He glanced at the cloud above them. It was a long way up. "I'm ready," he said.

They took off from the ground, Zire waving up at them, Thomas looking down but unable to wave back. He watched as Hezzoroch's lifeless body become smaller and smaller below, and felt a new pang of guilt and sorrow. The citizens of New Kadeon became a sea of ants moving in the direction of City Hall. It felt like he was abandoning them.

At the same time, Thomas felt a surge of excitement – not at flying but at being able to see his sister in person again! He stopped looking down, choosing to face the clouds above instead.

For her part, Velarr was being careful not to go too fast in their ascent (Rebecca had advised her against this). Of course it helped that she hadn't been sprinkled with sprite dust this time around.

Together they journeyed upwards, through the cloud's cool mist and onto its fluffy surface. Immediately, Thomas was struck by the beautiful marble city that lay ahead. Sunset was just beginning. Over the next twenty minutes Paarl would become awash in gentle hues of yellow, orange, and red – not unlike the leaves of the forest below.

"It's beautiful," he remarked.

"You've caught it at the best time." Velarr could see he was still quite sad. She had seen the same face on Rebecca a number of times, and was taken by how similar the siblings were in appearance. "You may continue to hold my hand if you'd like," she said. This was another thing on which she'd been instructed.

"Will I fall if I let go?"

"No, I can promise you won't fall."

He let go. Thomas was fortunate in that his current buoyancy level left him only knee-deep in the cloud. Rebecca, of course, had been up to her chin.

They walked to Paarl's gates. More Uru were poking up through the cloud and heading in the same direction, and a crowd seemed to be gathering there.

King Arros himself was among those waiting. The number of gold accessories he wore had been pared down since Rebecca had first met him, but he still had his crown and sceptre.

Velarr bowed and Thomas followed suit.

"Is it true Velarr?" he asked calmly. "Did this young boy defeat the Nasrati?"

'News sure travels fast here!' thought Thomas.

"It is true."

The crowd began applauding their approval, all looking very serene. Besides the King, several of them stood apart for the burgundy robes they wore. These Uru seemed to harbor doubt that a young boy could have accomplished such a feat. One of them raised his hand.

"Your Majesty, if I may? The Magic Council would like to meet with the boy."

"Oh yes, undoubtedly," he agreed. "As soon as possible."

Velarr grabbed Thomas's hand protectively. "Your Majesty, *Thomas* just lost a dear friend to the Destroyer, and narrowly missed the same fate himself. I respectfully request that their Magistrates meet with him at a later date."

As a sign that King Arros was becoming more independent in his decision-making, he didn't look to the Uraiel first before stating "Well that sounds reasonable. At a later date then. In the meantime, let me be the first to shake your hand Thomas."

The King leaned forward and shook his free hand while everyone else applauded once more, reminding Thomas of his encounter with the mayor of New Kadeon not so long ago. The crowd then parted to let King Arros leave. Velarr and Thomas also walked away, retracing the same route to Elori's place she had led Rebecca along before. When they arrived there his sister was already waiting with the door open, having seen them approach from her bedroom window. She raced out and threw her arms around Thomas.

"I'm so glad you're okay!" Rebecca exclaimed. "And look how buoyant you already are! When I first arrived only my head was above the cloud. Lucky!"

He chuckled at the thought of just her head walking thorough the streets. Then he felt guilty about laughing and burst into tears again.

"What is it Thomas? What's wrong?"

"It's been a rough day," said Velarr, steering him into the house and sitting him down in the living room.

Rebecca sat beside him. "Thomas? You're making me cry too, and if you don't tell me why, then I'll be crying for no reason!"

He gave her a half-smile. Rebecca often cried in sympathy with others without knowing why they were sad first. "It's Hezzoroch," he said softly. "He's…dead."

"Oh Thomas!" she hugged him again. He had told her loads about Hezzoroch during their communications. She knew he likened him to their own grandpa, who'd died last year. "It's not your fault, you know."

He shook his head. "Yes it is."

"No it isn't Thomas."

"Well then it's Will's fault!" he exclaimed, slamming the armrest. "It's either mine or his Rebecca!"

Velarr came back in the room with some hot tea. "Drink this," she instructed. "You'll feel better."

"I don't want to feel better."

He pushed it away but she handed it back. "Drink it."

A small sip and he found his body immediately warming up. The tea did indeed make him feel calmer at the very least.

"What was he like?" asked Rebecca tentatively.

"Who – Will? Confident, arrogant, cruel." He could picture Will staring down on New Kadeon, laughing as people were being hurt. The memory revolted him.

She bit her lip. "He's still our cousin."

"Will Hastings was our cousin!" The effects of the tea prevented him from screaming it out. "That person is gone now. All that's left is the Destroyer."

"We're here to *save* him Thomas!"

"We're here to save Fardoor now. I don't think he can be saved anymore."

"If that is what you truly believe," said Velarr "then it is likely Fardoor cannot be saved either. There may be no other way to defeat him than to separate the boy you call Will Hastings from the Destroyer stone."

"See Thomas? I still think it can happen. We can't give up hope now. From what I heard you did some pretty amazing stuff today. And I'm really happy you're here now. And, well…I've been working really hard too. I want to show you what I've learned so far." Rebecca started floating off her seat. Velarr's hand on her shoulder pushed her back down.

"Tomorrow, Rebecca. For now we could all get some rest."

Thomas chuckled in spite of himself "I'm really glad I'm here now too," he said sincerely. "And if you aren't giving up hope for Will then I guess I won't either." This was said to make his sister happy, but inside he wasn't so sure.

Just then Elori walked in the front door. Thomas turned at the sound and saw an elderly Uru with a long white beard and the same burgundy robes as some of the ones who had first greeted him in Paarl.

"Where is he?" he asked loudly. "Where is the boy who single-handedly defeated the Nasrati?"

Velarr went to greet him. "Elori, I was just saying that we should all be going to bed."

"Well at least let me shake his hand!" he scoffed, entering the living room. "Ah there you are dear boy!" He did more than shake his hand. He grabbed Thomas in a great big bear hug. Then, just so she wouldn't feel left out, he grabbed Rebecca and hugged both of them together. "The two of you are really quite something! I have no doubt you will help us prevail in the end!"

"The other Uru with robes like yours looked sceptical when they met me," said Thomas. He realized it was rude, but it was the first thing he thought of to say.

Elori let them go and sat down. "Oh – you mean when you entered Paarl? All members of the Uru Magic Council. I don't know if that has been explained to you yet. They have a hard time accepting you could succeed where we have so far failed. Sorry I was not there to greet you as well."

Velarr whispered something in his ear. "I see. My heartfelt apologies, Thomas. I looked forward to meeting Hezzoroch; I am sorry I never got the chance." He sighed. "Perhaps it is best we get some rest now."

Thomas finished his tea and let Rebecca lead him to the room they would be sharing. Another cloud bed had been set up. The novelty of sleeping on a cloud aside, it looked extremely inviting.

Rebecca shut off the light and climbed into her own bed.

"Do you mind if we keep the light on just a little?" he asked.

"Sure." She waved her hand and the globe on the ceiling gave off a dim glow. "That okay?"

"Yeah, thanks." A few weeks ago what his sister just did might have fazed him, but not anymore.

"Goodnight Thomas."

"Goodnight."

He closed his eyes. And thanks to the tea, he slept.

* * * *

That night, many Uru stayed up and watched the destruction of New Kadeon. Less than an hour after sunset, Will returned with his knights, bringing them thirty at a time until they numbered in the hundreds. By then the city had been emptied; only the buildings themselves remained. Within minutes the whole of New Kadeon was on fire. It burned so bright that it could clearly be seen from Paarl, even without the magical magnification devices many Uru were using. It was not long before the city was reduced to rubble. What remained could have been sifted like flour.

Elori was among those watching, joining a large group in the park where the cloud had been swirled to permit a direct view. '*It is good that Thomas did not see this,*' he thought.

But he did see it. In his dream Thomas witnessed every moment of New Kadeon's destruction over and over.

CHAPTER SEVENTEEN

Their time in Fardoor was coming to an end.

Thomas woke up with that feeling, and somehow knew it to be true. He wondered if Rebecca felt it as well.

No one mentioned New Kadeon that morning. Velarr and Elori thought it best to not say anything, comfortable in their knowledge that Thomas had not seen what occurred. He didn't let them know otherwise. In truth, although he did feel a deep pain, it was somehow more manageable than it should have been. Velarr expected this. The tea she had brewed was indeed magic, and worked to make strong emotions such as grief more bearable. As such, it was highly valued by the Uru. She herself drank this tea when both her children were captured by the Destroyer.

Thomas returned to his preparation with renewed fervour. The Eechawey texts had been carried up from New Kadeon and delivered to Elori's home. After breakfast he delved back into them, quickly scanning the ones he hadn't looked at for anything that might be useful against Will, not bothering to write anything down that wasn't.

"You can read this?" asked Rebecca upon opening one of the books.

"I can with this," he said and produced a wachaoum from the

white toga they'd given him to wear.

She already knew he used it for magic. "It helps you read an ancient language too? Who would've thought those stones Will found in the cave would be so important?"

"Yeah."

She continued thumbing through the ragged pages of incomprehensible text. "Oh! I have a stone to show you too," she said, pulling out the Verrakal crystal. "It's more of a gem, really."

"Will found that in the cave too."

She handed the crystal to him for a closer examination. Its violet color was more vibrant than the last time he had seen it. "You took it out of the Native decoration," he observed.

"Yeah, but I'm actually thinking of putting it back in and wearing it as a necklace like it used to be."

"What's gonna stop Will from just taking it from you?"

"I don't think he can - watch." She threw it across the room and it flew right back into her palm. "And that's without even trying!"

"But *I* just took it from you!"

"I handed it to you. That's different."

Eager to show him some of what she had learned, Rebecca did a bit of flying and some tricks with invisibility. She also demonstrated her ability to control wind.

"I can do some pretty impressive energy bolts too," she said "but I can't show you here."

"That was great what you just did," he encouraged.

"Thanks. It's harder for me, you know? I don't have any books to help. Almost everything I've learned started as an accident. Kind of trial and error." She gave him a hopeful look before asking "Do you think any of it will be useful?"

She wanted him to say yes. Before coming to Fardoor, Rebecca had always been protective of Thomas, sometimes to the point of being patronizing. Much as he hated to admit it, he did occasionally look to her for guidance. Now he sensed their roles had changed: Rebecca was looking to *him* for guidance, and he wasn't sure he had the answers.

"Of course it will be useful."

"Do you really think so?"

"I said yes."

"Okay, thanks. Now you show me something."

He just wanted to read, but she was insistent. He created the illusion of a sandy beach around them.

"Oh that is so cool!" his sister exclaimed. "Do another one!"

"*One* more." He closed his eyes and the beach was replaced with a tropical waterfall. Elori walked in the door and did a double-take.

She giggled. "Thomas created this illusion! Isn't that neat?"

"Yes, very interesting. But I am sure those books must contain spells that will be more practical in your fight."

Thomas made an 'I-told-you-so' face at his sister.

"Speaking of which," Elori continued "the Magic Council would like to meet with you in one hour. I took the liberty of telling them that would be acceptable."

They wanted to see him conjure the same magic he'd used against the Nasrati. He hoped he could do it again.

An hour later they went to the Chambers of the Uraiel. Located only a little ways from the Palace, it was much less conspicuous than that magnificent edifice. The front entrance was small and sandwiched between two other buildings. There was no sign overhead announcing its existence. Once inside, however, a long hallway took you to a rather large building hidden from the street. Rebecca had been here just once before, and the only thing she liked were the cloud sculptures in the hallway (more of Elori's creations, they mostly depicted famous Uraiel in various poses). The rest of the Chambers were dark and filled with strange smells. This was where the greatest Uru magical minds did their experiments.

The Chambers held an aura of secrecy about them, of which Rebecca didn't understand the purpose. *'Everyone knows the Uraiel exist,'* she reasoned *'and sure you don't notice the Chambers from the street, but any old Uru can see it when they fly overhead!'*

Elori led the Day children to a large room with blinds pulled over its few windows. There, the entire Magic Council (minus the four that had been banished) watched as Thomas recreated the ethereal dragon creature.

"Dragus maerrabi etheros!"

At first nothing happened. The Uraiel murmured softly amongst themselves. After twenty seconds the cloud beneath them moved and a shimmering creature emerged to fill the room. It had come from the ground as before, then travelled to where they were high above the land. When Thomas yelled "LIGHT!" the creature roared and exploded into hundreds of powerful beams just as it had done before. The light was not injurious to those watching, but rather passed harmlessly through them and the building itself. Some was caught by the Uraiel in what looked to be an ordinary glass jar, giving them great excitement.

The Day children were thanked for their time and ushered out. Elori stayed behind. In a matter of days the secret of this new magic was unlocked, and soon dozens of 'Etheros' staffs had been produced that were capable of creating the same light.

This was the calm before the storm. Over the next few weeks Rebecca continued practicing with the Verrakal crystal, while Thomas poured himself into scouring the Eechawey texts. Shortly after arriving in Paarl he had contacted Zire to make sure she was safe. At the same time, he sensed that Will had left many knights on the eastern side of the mountains. It was not safe to go down there. He missed Hezzoroch's funeral.

He recalled a story the old man had once told him:

"There was a time," he had said *"when the Forest of Laurea stretched all the way to the Jagged Mountains and right down to the ocean. It covered a vast territory but has been receding for quite a while now. The stone altar you saw on the plains tells you it was larger even in the time of the Eechawey, for they only placed altars in the forest."* He had paused for a moment, before solemnly announcing *"The heart of Fardoor is in Laurea."*

"You mean the Tree *of Laurea?"* Thomas had asked.

"Yes. The Uru believe the source of all life in Fardoor was the Tree of Laurea."

"Do they think it formed *all life or it was used as a portal like for us and the Eechawey? And what about your other ancestors, and the second portal?"*

"So many questions! And unfortunately I do not have the answers. Like the Uru, I do believe all life in this world is somehow connected to the Tree of Laurea. That is the Gaia force you can feel when using the brown stone."

"Well then why is Laurea receding?"

"The Tree is growing older, although it still has many years left. When it dies, though, so too will Laurea. When Laurea dies, so too will Fardoor. That is why we must prevent the Destroyer from finding the Tree."

When he and Hezzoroch had had this discussion, the story of the first humans in Fardoor arriving from a portal other than the Tree of Laurea was just that: a story. Thomas hadn't yet discovered the Tree in the Ocean. Upon finding it, though, he had to wonder about Will's real motivation. Was his intention to destroy the Tree and thereby all of Fardoor as well? Did he think the same thing could be accomplished by destroying the Tree in the Ocean instead? These were questions to which only Will had the answer.

Thomas couldn't find his cousin. Now that he was in Paarl, there was no need to hide, so he tried using his wachaoum to locate him. All he could sense were his knights.

Nor could he find the second portal. He had made several attempts since his arrival in Paarl, to no avail. "The Tree of Laurea is growing older," he muttered. "Maybe the one in the ocean is almost dead. Maybe *it* was the first Tree in Fardoor!" He contented himself with knowing that Will probably couldn't find it either.

Elori took their cousin's absence as a good sign. Most everyone was of the belief that the small victory in New Kadeon had earned them something of a reprieve. One third of his knights had been left in the foothills on the eastern side of the mountains. Laurea was left more open, although Queen Dalea still advised Velarr against any travel there. Thomas had the opportunity to talk to the Forest Queen using the communiglass, and she was full of praise for both Day children (Rebecca was embarrassed because she felt she hadn't actually done anything yet). Then yesterday, King Irith himself spoke to them:

"I wish to commend you, Thomas," he said, his young face still stern. "There have not been any Nasrati in Laurea since the attack on New Kadeon. That is a fact I cannot ignore."

Thomas didn't know how to respond at the time, so the Forest King continued. "I am now willing to accept your help, and offer both of you mine in return, Thomas and Rebecca."

Here his sister had butted in. "Thank you, Your Majesty."

He nodded slightly, still no smile. "However, I have not yet changed my mind on the Destroyer, your cousin. Know this: I will kill him if necessary."

The communiglass faded before the children could reply.

"What a horrible thing to say!" Rebecca fumed at the time. "We have to get to Will before the Forest King! Are you listening Thomas?"

Velarr had calmed her, assuring both children that the Uru would get them to their cousin first.

It had been left at that yesterday, but today Thomas was curious as to what their plan actually was. All Hezzoroch had told him was that the Uru would be giving them the signal.

Rebecca walked in where he was reading. The Verrakal crystal was back in the Native decoration and around her neck.

"Find anything good today?" she asked, referring to the texts.

"No, mostly blessings for crops and stuff in this one." He closed the book. "Hey Rebecca – has anyone told you exactly what the plan of attack is going to be?"

"Sort of. They said when the time is right we will all be flying down to Laurea. They feel that's where the battle will be taking place. A signal will be given to the humans to let them know."

"But how will the humans get to Laurea in time? It's so far away!"

"Hezzoroch never told you? Before Will's knights covered the forest, Queen Dalea was sending gnomes to New Kadeon with bags of sprite dust; there's a stockpile in each city. When the signal is given they'll use the dust to get there."

"I see."

"We're supposed to focus on Will and ignore everything else."

"I know."

"We're supposed to use the apples."

A light went off in Thomas's head. "The apples! I forgot all about them! We left them with Queen Dalea!"

"No, she gave them to Velarr for safe keeping."

"Okay, well just how are we supposed to use the apples? Throw one at him? *Here Will, take a bite – it's delicious!*"

Rebecca knew he was mocking, but that was in fact what Will had said to her in the cave. It was a bittersweet memory that seemed like ages ago. "You shouldn't joke like that," she said.

He stuck out his tongue. It was the first childish thing he had done in ages.

"I'm tired of feeling so…responsible, Rebecca."

"Me too."

"I want to go home."

"Me too."

That evening they watched the sun set together. It would be their last one in Fardoor.

* * * *

The sound of Elori running up the stairs woke the children up before he burst into their room and turned on the light.

"It has begun!" he exclaimed. "The Destroyer has moved his knights back to Laurea. He is preparing for battle!"

Rebecca rubbed her eyes. "When did this happen? I thought you couldn't sense him Thomas!"

"I couldn't." He grabbed his wachaoum and closed his eyes. "Will's in Laurea," he confirmed. "The Nasrati are there too! And…they're burning the forest!"

Velarr flew up the stairs and entered the room. "Laurea is on fire!" she said. "Paarl is being positioned overhead, Elori."

"They must release the rain."

The Uru wielded some control over other clouds. They could cause a torrential downpour if needed.

"It won't work," said Thomas. "This isn't ordinary fire; it has been created by the Nasrati. Ordinary rain won't put it out."

"I'll go tell King Arros. He needs to send Uru with the Etheros staffs to fight the Nasrati."

"Go," Elori affirmed. Velarr was gone as quickly as she had appeared.

"I don't understand!" said Rebecca. "If Will burns the forest, he may burn the Tree of Laurea as well! That's not what he wants."

"Maybe he's decided it *is* what he wants," her brother suggested.

The sound of a large firecracker filled the air, followed by a blinding red flash. "The signal to the humans has been given," said Elori as it was repeated multiple times. "We must get you to Laurea."

They jumped out of bed and raced downstairs still in their pyjamas. More bright flashes greeted them at the door, these ones ivory in color. The accompanying sound was something akin to a laser.

"More signals," said Thomas.

"No, that is energy fire. Paarl is under attack." Elori fumbled with the door so they could see outside.

The night sky was alight with blasts of energy being created by pillars on many of the city's buildings. They were its automatic magical defence, able to recognize the dark magic of the Destroyer and his army. Currently, they were all aiming at the same place.

"He's here!" yelled Elori.

Floating high above the city was a knight in full armor, his face obscured by the metallic black helmet he wore. His dark cape fluttered in the wind. A protective force field surrounded the knight, and he appeared unharmed by the hundreds of bolts that struck him.

"He has gotten stronger," Elori observed.

The knight hovered in one spot, unmoving. He took off the helmet and they could see it was their cousin.

"Rebecca…Thomas! Come join the fun!" he boomed. The voice was playful, yet menacing. "I know you're here!"

The Day children looked at each other with fear. "What's he doing?" asked Rebecca. "He's just hovering there."

"I don't think he can attack from behind his shield," said Thomas "but he can't let it drop either."

Elori began shooting at their cousin. It appeared as though thousands of other Uru had the same idea. A giant energy ball swirled into form and went hurtling at Will. It knocked him back a few feet, but his shield remained intact. "That was the Uraiel," muttered Rebecca.

He started gliding over Paarl, searching.

"This is bad," said Elori, still shooting. "We have to get the fighters outside of the city so they can go down to Laurea. If the Destroyer sees them making a break for it he may kill them before they can spread out!"

"Let me handle it," said Rebecca. She raised her hands and chanted *"The power of the Verrakal crystal! FOG!"*

The crystal glowed violet, and so did her hands. The cloud beneath them churned, then suddenly spewed forth a thick fog that rose hundreds of feet in the air before settling a bit.

Elori held out his arm and could barely make out his own hand. "Well done," he congratulated. "I hope they realize what the cover is for."

"I'll contact Velarr to let them know," said Thomas.

Had they been able to see him they would have observed his lips moving slightly as his eyes stared straight ahead. As it was, they didn't know what Thomas was doing until he announced delivery of the message a half-minute later.

"Excellent." Elori continued shooting in the air, although now he didn't have much of a target. All any of them could make out were random flashes of energy fire.

"I'm not going away because of some fog!" boomed Will. "Come out and play you two!"

A house two streets over exploded. "He's shooting back!" Rebecca exclaimed.

"The fog must be obscuring his dark energy from the city's automatic defences. We can't hit him accurately, so he can risk lowering his force field!"

All three of them had the same idea in creating their own protective field. No one thought of going back inside. A blurry shape suddenly flew past them. Several more followed in quick succession.

"What are those?" Rebecca asked with worry. "Are they Nasrati?"

"They aren't Nasrati," said Thomas.

"No. They're Uru fighters! They're all headed for Paarl's gates!"

"Please let them make it," she whispered.

Thomas reached out for Elori. "We should be going too. We can help."

"Not yet. You must stay with the Destroyer. Our fighters can handle the Nasrati thanks to your magic Thomas. No doubt the inhabitants of Laurea are already engaged in battle under King Irith, and hopefully the humans will be arriving there soon as well."

Through the fog they heard Velarr's voice calling them. "Are you there?" she asked from outside their force field.

"How did you find us?" Elori inquired as they let her in.

"Thomas maintained a connection leading me here. Thank you, Thomas. And thank you Rebecca for helping get our fighters out of Paarl."

As if on cue, at least ten more flew by.

"King Arros is sending all of them, not just the ones equipped with the Etheros staffs. The other Uru cities are moving into position as well."

"Then this really is it," said Rebecca. She covered her ears as another nearby explosion rocked them. Uru fighters continued to stream past. "How long are we supposed to wait?"

"Until your cousin makes his move," said Elori.

"But he could be gone already – we can't see him either!"

Thomas closed his eyes. "He's still here."

"Was that you Thomas?" called Will. "See I knew you were here! Now let's try getting rid of this fog, shall we?"

The mist began to swirl again. The crystal glowed around Rebecca's neck as she resisted his efforts. "He'll have to do better than that!" she said smugly.

"Just testing!" he announced. A field of dark energy suddenly moved vertically past them with a distinct humming noise. It pressed the fog she had created back down into the cloud. Immediately the city's defence system began targeting him again.

Now Will could see the Uru fighters streaming towards the city gates. "Naughty, naughty you guys!" he admonished before promptly disappearing. The barrage of energy bolts was stopped.

"Where'd he go?" asked Rebecca excitedly.

"He's just outside the forest," said Thomas.

Elori grabbed their shoulders. "Now is the time! You must follow him!"

"We don't have the apples!"

"I have them with me." Velarr handed each of them a little cloth bag containing one red and one yellow apple slice. "Guard them with care. I will be following you shortly."

Rebecca turned to her brother. "Are you ready?" He nodded. "Then take my hand!"

Thomas grabbed a hold with both his hands as he'd done with Velarr.

"Good luck!" called Elori as they lifted off the ground and soared high up into the air.

Rebecca waved at them before telling her brother to hold on tight, " – 'Cause here we go!"

They zoomed straight towards the city boundaries. More and more Uru continued to head in the same direction then sink down beneath the cloud once they had exited Paarl. The children followed them down through the cool cloud, emerging below to see they were almost directly above Laurea. Pockets of it were on fire, and large plumes of acrid smoke wafted towards them carrying with it the sounds of fighting. Tremendous rain clouds summoned by the Uru could be seen moving into position over the forest.

Will was firing at them from the ground. The Uru fighters spread out as they descended, but many were being hit anyway. A single blast from Will could take out several of them at once. A steady stream of knights could be seen going in and out of the forest, like ants at an anthill. Many of them were firing on the Uru fighters as well. They themselves were all aiming for Laurea.

Thomas felt a surge of power from the many stone altars nearby. "Take us to where he is, outside the forest!" he shouted over the noise.

"Okay!"

"Not too close!" He wondered if they'd been spotted yet.

They landed a few hundred feet away. Will stopped shooting at the Uru and disappeared, reappearing right in front of the Day children.

CHAPTER EIGHTEEN

"Finally! It's just the three of us again." Will's eyes were cold, full of malice.

"Will!" Thomas shouted. "Stop this!"

"Stop what?" He aimed a powerful blast at them, which they both blocked. "Still just testing," he said.

The Day children remained in a defensive posture. A rising wind began howling around them.

"This isn't you!" Rebecca cried.

"But it *is* me, I assure you."

She tried a different tack. "If you destroy the Tree of Laurea you'll be destroying Fardoor as well. There won't be a land for you to rule!"

He nodded. "Yes, I too believed that at first. But I've come to realize that Fardoor won't be destroyed without the Tree – it'll be changed, *better*."

Dark clouds had collected over Laurea and the downpour was begun.

Will laughed. "Pitiful! Rain will not put out these fires. See – they still burn bright."

Anger rose up in Rebecca. She'd had enough. Without saying a word she pointed at the falling rain. The crystal glowed and then so did the rain in response. Within seconds the fires were doused and the downpour stopped. Thousands of sprites lifted off the trees and hundreds of Uru entered into the forest.

It was Will's turn to be speechless. He stared at Rebecca, his blond hair blowing across a face twisted with malice.

She stared back, nervous. Thomas watched at the ready. The Verrakal crystal stirred and broke free from her necklace. Will reached out for it, but it flew right back to her and reattached itself. In the distance, they could see something large and rapidly approaching. It was the humans.

"Give it up," said Thomas. "Your army is outnumbered and the Uru now have weapons that can defeat the Nasrati. You can't win."

"I don't even need the Nasrati anymore!" he scoffed. "I've become too powerful! Both of you may have your tricks, but let's see some of the new ones *I've* learned."

Dark energy began forming a halo around him. The Day children fired their energy bolts but his blue force field sprang up and absorbed the shots each time.

"You didn't bring your friends, so I think I'll invite them," he said, looking up.

Two other unusual clouds now occupied spots next to Paarl, and Uru were emerging from these as well. He pointed at one cloud and made a pulling motion. It started falling to the ground.

Uru rushed to get out of the way. Rebecca and Thomas each tried to stop it but only managed to slow its descent. It still came crashing down, releasing a thunderous cloud of dust where it landed in the plains. They put up shields for protection.

"That's not the one!" exclaimed Will.

The Uru city stood still, new cracks running through many of the buildings, some of them collapsed entirely. It wasn't Paarl.

Their cousin reached up and pulled down the two other cloud cities, which had started moving off. Immediately the children saw that one of them was in danger of landing right on top of the first grounded city.

"Together," muttered Thomas. "One, two, three..."

He and Rebecca released their magic, she invoking the Verrakal crystal and Thomas connecting with the many stone altars around him. They succeeded in moving it a safe distance away. Despite the rough landings, the cities' magical defences began firing at the knights. The humans arrived and began engaging the army in making their way towards the forest. A mile away from this chaotic scene stood the Day children and their cousin.

"I'm not done yet!" said Will. Hundreds of his knights were coming out of Laurea and attacking the Uru cities. Sprites, gnomes, and Uru were following them out and attacking from behind. "I thought I'd wait for you two to see this."

The dark aura surrounding Will had grown. He laughed again and a blue light escaped his body and rushed through every knight. Each of them grew to giants of twenty feet, enormous weapons held in mammoth hands. A destructive rampage ensued, the ground shaking with their heavy footsteps. The children didn't know where to look: Will, or the chaos behind him.

He grinned. "Alright then, good luck to you both. I'm off to find the Forest King. No more hiding: today both he and the Tree of Laurea will be destroyed!" And with that, Will replaced the helmet on his head and disappeared.

It took a moment for the children to register what had just happened: an encounter with their cousin and they had barely done anything to stop him.

"I'll go into Laurea, you go help the cloud cities," ordered Thomas.

"No we have to stay together! Neither of us stands a chance against him alone." She aimed a wind blast at some giant knights exiting the forest nearby and they were blown several miles away. "They have enough help – our job is to deal with Will!"

Rebecca was right – this was just a diversion. Most of the humans and Uru were being kept from Laurea by the ongoing battle in the Uru cities. Buildings were crumbling all over as the lumbering giants levelled them with a single blow of their clubs. Paarl tried to raise itself up off the ground but only got fifty feet in the air before crashing back down again.

As big as the knights were, however, they were still greatly outnumbered. The humans were having some success in slowing them down with their stop spells, and every now and then one of the giants would come tumbling down under energy fire from the Uru.

"You're right," he agreed. "They're handling it."

"Take my hand," she said, holding it out for him.

"We don't need to fly."

"It'll be faster, and it might be better if we were invisible." She disappeared in front of his eyes. He felt a hand grab him and then he disappeared as well.

"Weird!"

"Can you sense Will?" she asked as they headed for the trees.

"Yes, go that way."

"I can't see where you're pointing!"

"Just go straight!"

They narrowly missed being flattened by three knights while entering the forest. Thomas aimed behind him and caused the ground to swallow the knights up to their heads so they couldn't move. "Keep going straight," he instructed.

As they journeyed into Laurea, he suddenly remembered the first time they had explored this forest with its strange trees and even stranger inhabitants. The familiarity ended there, however. Tonight the air crackled with energy fire and explosions that illuminated the forest despite it being a cloudy night. Muffled yells interspersed with sounds of clashing, running and breaking trees. Instead of cinnamon, there was the lingering smell of burnt wood.

Hectic displays of fighting impeded their progress. Two gnomes went running past them, chased by a twenty-foot knight. Rebecca thought she recognized them as Cog and Klep – the brothers they had met after being rescued from Will that first time. Thinking quickly, she cast a bubble that encapsulated the knight and froze him hovering inches off the ground. "We have to try and avoid harming them," she reminded her brother.

Off to the right, ten more gnomes had cast a sticky moss that magically held a knight against a tree, while a flock of sprites worked on his giant helmet. A Nasratum materialized and immediately turned several of the gnomes to stone. The remaining ones threw mushrooms that exploded in front of it but did no harm. Thomas was about to intervene as the gnomes and sprites began fleeing, but just then an Uru showed up and disintegrated the Nasratum with light from the Etheros staff she was holding.

They continued on their way, still invisible, with Thomas giving directions based on where he sensed Will. Both children helped where they could as they rushed on by. Twice they saw Nasrati attempting to restart the fires, but the spell Rebecca had cast on the rain prevented this. Most of Laurea had been spared from going up in flames.

They also came across one of the clearings with the stone altars. It was strangely devoid of activity but Thomas did see an unusual shimmering coming off the altar itself. When asked, Rebecca said she hadn't noticed.

"Maybe we should fly above the forest and then you can pinpoint where to go," she suggested. She had no idea how long they'd been searching for Will, but it seemed a long time.

"He keeps popping in and out of places," said Thomas. "That's the problem!"

"Then see if you can find King Irith! That's who he's looking for!"

"Good idea sis." He concentrated. "I can't find him."

"Try again!"

"He's not here!"

"Well then find Queen Dalea!"

"Stop flying Rebecca. She's underground; I'll take us there." He guided them on a diagonal path through the earth to the underground lair. They emerged from the ceiling, with Rebecca gently floating the two of them down.

The lair looked the same as they had last seen it, with its soft grass and floral trees. Although, not many sprites were flying about as they headed to the centre of the lair. Queen Dalea was standing at the stone altar. A pale green mist rose out of it and up to the earthy ceiling. A funny dance was being performed by the water sprites upon the stream that encircled this clearing, and Jorka was moving around the perimeter, catching the dust that fell from them and bringing it to the altar.

"Your Majesty!" Thomas called out.

Both she and Jorka stopped what they were doing and looked around. The children realized they were still invisible so Rebecca let go of her brother's hand and made herself reappear as well.

"Rebecca and Thomas!" called Jorka excitedly. Queen Dalea looked at him and he went back to collecting the sprite dust.

"How did you get here?" she asked, a sense of worry in her voice that they had never heard before.

"I brought us here, through the ground," said Thomas.

"You shouldn't have been able to enter this place. That means the field is too weak. There is too much dark energy in Laurea."

"It's Will. He's turned his army into giants and caused the cloud cities to come crashing down on the plains. Most of the Uru and humans are caught up defending them; they can't reach the forest."

"He's looking for King Irith," added Rebecca. "Thomas couldn't sense him."

The worry in Queen Dalea's voice was now on her face. "He's in the forest, guarding the Tree of Laurea. This spell is maintaining a cloak over that area. If you could not sense the King, then perhaps the Tree is still protected."

Jorka came up and sprinkled more sprite dust on the altar. He grinned at the children, then returned to the stream to collect some more.

"Maybe I can help strengthen the field," said Thomas. The Queen nodded, which he took as a sign to approach the altar. Rebecca stayed back and watched as he assumed a position across from the Queen, placing his hands on the stone as she had done.

Flashes of the Tree appeared in his head. It was in the forest, not far from them – how could he have missed it? He sensed King Irith there waiting, guarding. Queen Dalea was right – the field was weakening. There were open holes that someone with keen perception might exploit.

The Queen was chanting: *"Callaerros scurrabi, callaeros scurrabi."* He joined in.

Now Thomas could clearly see the Tree of Laurea in his mind's eye. It was hidden amongst the other trees. There was fighting occurring all around it, but nobody entered within a one hundred foot radius, as if that portion of the forest did not exist. *"Callaerros scurrabi,"* he said. The green mist rising from the altar became brighter. The spell was working; the patches in the protective field surrounding the Tree's perimeter were closing.

Seven Uru were battling with a knight nearby. The group was coming very close. *'It's okay,'* thought Thomas *'they won't notice it. They can't get through the cloak.'* The holes had almost closed. The knight swung his mace, missing the Uru, but sending an arc of energy that went right through a hole just before it filled in completely. It struck a tree within the protective field. Queen Dalea opened her eyes in horror.

"What is it? What happened?" asked Rebecca.

Thomas realized the enormity of what just took place: an area of Laurea that had previously not even seemed to exist had briefly popped into existence when that arc of energy entered it and struck a tree. Neither the knight nor the Uru had noticed but someone paying closer attention might have.

"The Tree of Laurea is no longer hidden," he explained. "Will is going to find it soon. We have to get there first!"

"Go now!" said the Queen.

Jorka waved at the Day children as Thomas grabbed Rebecca's hand and took them back through the ground.

"This isn't the right place," said Rebecca, after they had re-emerged in the forest. "I don't see the Tree of Laurea!"

Where they had come up looked like any other part of Laurea: trees with twisted trunks and thick branches with struts that reached down into the ground. There was no grassy clearing, and no unusual apple tree to be found. However, there were also no skirmishes. This area seemed to be oddly quiet when compared to the fighting that could be seen a hundred feet away on all sides.

"It's an illusion," said Thomas. "This is the Tree of Laurea."

He patted the bark of the tree next to him, and felt its tremendous power. A multi-colored flock of sprites descended out of its branches, with one of them coming forward and giving off a brilliant light. King Irith was left standing in front of them.

"Your Majesty, we're here because this area became unhidden a moment ago," Thomas quickly explained.

"I know," the young-looking King replied. "I saw it happen; no doubt the Destroyer will be here soon. *We must protect the Tree of Laurea at any cost.*"

Rebecca didn't like how he had phrased that.

"We'll help in any way we can," said Thomas.

"Good. Just protect the Tree from his attacks."

It was now only King Irith standing there, the rest of the sprites fluttering around him. The Day children nervously watched their surroundings, invisible. Fighting continued on all sides, but there was no sign of their cousin. A figure quickly appeared then disappeared in the distance. "I saw him!" whispered Rebecca.

He popped in and out again, closer and off to the right. Next thing they knew a dark knight was appearing/disappearing all around the perimeter of where they were standing, so fast that he couldn't be kept track of. Suddenly he appeared inside the hidden area and fired a blast of blue energy directly at the tree in which the sprites had been sitting. The children blocked it and King Irith blasted Will, knocking him backwards onto the ground where thick tree roots grabbed him and held him fast. At the same time the sprites zoomed over and lifted off his helmet, releasing silvery strands inside and out of it that caused it to disintegrate.

While the children watched the helmet, Will disappeared from under the roots and reappeared in the air. King Irith had been watching, though. This time he blocked the shots Will took at both him and the Tree.

"You die today Forest King, and so does the Tree!" Will exclaimed.

"It is you who will die!" he countered. They both had hatred on their faces.

King Irith took another shot but Will was too fast this time, vanishing instantly then reappearing with his back to the children. They both struck him full on, sending him flying. He vanished again in mid-air then began disappearing and reappearing continuously while the three of them aimed their energy blasts (always missing).

"Who else is here?" he asked, his blue eyes darting around each time he rematerialized. "Is that you Thomas and Rebecca? I hope so!"

A dark energy field surrounded him, then rapidly expanded to cover everything nearby in a thin black film.

Thomas felt very cold for a second, before being suddenly ripped loose of his sister as the field released its energy. King Irith and Rebecca were also knocked over and all the sprites fell to the ground. More sprites appeared from the branches of adjacent trees.

The Day children had become visible and Will blasted them before they could get up. Thomas slipped into the ground but Rebecca was hit with a glancing shot. "I knew it was you two!" he said, blocking an attack from King Irith. "And still in your pyjamas!"

"We don't want to hurt you Will," said Rebecca as she got up, limping.

"I'm afraid I can't say the same." He tried reaching into both their minds, but was again rebuffed by their golden shields. King Irith continued his attack, occasionally getting a glancing shot off Will. His armor seemed to prevent any real harm, however.

"I've called some of my own friends, you know," said Will.

Thomas realized the ground was vibrating with the thunderous march of many knights heading their way. He pounded it with his fist, creating a wall of earth a hundred feet high that encircled the immediate area. He hit the ground again and the wall moved out like a wave, pushing all the knights (and everyone else) out of Laurea while the forest itself rolled over it.

"It's just us Will."

His face skewed up. "Fine. Have it your way."

The battle began again as if a choreographed dance. Will disappeared and reappeared rapidly all over the place making surprise attacks on the children, King Irith, the sprites, and the Tree. It was hard not to get hit, and despite their best efforts he managed to take two branches off the Tree of Laurea. Thomas felt a shudder in the Gaia force each time. Rebecca went invisible and took to the air.

Her powerful winds were useless against Will and her well-targeted blasts of violet–colored energy were similarly ineffective as long as he wore his armor plating. His head was exposed, but she wouldn't risk hitting it. King Irith was mostly trying to protect the Tree while the sprites made several passes at Will. They stopped when he succeeded in taking some of them down with his dark energy.

Thomas wondered what the sprites were even trying to accomplish. He aimed his own shots at Will's exposed head, but their cousin was too quick and his aim wasn't as good as Rebecca's. Will materialized behind him and blasted Thomas before he could react.

"No!" screamed his sister.

Will smirked and shot where he thought her voice was coming from, narrowly missing her.

Thomas lay on the ground. He heard the roots grow over him - a shield from King Irith. He was wounded, blood trickling down his back. Curiously, there was no pain.

"LET ME HELP HIM!" he heard Rebecca yell.

Thomas was calm. It was the Tree of Laurea. He was connected to it – and through it, all of Fardoor. The stone altars were merely a conduit. This was the true power. This was the force of Gaia. He heard it speaking to him again, telling him how to heal, and…something else.

He went down into the ground and emerged outside King Irith's cover.

"Thomas!" his sister exclaimed in surprise.

Will also looked taken aback, and momentarily forgot to phase out. Thomas released a spell that distorted the air as it sped towards his cousin. This was what he had been told to do.

Will felt its force, then laughed when nothing happened. "Pathetic," he chided.

Thomas followed it with a powerful energy bolt. It hit Will square in the chest and knocked him over, surprising everyone. "He's stuck!" said Thomas. "He can't vanish anymore!"

There was a flash of fear across Will's face as he realized it was true. "NO!" he yelled angrily. A massive ball of dark energy began building from his hands, but he was struck by both King Irith and Rebecca before it could be released. Will held up an energy shield to avoid being hit. Even so, his armor protected him from any real damage.

As soon as he had become stuck, the branches of the trees had begun to grow out into a thick tangle. This was the King's doing, and it prevented both Will and Rebecca from flying overhead. "Protect the Tree!" he yelled at Thomas. He turned back into a sprite before Will could strike him. The flock began making more passes, this time protected by a green force field King Irith was creating. They aimed for the latches on his armor.

'Maybe I can help,' thought Rebecca. She dared going right up to her cousin while invisible, and magically released the clamps on one side. He spun around and shot but missed. She did the same thing on the other side and the sprites quickly moved in to sweep up the armor as it fell. They covered it in the same silvery strands, causing it to disintegrate as the helmet had done. King Irith reassumed his larger form.

Will was left standing in just a tunic. Far from an imposing knight, he now looked quite vulnerable. He surrounded himself in a blue force field. Thomas, Rebecca, and the Forest King focused their energy beams on him, causing the field to falter, then collapse. He shot at all three but was blocked. Rebecca slammed him into the ground with her wind. Thomas caused a giant earth-hand to rise out and hold him down.

"You can't win Will," he said.

"Come home with us," added Rebecca. "Please!"

"What home?!" he spat back as he burst back up. A thorn grazed his chest, shot from a brambly plant King Irith had made grow out from the earth. He struck the plant down, not noticing that three more had sprung up behind him. "Nice try, but I'm –" he stopped mid-sentence as several more thorns hit him in the back. They tore through his tunic and penetrated his flesh, working their way in deep.

Will opened his eyes wide and gasped. He shot at the King but the energy was weak and erratic. The poisoned thorns did quick work. He took one step and toppled over. King Irith moved in to finish him off.

"NO! DON'T KILL HIM!" Rebecca yelled, becoming visible again.

"I must," he said, and moved in closer.

She stuck her hand out and a gale-force wind swept him and the sprites away. As this happened, Thomas saw two Nasrati appear beside Will and disappear with him.

"The King will be back soon," he said to Rebecca. "We must leave."

She turned around and saw their cousin was no longer there. "Where'd he go?"

"The Nasrati took him, and I think I know where. Grab my hand; I'll take us there."

They went down into the ground and headed straight across the Western Plains, coming back up at the base of the Jagged Mountains.

This particular spot of the mountain range had no unusual markings to identify it; you could walk right by a thousand times without thinking twice. But Thomas could sense there was a small cave less than fifty feet up, and Will was in it. Far behind them the fighting continued.

"He's up there Rebecca."

Without saying a word she flew them up to the small cave. The Day children walked inside and saw Will lying on its cool floor. Crimson red blood seeped out from underneath him.

Several Nasrati had surrounded their cousin, but they immediately backed off upon seeing Thomas and Rebecca; it seemed as though they feared the Day children. A swirling vortex lay flat against the rock face behind the Nasrati, which they now backed up towards. One by one they entered and disappeared.

"So that's where they come from," said Thomas as they hurried over to Will. He was still alive, but his breathing was rapid and shallow.

"Will?" asked Rebecca. Even though he was now seventeen, she could still see their old cousin in his face. She started to cry.

"You've ruined everything," he whispered.

Thomas leaned close to his ear. "You must release the Destroyer stone Will. It's killing you."

"You killed me."

"No Will, we're trying to save you!" said Rebecca. "We just want you to come back with us."

He breathed in sharply, as if in pain.

"Quick Rebecca – the apples!"

She fumbled for a moment before taking out the two apple slices from the bag tied around her waist. First the red one was squeezed, the drops of juice landing in Will's open mouth. Nothing happened.

"The yellow one – from our world!" said Thomas.

She squeezed the golden yellow slice, which looked as if it had come from an apple just plucked minutes before. Again nothing. His eyes stayed closed and his breathing became even shallower.

"Try to remember, Will!" She looked to Thomas with panic. *"We have to help him remember!"*

"Okay." He closed his eyes and tried to think of what their cousin needed to see. When he opened them the dim cave had been replaced with the bright outdoors of their backyard in Muskoka. Their two-story house with its white walls and blue shingles was on one side and the woods on the other.

"Open your eyes Will," Rebecca whispered.

Surprisingly, he did. He looked around slowly, taking in the once-familiar surroundings. He felt the soft grass with his fingers and a tear rolled down his cheek.

Three things started happening at once: Will began growing younger, the thorns in his back worked their way out and disintegrated, and a dark liquid began seeping up through the skin on his chest. As the illusion around them faded, the liquid collected into a small ball, then hardened into a smooth, black rock. It rolled off his chest, across the floor and up into the vortex where it disappeared. And incredible wind blew past them into the vortex as it then collapsed, leaving a plain rock face in its place. Will looked up at his cousins. He was twelve once more.

"Is it really you?" he asked weakly.

"It's us," said Rebecca.

He didn't respond, but rather looked at his hands and touched his face. He looked around the cave, bewildered.

"Do you know where you are Will?" Thomas asked.

Again he looked around, slower. "Yes." He took a deep breath. "I remember everything. It was a nightmare."

The Day children looked at each other with concern.

"I tried to escape, I swear!" he went on. "The stone was too powerful." He turned his head away. "I'm sorry."

They lifted their cousin off the ground and hugged him.

"We knew it wasn't really you," said Thomas.

"We're so glad to have you back," Rebecca added. "I should never have left you alone in Fardoor."

"No, I should have gone back with you. Despite what I said, I never really blamed you Rebecca. Inside I knew it was my fault." He broke out in tears again. *"All those terrible things I did! All those people I hurt!"*

Hezzoroch's smiling face flashed in Thomas's mind.

"You were being influenced by the Destroyer stone," said Rebecca.

He looked away, angry. "I still did those things Rebecca! *I* destroyed cities! *I* separated families! *I* tried to ruin all of Fardoor! *Me!*" There was nothing the Day children could say to change that fact. He knew it and so did they.

"Fardoor will heal," said Thomas, feeling very grown-up "and so will the people who live here. But I think it's time we all went home now."

"I don't have a home," said Will with a bit more strength.

"Yes you do!" Rebecca exclaimed. "Your home is with us, in our world."

"I don't deserve to live with you guys."

"Yes, you do," they responded in unison, then they each grabbed one of his hands and led him outside. He was too weak to resist.

"Wait," he said softly. "My clothes are still in there." They took him back in the cave to retrieve his original clothes and sneakers, which had sat in a dusty pile for the last five years. Putting them back on somehow made his transformation complete. The Destroyer was gone.

CHAPTER NINETEEN

Dawn was breaking on the land of Fardoor. They had an incredible view of the Western Plains from their vantage point on the mountain, all the way to Laurea in the far distance. The three cloud cities still rested on the ground in front of it, but the energy fire had ceased.

"It think the fighting's stopped," Rebecca observed. "I suppose everyone is free of the Destroyer stone now, including the army."

The boys let her fly them to Laurea. Without the stone, Will had lost his powers, and Thomas wanted a final good look at Fardoor before leaving. It was one last, exhilarating flight that took nearly an hour at Rebecca's top speed. The Day children felt so free, so unburdened, it was hard not to yell in glee. Even Will began to warm up. His life as the Destroyer was fading, and he was once again becoming Will Hastings, the twelve year-old boy. They all felt the same excitement as when they had first entered Fardoor. It was a glorious morning.

As they neared Laurea they saw the devastation that had been wrought upon the cloud cities. Paarl was the worst hit, with half its buildings in ruins and smoke billowing from fires only just put out. Still, this fact seemed to be lost on the Uru cheering in the streets and on the grassy plains alongside the humans, gnomes, and sprites.

The cheer grew louder as the children approached. The people below waved up at them, and Thomas and Rebecca waved back. All over, the children who had been in the Destroyer's army were being reunited with their families after having woken up as if from a deep slumber. Strewn across the ground were their discarded pieces of armor, now normal in size. Thomas wondered if the people cheering recognized his cousin as the same person who had caused them so much suffering. For his own part, Will was staying silent.

Rebecca landed them on the grass next to King Arros and Elori, not far from the forest edge. Elori was the first to greet them, getting down on both knees and embracing the Day children.

"I knew you could do it!" he exclaimed. "Well done, both of you!"

King Arros was next, presenting them each with a small golden key. "You will always be welcome among the Uru," he said solemnly.

"Do you think you'll be able to get your cities back in the sky?" asked Rebecca.

He surveyed the damage. "Oh I believe we will be staying on the ground for quite some time. I welcome this opportunity to reconnect with the other people of Fardoor. We have been isolated for too long."

Will stayed back during all of this. For once he didn't mind other people getting all the attention.

The mayors of New Kadeon, New Gerron, and New Shale approached and offered their congratulations. New Kadeon's mayor produced a small glass globe that gave off rainbow sparkles in the sunlight. "Zire told me to give you this if I saw you," he said, handing it to Thomas. "It used to be Hezzoroch's. It's very old, I believe. She also wanted you to have this, which she made for you to remember them by." He pulled out a carefully folded fabric, onto which Zire had meticulously sewn three smiling faces and the library he had called home for so many weeks. Thomas accepted the gifts, and the mayors receded back into the large crowd that was forming around them.

Velarr was next, looking as if an enormous weight had been

lifted off her shoulders. Her long golden hair was in tangles and her light blue skin was marked by several cuts, but Rebecca had never her seen her smile so wide.

She too came bearing gifts: their old clothes, clean and neatly folded.

"Where did you get mine?" asked Thomas.

"They were brought up from New Kadeon when you came to Paarl."

An Uru boy and girl nervously approached and clung to her side. They looked to be between the ages of eight and twelve, but Rebecca had learned that appearances were deceiving with Uru, as their childhood lasted almost twice as long as humans'.

Velarr was beaming. "I would like you to meet my children, Prakell and Evarri." They didn't seem to recognize Will.

The hugging and handshakes that followed was interrupted by Noggin, Brufa and Jorka, who walked out of the forest in front of them.

"Hello dears!" called Brufa, looking jolly as ever if only a bit dishevelled.

Jorka bore the usual face-wide grin. His little eyes twinkled and he seemed to have grown some more hair out of his grey ears. "Rebecca and Thomas save Fardoor!" he said before spying Will. "Rebecca and Thomas find friend! Remember Jorka?"

The question was aimed at Will. Clearly Jorka remembered him from their encounter five years ago but it was doubtful if he comprehended what had happened to him since.

"Um, yes I remember you Jorka," he said quietly. "Nice to see you again."

He took all three of them up in a big bear hug. "Jorka miss you!"

"We missed you too," said the Day children. "And it's good to see you Noggin and Brufa," added Thomas when Jorka let go.

Noggin tipped his pointy red cap. "Glad things worked out. The Forest King and Queen should be here at any moment."

A hush fell on the crowd as a flock of sprites fluttered out of Laurea. The King and Queen took on their larger forms with a brilliant green flash, while the rest continued flitting about overhead.

The Day children were very nervous as to how King Irith would react to Will, and took a slightly defensive posture in front of him.

"There is no need for concern," said the King "I come as a friend." Queen Dalea smiled at them, and they relaxed. "I do have a question for your cousin, though: I sense that the Destroyer stone is no longer in Fardoor, but can you tell us where it came from?"

Will stepped forward. "I…I'm not sure exactly. I know it wasn't formed in Fardoor; it came from another world. I remember going there many times, and taking the knights there as well. It's a dark place, and cold. It's where the Nasrati come from. They are the stone's keepers but not its master. What you saw of them here was…more like their shadows. In their world they are as real as any of us."

Excited whispering followed Will's speech as the information he had conveyed made its way through the crowd.

King Irith pondered what he had said. "I do not know of this world. But tell me: is the portal between it and Fardoor still open?"

Will shook his head. "No sir."

"We saw it Your Majesty," Rebecca interjected. "It wasn't a tree – I don't know what it was. But it collapsed after the stone fell back into it."

"There may be a time when it reopens. For now, we are safe again. And I thank you for your help, Thomas and Rebecca. Please accept this gift." He plucked two golden leaves from his crown and handed one to each of them. The crowd applauded.

"There's something else you should know," said Thomas. "I felt a powerful magic deep in the ocean. It was a tree, and I think it may be another portal to *our* world. I only found it once and never again."

"I remember looking for it too," said Will. Another murmur passed through the crowd.

"The tree you speak of has been lost to us for thousands of years," said Queen Dalea. "This is a good sign! It means Fardoor is reawakening!"

That was the strange feeling Thomas had been having since they left the mountains! Fardoor was reawakening. The Tree of Laurea was reawakening! "Look!" he pointed out. "The forest is expanding!" Small green shoots had sprung up from the ground several feet from the forest edge.

"I believe this world has more life left in it than we previously thought," said Queen Dalea.

Rebecca smiled. "Your Majesties, I think it's time the three of us got back to our *own* world."

"As you wish," said King Irith. "But should you ever return..." he warned "...know that you will be welcomed as friends in the Forest of Laurea." Next he turned to the crowd. "From now on *all* humans and Uru will be welcome in this forest."

The crowd applauded, and King Arros went to shake the Forest King's hand. "That's good because we may be living beside you for the foreseeable future!" He was of course referring to the Uru cities, which remained firmly on the ground just outside Laurea. "There is one more thing before you go Rebecca. The Magic Council has requested that the Verrakal crystal remain in Fardoor."

"Oh! Of course," she said, having forgotten all about it. "May I keep the necklace, though?"

"Certainly," said Elori. "In fact, I have brought another stone to replace it with." She handed him the necklace and he carefully removed the Verrakal crystal. In its place he set a pale blue gem. "It isn't the Verrakal crystal, but you also will not find one like it in your world. These rare stones are cultivated in our clouds."

"Thank you Elori." She put it back around her neck. "I sure am going to miss flying!" she laughed.

"Are you ready?" asked Queen Dalea.

"Ready," they all replied.

"Then the King and I will take you to the Tree of Laurea."

They turned around and headed into the forest. Rebecca gave one last hug to Elori and Velarr, and Thomas thanked them for their hospitality. The three children followed the Forest King and Queen. Noggin, Brufa, and Jorka came along for the walk. Jorka insisted on holding one hand each from Thomas and Rebecca, and Rebecca held Will's. The flock of sprites flew overhead, some of the younger ones choosing to land on the children and get carried along for the ride. Thomas could hear them giggling beside his ear. He could also hear the sounds of the forest come alive again. Birds were chirping, insects humming, and small animals chattering.

Despite it being well into autumn, Laurea was as green as ever; perhaps it always stayed green. The occasional burnt patches they passed along the way were showing signs of new life already, with small white flowers dotting the scalded trunks. This truly was a magical place.

Rebecca was rediscovering some of the landmarks they had noted the first time they had been here and tried to create a path back. "Look – there's an arrow we carved!" she commented, then "There's the tree that looks like a ballerina!"

"Not *that* one again," Thomas groaned.

Jorka just smiled and nodded the whole way, while Will kept quiet. After a long walk they came to a part of the forest that looked like any other, except the tree just ahead appeared to be missing two branches.

"It's the Tree of Laurea," said Rebecca.

Thomas knew – he could feel it.

King Irith waved his hand and the illusion melted away. They were back in the clearing with its long, wavy grass. Sunlight poured down on them and on the Tree of Laurea which stood at its centre, the stumps of the missing branches already sprouting new shoots.

"It's really here," whispered Will. "We're really going home!" He let a tear escape despite himself.

"Well dears, I hate long goodbyes," said Brufa. "So just give us a hug." She embraced each of them in turn, even Will.

Noggin stepped up and shook their hands as the sprites lifted off the children's shoulders, some of them saying goodbye in their pipsqueak voices.

"Rebecca, Thomas, and friend go home now?" asked Jorka. He knew the answer already, and began to cry a bit.

Rebecca, of course, followed suit. "We won't forget you Jorka. You were a very good friend to us."

He wiped his wrinkly grey face and then declared "Jorka have something for Rebecca and Thomas." Out of a pocket from his frock he pulled the plastic bag they had carried their lunch in, as well as the flashlight. "Jorka save it for Rebecca and Thomas."

Will looked confused.

"Um, thanks," said Thomas, accepting the flashlight. "Still works," he muttered.

Jorka was looking at him expectantly, continuing to clutch the plastic bag with two hands.

"Why don't you keep the bag as something to remember us by?" Rebecca suggested.

His tiny eyes opened wide, as if having just received a valuable treasure. He scooped all three of the children up in another bear hug.

The Forest King and Queen waited patiently during all of this. "I have one more thing to ask of you," said King Irith when Jorka had let go of the children. "I ask that you promise to keep this world and this portal a secret."

"I promise," they each said.

"I doubt anyone would believe us anyway," Thomas added.

They all said one last goodbye, then the children trudged through the tall grass to the Tree of Laurea. Several red apples lay under the shade of its wide branches as if waiting for them. Many more remained among its thick, green leaves. Thomas picked one up and they each took a bite in turn, savouring its delicious taste.

"I'll go first," said Will. He walked up to the Tree slowly, then before touching it quietly told them, "Thanks for coming to get me." He placed a hand on the trunk and disappeared in a flash of brilliant light.

"My turn," Rebecca announced. "We had some fun, huh?"

"Yeah."

She took a deep breath, then walked up and touched the Tree. Another flash of light and she too disappeared. Thomas looked over his shoulder and saw everyone still watching, although the King and Queen had changed back into their sprite form and rejoined the flock. Through the brown stone he remained connected to the Tree of Laurea and all of Fardoor. He soaked it all in one more time, wondering if he would ever be back or have this feeling again.

"Ah well," he sighed, then walked up and placed his own hand on the rough bark.

* * * *

They were back in the large cave with its pale grass, pale tree, and pale glow. Everything was still. Rebecca suddenly got all excited. "We're home!" she exclaimed. "I wonder how much time has passed? What if it's been a while since we left?"

"I hope your Mom and Dad aren't too worried," said Will.

"What are you doing Thomas?"

"I'm looking for the sprites that were here. They're probably up in the tree." He thought he caught some movement among the leaves.

Rebecca grabbed his hand. "Come on."

"Okay," he reluctantly agreed. As soon as he had re-entered this world he'd felt a sense of loss – no longer did he have that profound connection to what Hezzoroch had called the Gaia force. There was something about Fardoor that had made it possible there only. His hope of being able to do some magic in their own world faded.

Rebecca knew what he was thinking. "It doesn't matter," she said. "Let's just go."

They smiled at each other. The three of them made their way to the staircase along the wall, then up it and through the tunnel. They exited the caves to find a bright summer day in the Muskoka woods. It was the maple trees and poplars that made them really feel like they were home again.

A blue jay flew down and rested momentarily in front of Rebecca. "Ooh a beautiful blue jay!" she exclaimed.

The boys laughed and started down the path to their house. Rebecca joined up and they walked side by side with Thomas in the middle, an arm around each of their shoulders. All three of them were filthy from the caves, but Rebecca didn't care about her appearance. Will was content to let some one else lead. And Thomas, well he was relishing just being a ten year-old again.

"Rebecca, Thomas, William! Time to come in!" called a voice.

"Mom!" said the Day children.

"We haven't been gone long at all!"

They all laughed and raced towards their home.

"It certainly was an exciting adventure for Hastings and Day!" said Will proudly.

"Day and Hastings," Thomas corrected. "There's two of us!"

ABOUT THE AUTHOR

Daniel Tascona is a young physician from Barrie, Ontario. He is fortunate enough to live next to poplars, maples, pines, and birches. This is his first book.

CPSIA information can be obtained at www.ICGtesting.com
Printed in the USA
LVOW06s1251200814

399908LV00025B/97/P

9 781461 109174